THE LAW OFFICE MURDERS

Victor Moss

ISBN: 979-8-3304-8318-1

Printed in the United Stated of America

PRAISE FOR "THE LAW OFFICE MURDERS"

This is a book that will keep you addicted to reading. The characters are good, and the twists and turns are expertly crafted. This book is a must-read, especially for people who love crime thrillers!

By Edward Gray

It is a masterclass of suspense and storytelling. This author has the ability to take the readers deep into the dark world of Denver. The plot is as intricate as it is unpredictable! Will definitely recommend it to others.

By Philip Haywood

Victor Moss has really outdone himself, offering this thrilling narrative. I absolutely loved vivid descriptions and complex characters create a world that feels both real and terrifying. This book is a must for anyone who enjoys a smart, well-written mystery with plenty of surprises.

By Bec Johnson

Also by Victor Moss

The Coffee House Murders

Country Club Murders

The Soul Named Samantha

No Return Home

The Murdered Wife

Beware the Wolves:
A Soviet WWII Love Story

No Return Home: Sequel to Beware the Wolves:
A Soviet WWII Love Story

Disclaimer

This book is strictly a fictional account of the police officers and detectives of the Denver Police Department including descriptions of physical settings and the Department's rules and procedures. This book is strictly for entertainment. All characters are imaginary, and any similarity to actual persons is simply a coincidence.

The author is not aware of any criminal or corrupt cops as described in the book. Instead, the author has deep admiration for the hard work and dedication of the men and women who chose to serve and protect society even though their lives may be taken away from them in an instant.

Dedication

To my wife, children and grandchildren who have given me support and encouragement to keep writing.

Acknowledgments

I thank my daughter, Katherine Stafford for her advice and suggested corrections. I also thank my sister and her husband, Mary and Duane Janssen for their encouragement and their useful comments and suggestions.

But above all, I have enormous praise for my wife, Rita Moss, for her support and the many hours she spent reading and discussing each segment. Her suggestions and editing were truly invaluable.

Contents

CHAPTER 1

Present day: Denver, Colorado

A WOLFISH smile broke out on his clean-shaven angular face the instant Elizabeth Durand Esquire strode into his office and slammed the door shut behind her. He expected her. The rest of the attorneys and staff had left for the day, and the building was locked tight. Being Friday, the staff did not waste any time leaving for the weekend. For Elizabeth and her boss, it was now playtime—their special time to be together. The excuse for working late was that there was just too much work at the Visser, White, and Garza Law Offices, LLC.

Elizabeth returned a sultry smile, her brown eyes sparkling. She sidled over, her generous hips swaying, towards handsome Baxter Visser as he sat behind his huge cherrywood desk. He slid his high-back Corinthian leather chair from his desk just in time for Elizabeth to fall into his lap. They kissed passionately, his hands all over her curvy body. One kiss followed several more before Baxter motioned toward the wide tan leather sofa that stood against a walnut-paneled wall of the large office.

"Yes, yes, yes, let's go," she responded breathlessly. In a state of arousal and hard breathing, they made it to the couch. Their clothes went flying. Elizabeth barely had a chance to lay down before Baxter pounced into the waiting arms of his beautiful and highly seductive associate.

They were in the act of overwhelming lust when suddenly the door swung open. Elizabeth twisted her neck to see what was happening. Her eyes widened in terror as a black-clothed figure flew towards them. She screamed a blood-curdling shriek. Baxter crooked his head toward the assailant and strained to lift himself off the woman. It was too late. Elizabeth saw a wisp of smoke as the gun with the silencer exploded. Baxter collapsed, his weight pinning her to the couch. A second later, still screaming, the gun went off again.

She was dead.

CHAPTER 2

IT WAS SATURDAY, their day off. Homicide detectives Nora Ricci, Clint Hawk, Mortimer Holliday, and several others from the Homicide Unit of Division 6 of the Denver Police Department were at a BBQ hosted by a co-worker, Detective Stan Orlinski. Shaded by Wasatch maple and ash trees, the air redolent of fragrance due to an abundance of flowering plants, the early August afternoon was delightful. The temperature was perfect, as were the beer and the brats.

The event was suddenly interrupted for Nora and Hawk when Lieutenant Perez, holding a bottle of Warka, a Polish beer, in his hand, walked up to them. He apologized for what he had to do and informed them that he had just received a call from dispatch. "Two individuals were found dead in a law office in the Capitol Hill area. I want you both to investigate. They're waiting for you right now."

Mortimer Holliday, the tall, lanky, almost cadaverous detective who had only recently transferred from the Tampa Police Department, asked Perez if he could accompany them since he liked working with the two and was bored with the party.

Nora looked disappointed. She came with a date, and now he'd be left alone. Hawk, on the other hand, was relieved to leave the party. He was pissed ever since Nora walked in with Seth Morgan, although he tried to hide it. He assumed that they'd be coming together today. He felt foolish for having to give excuses as to why Nora came with someone else—another detective from another unit. He shrugged it off, knowing that it was his fault. But no matter how much he tried to convince himself that it was for the best, he felt betrayed and jealous.

The three detectives, Hawk, Ricci, and Holliday, dressed in casual clothing, rushed off to investigate the deaths. It was awkward for Nora and Hawk to be now confined in the same vehicle. But they were partners, and both were professional enough to separate their personal feelings from what had to be done at work. At least, they realized that that was how it should be. Unless their relationship became a huge issue that made the situation miserable, one of them would need to partner with someone else or transfer out of the unit. At the moment, neither wanted to do that.

As he steered his Jeep, Hawk's breath was labored. He felt a pit in his stomach. He tried to think about something else, but the thought of Nora arriving with another man ate at him. He wanted to talk to her privately and explain his feelings, but Mortimer was tagging along again. *But maybe it's better this way; otherwise, I might blab something to Nora that I'll regret.*

No one said a word; there were just a lot of heavy sighs. Mortimer, who usually ended up in the back, now sat beside Hawk since Nora chose to sit behind him. He looked perplexed, trying to understand why neither Hawk nor Nora said anything. It was unlike Nora, who was always chatty and laughed a lot. He missed their banter and camaraderie. And he meant to find out why Nora came to the party with someone else because he thought they liked each other. But before he was able to ask, Hawk broke the silence.

"We're not too far from the law office building. I remember it well. It's in a converted 1890s three-story, red brick mansion. I've been inside it a few times while on patrol duty." Nora cleared her throat but didn't comment.

Hawk continued, "As a matter of fact, we were called out to the place several times. At one time, the front windows were shot out. Another time, a brick was thrown through a window. A third time, the fancy office sign was egged. But most of the time, we were called because some disgruntled client or someone they sued was disruptive and threatening. It seems to be more the case with divorce lawyers. If they're any good, they put up with a lot of crap. They deal with human emotions at the basic level—children, property, and all sensitive issues. A friend of a lawyer told me that when a client hires a divorce lawyer, the hatred the spouse feels for the other is transferred to the lawyer. The lawyer then becomes the enemy. It somehow becomes all their fault for the marriage break up."

"What you're saying is that if these people were murdered, then we may be looking at a lot of suspects," Mortimer said.

"It might very well be. I know that one of the lawyers is an overly aggressive and ruthless divorce attorney. We were called to stop a disturbance or two specifically because he managed to take the spouse, usually the husband, to the cleaners."

"Cleaners? I don't understand."

"Took everything they had away from them."

"Yeah, Mortimer," Nora couldn't stay silent any longer, "If your marriage doesn't work out with Josephine after you inherit millions from your aunt, you may need a lawyer like that so she doesn't wipe you out."

"Oh, I don't think I need to worry about that. She told me she is wealthy and doesn't need any more money."

"You just believe what she told you, but you don't know her well, do you? She just became interested in you on that cruise ship after you told her about your wealthy aunt. I know you are not interested in running a background check, but you should."

"Oh, I told you that I wouldn't do anything like that. She wouldn't like it at all." Mortimer then began to sneeze, one after another, a mannerism whenever he became stressed.

Hawk's eyebrows shot up after hearing Nora's comment. That managed a silent chortle from him. He knew that she believed Josephine, whom no one had ever met or seen pictures of, was perhaps a con artist. But he was surprised that she threw it out like that, so bluntly.

Mortimer didn't even flinch. Instead, he abruptly changed the subject. "This is quite an area with all these old mansions around. It must've been something in the old days. What's the history here, Nora?"

Now that Nora had her say about her concern regarding Josephine, she did not feel like giving the man any more history lessons about Denver as she had done in the past. "Why don't you ask Clint about it."

Mortimer looked at the man, "Oh, what can you tell me about the area, Clint?"

Hawk did not want to explain anything to Mortimer either. At times, the man could be very irritating, and this was one of the times— or maybe he was just irritated with Nora."

"Clint, please tell me. I'm curious about the history here."

Deciding to keep it brief, Hawk said, "There is a lot of fascinating history here because these magnificent mansions were built by many silver barons in the late eighteen-eighties and early eighteen-nineties. But a few years later, a silver crash and a depression followed in 1893. Most of the barons lost their homes. Since then, many mansions were torn down to make room for offices, and some were converted to apartments. But as we drive around, you'll see several still standing and keeping up well. Still magnificent."

"Yeah, I see a few. It's a real shame, though, that so many were destroyed. You're right. I can see all the office buildings and apartments interspersed among the grand houses. I would have loved to have lived here in that era."

The Jeep stopped across the street from Visser, White, and Garza Law Offices. The medical examiner's van and a patrol vehicle were parked in front. A crowd milled around the place, phone cameras recording. They waited for the heavy one-way traffic to pass before they slid out of the vehicle. Nora commented in a flat voice, "Let's hope the deaths are of natural causes, but somehow, I have a feeling that we'll have another complicated homicide to deal with."

CHAPTER 3

THE LAW OFFICE was in a converted mansion on Logan Street near the Governor's house. The huge building, built by a railroad magnate, displayed Italianate architecture, red brick fronted by a wide portico across the entire width of the house. Five cement steps led up to the porch. A newly constructed handicap ramp was built to the side of the steps.

A massive oak door with a colorful geometric stain-glassed panel, guarded on each side by a topiary plant, was wide open as the three detectives approached. They entered the highly polished tiled foyer, and Corporal Hopkins met them with the usual sneer on his expressive, narrow face. Hawk expected such a reaction from the man, although he did not feel the scorn was as hostile as usual. The rivalry between them began while they were at the police academy. Each tried to outdo the other. Unfortunately, Hopkins failed several examinations—for sergeant and for a detective. He resented Hawk's advance to detective, while the highest rank he achieved was that of a corporal.

Hawk hoped that by now, Hopkins would let bygones be bygones. Just last week, Hopkins put his life on the line to help capture a killer while Hawk and Ricci were pinned down by an assail of gunfire.

If it was not for Hopkins, either he or Nora, or both, might have been shot by the assassin arranged by a vengeful, incarcerated corrupt cop in a previous case. His killer's job was to eliminate them as witnesses. Hawk appreciated Hopkins' bravery and thanked him for helping them out of a tight situation.

"Hello, De-tec-tive Hawk," Hopkins said. But this time, his voice did not carry the usual sarcastic tone. Instead, his scowl turned into a wide smile. He nodded to Nora and Mortimer.

Surprised at the turnabout in his demeanor, Hawk said, "Hello Dave, "What do we have here? More dead bodies, we're told."

"Yeah, you got that right. But before you go in, I'd like to tell you that I've been made sergeant…will get my extra stripe on Monday. So, you can call me sergeant after that."

"Hey, that's terrific. We need to celebrate over a beer. You're on your way up now…before you'll know it, you'll be my boss someday."

Hopkins laughed, "Sure, sure. That'll be great. I'd give you hell."

Hawk returned the laugh.

"If you boys are through chit-chatting," Nora said, "we better get to work. Who found the bodies, Corporal?"

"The two ladies from the janitorial service. They clean the offices on weekends." Reviewing his notes, he said, "A Lupe Gutierrez and a Dominga Lucero. They're waiting in the conference room for you," pointing to a door a few feet away to the left.

"Did they tell you anything about what they saw?"

"Detective Ricci, they were so shocked that Mrs. Lucero almost fainted upon viewing the dead bodies with all the bloody mess. They didn't stick around, ran out the door, and called 911."

"Bloody mess? So… they were murdered, then?"

"Oh yeah, Detective Ricci. No doubt about that."

"Thank you, Corporal," Nora said.

"Where're the victims?" Hawk asked. "Are they together?"

"Oh, yeah. They're as together as they could get." He tried hard not to chuckle. "You'll get a kick out of it, Hawk. They're in the office at the end of this long entryway. You'll see them one on top of the other."

"On top of the other?" Hawk asked. "The killer left them that way on purpose?"

"You just have to see for yourself," Hopkins could not hold back a laugh.

"Oh, I don't understand," Mortimer said. "Why would someone want to stack one body over another? Must be a message there." He scratched the back of his bony head, his eyebrows knitted. Hopkins could not help but laugh again. To avoid further embarrassment, he walked out onto the porch and yelled at the crowd waiting outside, ordering them to leave.

"I can't believe that he's laughing about dead bodies," Nora said, looking disgusted. "What's wrong with him?"

"You know that we become desensitized in this job," Hawk commented as he shrugged. That was the first direct communication with Nora all afternoon.

The detectives walked past a white marble-clad reception desk that stood diagonally off the side. Nora admired the impressive walnut wainscoted walls that matched the dark wood of the floor, crown, and doors. When they came to the glass-walled conference room, Hawk poked his head in, thanking the two women for waiting. He told them that they'll be back to talk to them shortly. They half-heartedly nodded their agreement.

As they entered the office, a coppery waft of blood and death assaulted their senses. The Medical Examiner, Dr. Janeel Thompson, awaited them inside. With a genuine smile, she said, "Here we go again, detectives. I don't know why I see you so often these days. There're just too many murders lately. I called Forensics, and they should be here any moment."

As soon as Mortimer saw the bodies, he blurted out, "Oh, my. Um…They're naked. Oh, Josephine will not like me looking at naked people now that we're engaged." He stood off to the side, lifted his head, and closed his eyes. Once again, as with every crime scene, he seemed to go into a trance. His excuse for such behavior was that he could feel the negative vibes in the room and get a better picture of what might have transpired. Hawk and Nora didn't believe him, but occasionally, he came up with something helpful.

Janeel chuckled, sending her plump belly into a jiggle. "He's at it again," she whispered. "Strange behavior, if you ask me."

Hawk and Nora were listening to Janeel, but their eyes fell on the man and woman, the woman underneath the man. "Oh," Nora said. "Embarrassing position to die in."

"*Flagrante delicto,*" Janeel said.

"What?" Hawk asked.

Janeel laughed. "Fancy term for getting caught with their pants down or caught in a compromising misdeed." She laughed again, incredibly pleased with her Latin words. "What a shame. They were such an attractive couple." She looked at Nora, "Just as the two of you are," laughing again.

That statement upset Nora, who was no longer sure she and Hawk were a couple. Hawk was used to Janeel's friendly teasing, especially about his and Nora's belongings. But he also wondered if they would ever be together in a relationship. It saddened him, and he wished he could commit to it and get serious about it. *I have a lot of thinking to do since Nora is pushing me on this.*

Setting aside their thoughts, Hawk and Nora bent over the bodies to look at the wounds. "Interesting…a bullet into each one of their foreheads," Nora said. "In close range, I'd say."

"Yup, that's what it looks like to me," Janeel said. "Obviously, they were frightened before they were shot."

"Why do you think that?" Hawk asked, still studying the point of entry and where a bullet might have eventually lodged.

"Look at the frozen expressions on their faces. They died in fear. Both heads were turned toward the door when they were shot. And if that wasn't enough, the man was hit hard over his head. Look here." She pointed to a gash on the side of his head. "Looks like something blunt, but not too wide, hit him."

Upon hearing Janeel, Hawk looked around to see if there was anything in the room that the killer might have used. There were several objects, but none with any visible blood on them.

"Wanted to make sure he died," Mortimer said, finally deciding to approach the bodies. "I sense that the shooter suddenly ran into the room, and these two had no time to untangle themselves. He then quickly shot them, but the man must not have been quite dead, so he hit him on the head. Probably used the handle of the gun."

"No, Detective Holliday," Janeel said. "When that bullet struck his forehead, he died instantly. It went right through him…look at the back of his head and the mess on the back of the couch."

"Oh, I didn't notice it at first. I should've looked more carefully before saying anything."

"But I think that Mortimer is right as to the shooter," Hawk said, "He or she must have run in with some speed, surprising the victims and shooting them before they were able to defend themselves."

"Well, it's hard to move around when that man, probably weighing two-hundred pounds, is dead weight on that slim woman," Nora commented in disgust. Then she thought of what she said. "Excuse the pun, ha-ha." Hawk walked away. Janeel laughed heartily as she began to stretch a cover over the bodies.

"Oh, I don't understand?" Mortimer said. "Where's the pun?"

"Dead weight, get it, get it?" Nora asked.

"Oh, I guess I get it. In other words, the man who is dead is weighing her down. Is that a joke?" Mortimer's long, pale face was as serious as always. No one in the Unit had ever seen his smile, let alone laugh. He told them many times that he does not get jokes.

"No, Mortimer…I guess, not really…forget what I said."

Nora and Janeel smiled while Hawk kept his eyes on the gash on the man's head. "What are you thinking, Clint?" Nora asked.

He looked at her in those dark blue expressive eyes. He realized he couldn't be upset with her for long but was still not quite ready to warm up to her entirely. He hesitated a moment before he answered in an even voice. "Nora, I'm trying to figure out why the guy was hit on the head. If, as Janeel says, the man died instantly, then why was he struck?"

"Are you thinking that it was personal then? He clobbered him out of sheer anger?"

"Yeah, indicates to me that it was extremely personal with the killer."

Nora said, "That's what I think as well." She turned toward Janeel. "Were you able to find where the slugs landed?"

"Yeah. Both slugs went right through the heads and through the soft material of the sofa. They must be lodged in the wall in the back. I'm certainly not going to be digging through these brain parts. Let the crime lab people do that."

Hawk was on the phone while Nora spoke to Janeel. After he clicked off, he said, "I called Chet Watkins from the crime lab to try to come over personally. He's the best they got, and I believe this case will require the best, not the weekend crew. Said he'll do it. Could use the overtime. I'll ask Hopkins to tape this room off. We don't want anyone traipsing around."

Nora asked Janeel, "Do we know who the victims are? It's not like they have IDs in their pockets." She chuckled. "I assume the guy is attorney Baxter Visser. At least that's what all these diplomas on the wall say."

"It is. I recognize him from the time I've been here before," Hawk said, his voice a little more normal. "But I have no idea who the woman is."

Janeel said, "According to the women from the janitorial service, they believe that they are both lawyers with this firm."

Nora said, "We're through here, don't you think? Mortimer, are you ready to go? Did you see enough?"

"Oh, my, I saw more than I wanted to see. I decided not to tell Josephine about it. She would not approve of such behavior." Nora and Janeel gave each other a glance and shared an amused smile. Hawk still did not feel like smiling.

Looking at the Medical Examiner, Nora said, "Okay, Janeel, we've seen what we needed to see for now. The bodies are yours as soon as the crime lab takes photos."

"I hope they're here soon. I really need to get back. Oh, I hear the crime lab people coming in now."

"Okay, then Janeel," Nora said, her voice missing the usual ring. "We'll wait for your report. Thanks."

"Are you folks all right? Something's going on with the two of you. You're not sounding like your normal selves. What's up?"

"We're just fine, thanks Janeel," Hawk said.

The detectives left the crime scene and entered the conference room, where the two women waited patiently.

CHAPTER 4

LUPE GUTIERREZ and Dominga Lucero took deep breaths when the three detectives entered the room. They did not know what to expect. They have already waited almost an hour, a time that they would probably not get paid for. They needed to finish cleaning the office building and move on to other jobs.

Mostly, they feared what might happen to Lupe. She was undocumented, and would this bizarre incident bring her down? Would she be arrested and placed in detention at the Aurora Immigration Detention Center, as was her cousin? She sat waiting, praying that they would let her slide since they were city cops and not ICE. *I should've run away after I saw the bloody bodies,* she thought. *Since Dominga was a citizen, she should've handled it herself and not even mentioned that I was there.* But she wanted to do the right thing and wait for the police as instructed by the 911 operator. *Oh, Dios Mio. Why did I wait?*

But not all might be lost. Seeing how distraught and frightened Lupe became, Dominga Lucero came up with a plan while they waited for the detectives. She was like a mother to Lupe and took her under her wing, becoming very protective of the poor, young, hard-working Guatemalan.

"Lupe, don't worry, try to remain calm. Everything will be all right. I'll just tell them that you saw nothing. I'll tell them that I was the first to enter that room, and when you tried to come in, I wouldn't let you because of the horrible scene. I'll tell them that I took you by the arm and led you out to the porch. Remember, it was me who called the police."

With that plan, Lupe calmed down a bit as she furtively watched the detectives enter. The younger man and woman both looked pleasant enough, but the tall, lanky man looked stern and a little scary. *If anyone puts me away, it would be him.* For some reason, his eyes bored into hers. *He knows something about me. Oh God!* No matter how she tried to act cool, her small, callous hands trembled. The younger detectives sat down across from them at the highly polished mahogany table, the one that she polished just last week. The tall, odd-looking one remained standing and fixed his eyes on her. She began to feel nauseous.

She wiped sweat from her forehead as the handsome detective smiled at her and began to speak, "Thank you so much for your patience and waiting for us. We know you have a lot of work to do, and we apologize for the delay. Sometimes, civic duty is not easy to bear. Now, ladies, could we start by you showing us your identification for our report?"

"I'll be glad to, officer," Dominga said, "Here's my license. But my co-worker here didn't even go into the room. I went in first and was so horrified that when Lupe was about to enter, I pulled her away. She didn't see anything. You don't need her information, do you?"

Mortimer cleared his throat, "Yes, we certainly do. We need to see both IDs."

Nora and Hawk saw the frightened eyes of the young woman. They immediately surmised why her friend protected her.

Gently, Hawk asked the girl, "Just tell us your name, date of birth and your address. We need that simply because you were in the building." She complied in a soft, shaky voice. Hawk continued, "Did you go into that office where the bodies were found?"

Lupe nervously answered in a heavy Spanish accent, "No, no, I didn't…no. I don't know what was in there except for what Dominga told me."

"Oh," Nora then asked. "What did she tell you exactly?"

"That there is something really bad in there. There were two dead people covered with blood. Just like she said, she pulled me away, and I thank her for it." Her hands were quivering as she wiped more sweat off her forehead. It became obvious to Nora that Lupe did see the bodies, and she was sure that Hawk and Holliday felt the same way. Even Janeel said that the women saw the bodies. But there was not much to gain from what she saw. She felt sorry for her and took onto herself not to push the issue with her identification.

"Detective Holliday, since she didn't witness anything, I don't believe we need her ID. What do you think?"

"That's not procedure. The young woman doesn't have an ID. It's obvious. So, you and Clint decide if her name and address are enough."

"That's fine with me," Hawk said. "Now, Mrs. Lucero," he was looking at her Colorado driver's license, "Which company employes you?"

"It's the Bandera Janitorial Service. I've been with them one-hundred years." She chuckled.

Hawk and Nora chuckled back, "We don't believe that for a minute," Nora said. "You're too young for that."

"Thanks," Lucero smiled. "It's been twenty-three years next month."

"Good for you," Nora said. "How long have you been cleaning this law office?"

"I think my boss signed a five-year contract with Mr. Visser. That should be up in about four months."

"Oh, you knew the attorney, Visser?" Hawk took over the questioning, ignoring eye contact with Nora.

"Yes, sometimes he worked on Saturdays, and we had to clean around him. He was not a very pleasant man."

"Oh, why do you say that?"

"He was very rude to us. We had a job to do, but he yelled at us for bothering him while he worked. Told us to hustle. But then, if he saw something that wasn't up to his standard, he complained that we were sloppy. We always hated it when he was in. And it affected our work because of the stress we felt. He was very arrogant and didn't care about us poor working folks."

Hawk looked at Lupe, and when their eyes met, Lupe stopped breathing for a moment. "Lupe, how was your relationship with Mr. Visser?"

"Um…I didn't talk to him at all. Ah…I agree that he was never pleasant, and I heard him shout a lot about this or that. It was Dominga that always dealt with him when he was in."

Nora took over now, "Mrs. Lucero, did you recognize the bodies."

"Yes. Well, Mr. Visser, for sure. But I think that the woman was a lawyer here also. I recognize her from a photo in one of the offices upstairs. It's in a newspaper article that is framed and hanging on the wall. She helped in a charity or somethin'."

"Can you show us the office?"

"Sure. Does Lupe have to go?"

Nora looked at Lupe. "I suppose not, but we may need to talk to you again, although it's doubtful."

Lupe's heart stopped. She took a deep breath and softly muttered, "I don't mind." She prayed to the Virgin Mary that they would leave her alone.

Suddenly, Mortimer spoke up. "I do have a question for you. Has your friend here gotten into an intense argument with any attorney in the building?" Nora did not know where he was going with that question.

"No, Dominga is always very pleasant, even though some people are rude to her."

"In that case, Mrs. Lucero, how often did you have a heated argument with attorney Visser?"

"No, never. I never talked back to him."

"But you admitted that you didn't like him."

"Not especially, no."

Based on experience with Mortimer Holliday, Hawk knew that he accused suspects of the crime out of the blue without any evidence to substantiate his accusations. Mortimer's theory was that if you catch people off guard, sometimes, they betray their guilt. But he and Nora disapproved of his methods. It only ruined an opportunity for further questioning. So, Hawk interrupted Mortimer by saying, "I think these ladies need to get back to work. They've been very patient with us." Mortimer became upset that he was cut off.

"Yes," Nora said, "But I do have a question for you ladies. "What door did you come in this morning?"

Mrs. Lucero said, "The back door."

"Was it locked?"

"No. We thought that was strange," Dominga said. "We saw Mr. Visser's car in the lot and figured he was in. But he never leaves the door unlocked when he's alone. The alarm was turned off, but we didn't think anything of it since we thought he was in."

"How about the front door? Was it locked?"

"Yes, I had to unlock it to get to the front porch for fresh air."

"Thank you. If you just show us the female victim's office upstairs, you can return to work. Just don't clean Visser's office or the one you'll show us."

Dominga led them to the office belonging to Elizabeth Durand. The detectives entered it, and Dominga went back downstairs to join

Lupe. A few minutes later, they could hear the vacuum. After spending a few minutes in the office, Hawk said, "when we come back on Monday to interview the staff, we need to search the place thoroughly."

"Why's that?" Mortimer asked.

Hawk was surprised by the question. To him, it was obvious that the place needed to be carefully searched. "There may be something here that leads to the killer. Perhaps there's something helpful on the computer."

"I doubt if they'll let you look at the computers," Nora said in a cold voice. "There's probably a lot of privileged client information on it."

"Yeah." Hawk hated to say it, "You're right. We may have to get a court order if need be. Anyway, let's look around and get an idea of where the killer came from. The cleaning woman said the front door was locked, but the back one was not. Just to make sure, let's see if we can spot any sign of a break-in."

Nora and Mortimer stepped outside and carefully walked around the perimeter while Hawk glanced into the offices. He took a quick look in the closet holding the upstairs furnace. Then he walked down and checked all the rooms. He found the door to the basement and descended the rickety steps.

There, he saw a dusty old blue metal chest by the furnace, like the one he took to college for storage years ago. Looking closer, he noticed a clean spot the size of someone's rear that must have wiped the dust off. He whipped out his camera and took several pictures of the spot from different angles. *Someone recently sat on this chest. Maybe the killer was waiting for everyone other than the dead couple to leave.*

As he ascended to the first floor and began heading toward the foyer, he took a quick glance at what he assumed to be desks used by secretaries. Hearing the deep voice of Chet Watkins, he hurried to meet up with him. The cleaners were just beginning to go upstairs, dragging a vacuum cleaner and bucket of cleaning supplies. As he approached the entrance, he spotted Watkins standing beside Nora and Mortimer. Corporal Hopkins was standing by the front door, talking to one of Chet's assistants. He and the woman were laughing away, the woman throwing her blonde head back as though Hopkins told her the funniest story she had ever heard.

"Hello, Chet," Hawk said, shaking his hand. "Glad you're here. I hope you'll find something of value for us. That office there," pointing to the door at the end of the hallway, "is where the crime scene occurred. The bodies are gone, though, picked up by Janeel's assistants. When you're through there, would you do the furnace room in the basement? Particularly the old chest down there and around it. Maybe there's a hair or something. I think the killer might've hidden there and waited for the opportunity to come up and kill the victims. There is a prominent impression of a butt in the dust. I'd like some measurements of it, just in case."

"Really!" Nora said. "This I gotta see you walking around with a tape measure in your hand measuring asses." She laughed as did everyone else."

Hawk smiled back, "Ha, ha."

Mortimer said, "Oh, I don't think that's funny. I'd hate to do that job."

The laughter became contagious as both Nora and Mortimer went down to check the butt outline for themselves.

The crime lab crew went to work, and Hawk waited for his partners to return. As he stood there, he reenacted in his mind how the crime could have occurred, only to be interrupted by Nora.

Nora said, "You're right. It looked like someone had been sitting there. Anyway, I'm ready to leave. Who's going to notify the families?"

"I suppose that we must do it…damn! I hate that."

"Yeah, I know…it's tough. But as far as I'm concerned, the spouses should be considered prime suspects considering the victims were killed while screwing." She glanced at Mortimer, who was standing off to the side with his eyes closed.

"Maybe you're right, Mortimer. Maybe the killer was trying to send a message."

Mortimer's eyes flew open, and he asked, "What would that message be, Nora?"

"Maybe it wasn't so much a message but a cruel act of revenge and satisfaction for killing them while they were in that position. Perhaps he or she tried to time it exactly right."

Hawk listened to Nora but did not comment. Looking at him, she asked, "Well, what do you think, or would you still rather not talk to me?"

"What do you mean? I've said plenty to you."

"Yeah, barely."

"Okay, I'll tell you this." Taking a deep breath and exhaling hard, he said in a level voice, "What you said makes sense, and we need to pursue that angle with the spouses. So, we might as well do that right away if we're sure of their identities. It wouldn't be cool to upset the wrong spouse."

Nora snorted, "Yeah, that'll be terrible, but we did find Visser's ID in his pants pocket. And the purse in Durand's office had her license with a photo. Don't you think that's enough?" Her voice hardened.

"All right, then, let's track them down."

CHAPTER 5

BASED ON the victims' addresses as listed in their driver's licenses, the three detectives headed first to Durand's house and afterward would see Mrs. Visser, a job they did not look forward to. Once Hawk's Jeep was in motion, Nora updated Lieutenant Perez as to where they were now proceeding.

"How is the party going?" Nora asked Perez.

"It's winding down, and several people have left, including Captain MacGregor and her husband. We'll be leaving soon ourselves, but your date is still here. Looks bored."

"I'll give him a call as soon as we hang up."

She called Seth and told him to go home because they must follow up with the families of the victims. "Don't worry, I'll make it home on my own."

"Just give me a call when you're through, and I'll pick you up, no problem. We can go out to dinner or something."

"Okay, I might take you up on that, Seth. I'll let you know. Thanks a bunch...sorry about how our date has gone."

After Nora finished with her calls, she and Hawk sat mulishly silent. Neither felt like chit-chatting, especially not Hawk, who became very irritated with Nora's conversation with Seth. Nor did the two even discuss the case as they normally would have done. Both still sighed, deeply and often, indicating their misery. Mortimer also sat quietly, trying to figure out why they were so upset. Was it the murder scene they had just left behind, or was it something personal between them?

Feeling the tension, Mortimer decided to find out. Never one to exhibit much tact, and with the habit of blurting out whatever was on his mind, Mortimer broke the silence. "Clint, are you upset that Nora brought someone else as a date to the BBQ?" He did not wait for his answer, although he heard Hawk exhale forcibly and mumble something that was inaudible.

Instead, he twisted his neck and glanced at Nora. "I know the problem between the two of you and why you and Clint are not discussing the murders as we should be right now. Nora, what you did was a shocking surprise to everyone." Nora's eyes went wide, but she did not say a word. "So, Nora, why are you so quiet? You are the one who came with that man. By the way, I didn't like him because I thought you should've been with Clint. It baffled me to no end. I thought that you and Clint were sweet on each other, or at least you acted that way. So why did you do it? I need to know so that I can tell Josephine all about it. This is hard to explain."

Nora's heart beat faster as her anger rose. *That's none of his damn business, and especially not that of his weird fiancé.* She wanted to lash out at Mortimer but took some deep breaths to calm herself. She felt bad for the awkward man with bizarre habits and did not want to chastise him. Forcing herself to answer in a calm voice, she said, "Mortimer, please, this is between Clint and me. We have a different view of what we want out of life."

"Like what?"

Nora again took a deep breath, exhaling loudly. *Mind your own freaking business, you fool.* She did not say anything to him for a while, then decided that she might tell him exactly why, using this opportunity to remind Hawk why she came with Seth.

"All right, you want to know, I'll lay it out for you. I told Clint that I wanted a more serious relationship. After all, I'll be in my mid-thirties soon enough. We are good for each other; unfortunately, Clint has a big problem with commitment." Hawk grunted. "Those were his own words, not mine. He doesn't think he's ready to get serious. He likes the fact that so many women seem to fall all over him. They flirt with him, and it boosts his ego. Besides, a family would interfere with his fun. Just look at this, Mortimer. As I sit in the back of his Jeep, I see toys behind me. There're two tennis rackets and a set of golf clubs. And don't forget the ski rack above us and the bike rack behind us. He just wants to play. But he's getting older also and needs to start thinking of where he wants to be when he's old."

Hawk snorted but remained silent. *Don't say a word. Not a damn word. Let her vent,* he told himself.

Glaring at the back of Clint's head as he drove, Nora was disappointed that he did not show any reaction, at least what she'd be able to see from the back seat. *Yeah, just keep quiet, you coward. You know I'm right. I must realize that it may be all over between us, and I must still try to work together as your police partner.* Deep in thought, she idly glanced out of the side window, not paying any particular attention to what she saw. *Or maybe I need to show some patience, and Clint will come around.*

Turning her eyes toward Mortimer, she hoped that he would make a comment to bolster her perspective. But he just looked clueless, as he often does. Then, the vehicle hit a pothole in the road, and Mortimer's head, resting on a long, thin neck, struck the headliner of the Jeep. His annoyed expression made her smile as he rubbed his butch-cut graying hair, then looked up at the spot he hit. She liked Mortimer. He was a good soul, just a little eccentric, perhaps. But at times, his antics made her laugh, and sometimes, he made her mad.

Today, he wore a colorful light-green Hawaiian shirt with pink flamingoes scattered about. The shirt looked a little tattered at the collar. Old, just like most of the clothes that Josephine bought for him in either consignment shops or thrift stores. Based on how he described it, it appeared his fiancé would not let him spend any money. And who knows what he'll wear tomorrow or Monday?

After thinking about what Nora said, Mortimer finally commented, "Nora, perhaps you're rushing things a little. Give him some time to decide." Turning his head toward Hawk, he asked, "Isn't that right, Clint?"

"Mortimer, please. I don't feel like discussing any of this. Let's get off the subject." Disappointed, Nora hoped that Hawk would have said something encouraging.

Mortimer continued, "Nora, I still don't like Seth Morgan, and you and Clint need to work it out. But I would like to discuss the murders. The bodies were found in the act of copulation, so I think it was a crime of passion. One of the spouses either he or she, shot them in such a way as to make a strong point. What do you think about that theory, Clint?"

Hawk cleared his throat, "Yes, that's certainly a possibility, maybe even a probability. Let's see how the spouses react to the news."

"They should be frantic by now since they most likely hadn't heard from them since yesterday."

"I would certainly imagine," Hawk said. "Unless, of course, one of them already knows what happened because he or she was the killer."

CHAPTER 6

THE DURAND house was one of the "cookie cutter" type houses in a quiet suburban neighborhood of Parker, Colorado. Even though there was a variation of house styles, they all seemed to be similar. The houses on the block were neat and orderly. The lawns were impeccably cared for, and the homes were painted in various shades of earth-tone colors.

It was a long drive from downtown Denver to Parker, taking at least forty minutes. A miserable ride for both Nora and Hawk. Nora wanted to explain why she invited Seth to the BBQ and have a meaningful discussion with Hawk. Hawk was leaning toward telling Nora that he did not want to lose her and explaining that he might even get counseling for his abnormal fear of commitment. The thought of living with the same person for the rest of his life continued to frighten him. One thing that held him back was his frequent fantasies of Marcie Turner, whom he first met the day he entered the Homicide Unit. He fell for her then, and she for him, but once again, he was unable to commit himself to a lasting relationship. She begged him to follow her to California, and on occasion, he thought that he should have. The thoughts of Marcie made him question if Nora was really the one for him.

But both remained silent, occasionally letting out an involuntary sigh. If it had not been for Mortimer in the car, perhaps they would have had a real conversation about where they go from here, both in their personal and professional lives. Each knew if they did not come to some understanding, one of them would have to transfer to another District. Nora would most likely go back to Internal Affairs, which she left to be able to work with Hawk.

They walked past the three-car garage and turned the corner toward the attractive inlaid wooden door with stained glass panels on each side. The stenciled walkway was lined with a variety of mum plants. Nora pressed the doorbell, and instead of the usual ring, they heard Beethoven's Fifth Symphony. No one came to the door, so she pushed the button again. As before, the Fifth Symphony sounded. Finally, the door was jerked open by a bare-footed, wide-shouldered, muscular man dressed in khaki cargo-style shorts. His white T-shirt was emblazoned with the name "Duros Bar and Grill."

In a harsh, nasal voice, the unshaven man with ruffled hair barked, "What do you want? Can't you see the sign, 'No Solicitors'? Now scram!"

He began closing the door when Hawk jammed his Brooks running shoe between the door and the jamb. In an angry motion, the man swung the door wide open. With slitted eyes, face reddened, the pecs on his chest flexed as he made a move toward Hawk. Hawk had his badge in his hand and shoved it in his face. The man backed off.

"Now, may we start over," Hawk said. "You didn't give us a chance to explain who we are and why we're here. I'm Detective Clint Hawk." He pointed toward Nora and then Mortimer and introduced them as well.

"Okay. So, what do you want?"

"Are you Mr. Norman Durand?" Immediately not liking the man, Nora asked with a cold edge to her voice.

"Yeah, so?"

"May we come in?" Nora asked.

"No! What's this about?"

"All right, then, Mr. Durand, we'll talk out here on the porch. We have some bad news about your wife."

Apprising Nora with a cautious gaze, Durand showed little concern. He asked, "What about her? Was she in an accident or somethin'?"

The man irritated Mortimer. He did not like his attitude and didn't care how he broke the news. "Yes, it was something, all right. Your wife was murdered."

Durand, who was about as tall as Mortimer, looked him in the eyes. "I sure hope you're kidding. I just saw her eating breakfast in the morning, or was it yesterday morning?"

Nora said, "Mr. Durand, this is not something we should be discussing out on the porch. We better come in."

"You're serious. Someone killed her?"

"Yes, we're so sorry for your loss."

With a tightened jaw, Durand looked away from their peering eyes. He threw his large head back as far as he could, drew in a deep breath, and closed his eyes. After remaining silent for at least a minute, he looked at Nora and said, "Okay, come in."

The house was a mess. An assortment of shoes, both male and female, were strewn about the hardwood floor in the entryway. A windbreaker jacket lay on the first step of the light-brown carpeted staircase leading upstairs. The dining table was stacked with piles of papers, a large calculator sitting on one of the stacks.

They walked down the hall into an open family room-kitchen combination. The brown and taupe granite countertop was cluttered with newspapers, unopened letters, and groceries that had yet to be put away. The place stunk with garbage or something else unpleasant. Suddenly, a large gray and white cat scurried between Hawk and

Mortimer toward the kitchen area, startling both men. Mortimer sucked in a deep breath as he jumped.

"Oh, don't mind old Sylvester. He doesn't like people much, and I guess you frightened him." Nora now knew what the stink was. *They hadn't cleaned out the kitty litter in days.*

Durand shoved a magazine and some blankets from the white leather couch onto the floor and told them to sit. Hawk and Nora noticed the cat's hair but sat down anyway while Mortimer, as usual, continued to stand. Durand brushed off the hair with the side of his large, meaty hand. He then sat down across one of the two black leather chairs that were separated by a glass coffee table from the couch.

"Excuse the mess. We just don't seem to have the time to clean up. Elizabeth is always working, and so am I. Neither one of us is much interested in housework."

"No problem," said Hawk. "We've seen worse."

The three detectives studied Durand to gauge his reaction to the news of his wife's murder. They knew that everyone grieves in their own way, but if the man was overly upset, he wasn't showing it. Nora thought it was odd that he talked about the cat and the messy house but so far did not ask about the death of his wife. Hawk had the same thoughts.

The man was silent for a minute before he asked, "Well, aren't you going to tell me how my wife died? I bet it has something to do with that sleazy lawyer that she works for. Am I right?"

Nora asked, "Why do you say that?"

With a raised voice, he said, "Because they'd been screwing each other for months. That's why. Anyway, when was she murdered? Must've been this morning."

Hawk asked, "Did you see your wife last night?"

"No. I assume she finally made it home after screwing that sonafabitch."

"You assume?"

"Well, yeah! You see, I own a bar and don't come home sometimes till after it closes at 2:00 o'clock in the morning...especially on a Friday night. I got to be there most of the time. Otherwise, the staff steals me blind, giving away free drinks and helping themselves to a bottle of booze to take home. You wouldn't believe how much meat is stolen out of the freezer every year."

"Didn't you notice whether your wife was home last night? Nora asked.

"No. Lately, we haven't been getting along. I let her sleep in the master bedroom, and I sleep in one of the other bedrooms. She likes it that way...or at least she liked it that way." The expression on his face turned to one of sadness as he bit his lower lip.

"Why, had you not gotten along?" Mortimer asked.

The man looked incredulously at the detective. "Man, why do you think? Her screwing around, that's why. You wouldn't sleep with your wife or girlfriend if you knew that's what she's doing, would you?"

"Oh." Mortimer said, "Josephine wouldn't do that. I don't need to worry. But how do you know she was...having an affair with the lawyer?"

"Because I just knew it. She had really changed a few months after she started working at the law firm. She kept talking about how smart and good-looking her boss was, and then she didn't mention him at all. That raised my suspicions. Then she lost interest in sex with me. Started to treat me like a nobody. We fought all the time, and I accused her of screwing her boss." He looked at the three detectives, taking a deep breath. "And do you know what? She admitted that they were having an affair, and there was nothing I could do about it. I felt like slapping her around, but I reined in my temper."

Nora asked, "And what did you tell her then...anything?"

"I told her that I wanted out. I want a divorce, and then she can go screw herself for all I cared."

"What was her response?"

"She laughed. The bitch laughed and said that she'll be happy to get the divorce and that her boss will make sure that she'll wind up with this house and my business, and I'll be out on my ass in the street." Anger sparked in his squinting black eyes while his face reddened. They could see him working his way up to rage. He lifted his head again and took some deep breaths before he spoke. His voice was soft when he said, "You know, I'm the one that paid her way through law school. If it hadn't been for me, she would still be trying to figure out what she wanted to do with her life. Her parents paid for a college degree in political science, but she couldn't find a job after college."

He looked directly at Nora, "Elizabeth was just used to a free ride on everything and getting what she wanted. I often wondered what kind of lawyer she'd make. I think the only way she kept her job was by screwing her boss."

"Then her being murdered doesn't upset you too much?" Hawk asked.

He thought for a moment. "Well, I hate to see her dead, but…" His voice broke down, and for the first time, they noticed his eyes became misty. Remaining silent, he sat motionless as though in a trance, staring past them at a print of the Teton Mountains of Wyoming. *Is that for real?* Nora thought.

A moment later, in a sad voice, he asked, "Will you tell me now how she died?"

Nora said, "She and Visser were shot to death last night in Visser's office."

"Last night, was it? They were on the couch together, weren't they?"

"Why do you assume that?"

"Because that's what they do…or did, I guess, every Friday."

Hawk asked, "How do you know?"

"Because while we were yelling at each other, she told me and laughed about it. So, am I right? They were screwing when they were shot?"

"You're right," Hawk said. "Didn't that make you mad as hell?"

"Yeah. Mad as hell, all right. I thought hard about driving downtown and beating the crap out of both. But I've taken anger management classes, and they taught me some techniques that seem to help me. Anyway, I thought that I'd lose everything if I did a stupid thing like that, including my liquor license and my livelihood. Besides, I realized that our days of marriage were pretty much over, so I let her do what she wanted to. Like a fool, I thought that once she matures and gets over her affair with the lawyer, she'll come to her senses and crawl back to me like she's done once after doing it with someone in law school." He suddenly glanced at his watch. "Listen, I don't have any more time to give you. I've got to get to the bar. Saturdays are busy."

"One more thing, Mr. Durand," Hawk asked, "Do you own any guns?"

He looked hard at Hawk. "You think that I shot them? You're crazy. I wouldn't have done anything like that…because, as I told you, I'm at the point that I really don't care that much what she does. Whatever love we had, if any, between us is long gone."

"But that doesn't answer my question about the guns."

"Hell yeah, I have a couple. I've got a nine-millimeter and a twenty-two that I use for target practice. And I've got a forty-five at the bar."

"What time did you go to your business yesterday?"

"Look, I know you're thinkin' that I killed Elizabeth and that lawyer, but I didn't do it. I was at the bar from 4 o'clock to closing. I came home at about 2:30 and collapsed into my bed. I had no idea that Elizabeth wasn't home."

Nora said, "Thank you, Mr. Durand. If we have anything else, we'll get back to you."

"Oh, I'm sure you will."

CHAPTER 7

THE DAY caught up with Ricci and Hawk. At the BBQ, they each consumed a bottle of Warka Polish beer without much food to go along with it. After Hawk saw Nora enter with Seth, he lost his appetite and only ate one-half of a brat sandwich. Nora spent her time socializing and introducing Seth to her coworkers and didn't bother to eat anything before Perez sent them out to investigate the homicides.

With an empty stomach, and no matter what they say about being used to seeing death, the scene with the bodies of Visser and Durand had affected them emotionally. Their brains were tired. Unfortunately, it was not over yet. They still had to see Angie Visser, the victim's wife, to relay to her the awful news and to study her reaction. The house was half an hour away, and they hoped that the widow would be home.

Only Mortimer seemed pumped. He did not drink alcohol, only water, and managed to polish off three bratwurst sandwiches. He called Josephine, explaining what they were doing, and told her he'd be late for dinner. After which, he hopefully asked Nora and Clint, "Maybe we can stop first and grab a hamburger or two."

Hawk rolled his eyes as this request by Mortimer had become his standard operating procedure. He was always hungry and looked for ways to eat without Josephine knowing. It wouldn't have been so bad if he actually paid for his meals, but somehow, he managed to get Hawk or Nora to foot the bill. Most of the time, they had no problem with that because they felt sorry for him. His hunger stemmed from the fact that Josephine was a vegan, and Mortimer always complained about her cooking or the lack of it.

Nora said, "Sorry, Mortimer, it's been a long day, and I want to get it over with. As soon as we inform the poor Mrs. Visser that her husband died, I want to head home."

"Oh, I guess that's okay. How about you, Clint? You want to get some dinner afterward?"

"I agree with Nora. It's been a long, lousy day, and I, too, want to go home."

"Oh. Maybe next time, then. How far is it still to the Visser house?"

"We have another twenty minutes of driving, I'd say," Hawk replied. "We have to get to the Belcaro area of Denver."

"I bet that's another nice area," Mortimer said.

"Oh yeah," Nora said. "I wouldn't mind living there at all."

"But the area we were in…Parker, you called it…what's the history behind it, Nora?"

Here we go again. Every time he's in a new area for him, he wants to know its history. Well, look it up yourself, Mortimer. "Nora, please, or you, Clint, I really would like to know unless you don't know yourselves."

"All right, all right. I'll tell you what I know, and it isn't much." Nora exhaled as she ran her fingers through her thick, dark hair, thinking what to say. "To keep it short, we've traveled north on Parker Road, known as Highway 83, before turning onto E-470. If we continued further on Parker Road, we would more-or-less follow the old Cherokee Trail, which ran alongside Cherry Creek to its confluence with the Platte River. That trail was a long trail that began somewhere in Arkansas and was used for centuries by the Natives and

36

later by the white hunters and mountain men. Most traffic came, though, after gold was discovered in the San Francisco area in 1849."

"Oh. Why is it called the Cherokee Trail?"

"As far as I remember, it's because the Cherokees used it mostly from Oklahoma on their way to California to prospect for gold."

"Oh, I didn't know that the Natives looked for gold."

"Yes, I was surprised at that when I researched the trail. But the Cherokees were only a fraction of those who used the trail. The trail became one of the routes used by prospectors from all over to get to California."

"That's interesting. Clint, did you know that history?"

Hawk cleared his throat. "No, I didn't. Nora certainly knows her stuff."

"Don't flatter me, Clint, but I hope I'm giving you the right information. It's been a while since I read about it."

"But what about Parker?" Mortimer asked.

"It all began when a man by the name of Butters put up a small one-room cabin along the trail, about a mile from what is now Mainstreet. It became like a post office for travelers where they left messages for other travelers. He also had some provisions that he sold out of that cabin. This was about 1864. He was a squatter on the land, and a few years later, he exchanged his cabin for some livestock, and the new buyers moved the cabin to Twenty Mile Road. A monument and a rebuilt structure still remain today located on the Twenty Mile Road."

"Twenty Mile Road, huh ? That's an unusual name."

"Well, it was exactly twenty miles from Denver. The people who moved Butter's cabin later enlarged it and put up a hotel for the travelers. Later, it was sold to James Parker, who began developing the area west of Highway 83. His brother, George Parker, put up several structures east of the highway."

Nora was suddenly tired of talking. "Mortimer, just look all this stuff up. To me, it's like a hobby to see how towns and cities grew from vacant land, and you might enjoy it also."

"Oh, that's very interesting. You're right, and I should start doing something like that. I'm sure that Josephine wouldn't mind if I do it from home, and it doesn't cost anything."

Hawk shook his head in disbelief. "Mortimer, you need to talk to her and explain how you feel about things before you actually get hitched."

"Oh, that won't work. As soon as I tell her what I'd like, she raises her voice and tells me that it isn't good for me."

That statement infuriated Nora. She really would love to meet that woman and give her a piece of her mind. Of course, she would not do that. She had hoped that at Orlinski's BBQ she could finally meet her. But Josephine didn't come because, as Mortimer had warned them, she doesn't like to be out with people.

"You have a problem, my friend," Hawk said. "Better work it out before it's too late."

"Oh, I believe that Josephine is just trying to keep me healthy and safe."

Miffed by that naïve statement, Nora wanted to scream at the man to wake up and wise up. She wanted so badly to lay it on the line that he was the biggest fool that she had ever seen when it came to Josephine. Wise, she kept her mouth shut and decided that it really was not her business to interfere.

"Come on, guys, change the subject. What did y'all think of the husband?"

Nora laughed for the first time that afternoon. "Y'all! Wow, Clint, your Texas is showing."

Hawk was happy to respond with a laugh. "Yeah, occasionally, it comes through. I'd love to be back in Tyler, Texas, with my folks right now. My dad made the best ribs, and as a kid, I never appreciated it until I tasted some of the others. I miss my folks and the ribs. I really should visit."

"I know what you mean," Nora said. "My mom makes the best chicken marsala I ever tasted."

"I'd love to try it."

Nora laughed, "If only you'd be that lucky, bud."

"Well, maybe someday you could set it up for us. I'd be pleased to drive down to Pueblo."

Nora remained silent, but Hawk's comments pleased her. She smiled with inner satisfaction.

After a short trip on E-470, Hawk exited onto I-25. Luckily, traffic was light, and they proceeded smoothly. In another fifteen minutes, he exited onto Colorado Boulevard. There, the heavy Saturday traffic slowed to a crawl. As it opened a bit, Hawk quickly reached Exposition Avenue, where he turned west into the Belcaro area. After a few blocks, Visser's home came into view.

The place was a mid-century ranch home with a double-wide garage. The houses in the block were all set back quite far from the street, leaving huge front yards—most of them set in an acre of green Kentucky grass. The Vissers divided their front yard with luscious grass and junipers closest to the house. Xeriscaping prevailed in the other half with gray river rock, large black lava boulders, and a few non-thirsty bushes to add a spot of color to the rocks.

Hawk parked the Jeep on the long and wide cement driveway. A Ring doorbell was prominently displayed to the side of the walnut-stained double doors, indicating that the occupants of the house could be aware of their presence. Nora pressed the button just to make sure. They heard the bell and then a woman's voice shouting, "Hang on, I'll be there in a sec."

CHAPTER 8

THE DOOR was pulled open by a slender, somewhat attractive, physically fit woman in her early forties, dressed in a white tennis outfit. She seemed anxious to see them after spotting their badges attached to the belts. Angie Visser exclaimed, "My god, that was fast. I just called the police station. I believe something awful happened to my husband."

Before Nora or Hawk had a chance to explain the purpose of their visit, the woman stepped out onto the porch to join them as the three detectives stepped back. In a frantic, raised voice, speaking rapidly, her arms flaying and on the verge of hysteria, she declared that she had been trying to reach her husband since breakfast.

"I called him again before I left to play in a tournament at the Country Club this morning. I kept calling his office number and his cell number a thousand times and then again after my last tennis match. Right before coming home, I ran by the office and tried to get in to see if he was there. His Range Rover was parked in the back, as was another car, so I assumed that he was busy working, and I didn't want to disturb him. So, I left." She pulled in a couple of breaths, her chest heaving, then continued, still not giving the detectives a chance to ask any questions. "After I came home, I tried to call him again a couple more times, but after no response from him, I thought that I better call you folks to do a check since he'd been threatened so many times." She hesitated for a moment, "Don't tell me you checked on him already? Then why didn't he call me?"

"Mrs. Visser, we do need to talk to you, but not on this porch," Hawk said. "May we come in?"

With a puzzled look on her flushed face, she asked, "You're not here about my call for a welfare check, are you?"

Suddenly, deep creases appeared on her forehead over her upturned nose. Her jaw tightened, and she sucked in a deep breath through her mouth as she invited the detectives inside. With obviously heavy breathing, she led them into the good-sized living room with its eight-foot ceiling and a large picture window looking out toward the street—typical for homes of that era. Two sofas sat across from each other, centered by a flagstone-lined fireplace. While they walked, Hawk glanced at her round rear, having a professional excuse that he wanted to see if it could match the imprint in the dust on the chest in the law office basement. He thought that it might. He did the same, though not as long of a view, with Norman Durand's bony rear. *This is crazy. Unless I get an exact measurement, my eyeballing makes no sense.*

"Please sit," Angie said, her voice brittle. "I'm afraid I can sense why you're here." She let out a deep breath as she looked directly at Nora. "He's dead, isn't he?"

"We're so sorry for your loss. He died last night."

"Oh God! My sweat, Jesus…how did he die?"

"He was murdered, Mrs. Visser."

"Oh God, my God." She looked at Hawk with what he thought were accusatory eyes as though he had something to do with it. "Any idea as to who did it?" A pool of moisture welled up over her eyes, and a tear drifted down her dimpled cheek on her round face.

Hawk said, "Mrs. Visser, we have no clue at this time as to who is responsible. But we won't rest until we find out who did it."

She lowered her head, her eyes closed. She appeared numb as she sat unmoving for a couple of minutes. Then once she opened her eyes looking at Nora, she mumbled, "It must be one of the vengeful husbands—a respondent in a divorce case, not happy with the judge's decision. A lot of those men blame everyone else but themselves, especially the lawyer." Then, taking a hard look at both Hawk and the standing Mortimer, she said with disgust, "My husband was always getting threats from disgruntled men. It was a constant worry that some idiot would harm him or our children." All remained silent for a few minutes again while the woman sniffled, trying to hold back tears.

Hawk asked, his voice compassionate and understanding, "We know that losing your spouse is dreadful and exceedingly difficult. It feels like the end of the world to you, I'm sure. We realize that you need some time alone with your family, but would you be up to answering a few questions that may help us find the killer as soon as possible?"

She stared at her bare feet for a few minutes. Looking up, she said, "You're right. I do feel as though my world is gone. Oh God! What am I supposed to tell the kids? What am I going to say to them?" Her voice trailed off at the end to a whisper. At the mention of her children, a steady rivulet of tears cascaded down her suntanned cheeks. Snot began to run from her nose. Wiping it off with her hand, she started to get up, "I need to get a tissue. I'm sorry."

Nora said, "Here, let me get you one out of my bag." She quickly reached into her purse, pulled out a small packet of tissues and handed it to Angie Visser. "How many children do you have?"

Sniffling and wiping her nose, she thanked Nora. After a long pause, she took a couple of deep breaths and said, "I have three, two girls and a boy, ages fifteen to eighteen. They all had sleepovers with their friends last night and haven't come home yet. Oh God! I need to notify their grandparents as well. They'll be devastated...." She looked at Hawk, "Okay, if you need to ask me a few questions, go ahead, but please just a few. I'm not thinking straight right now." She again paused, lifted her head with her eyes shut, and cradled the side of her face with her right hand.

Seeming to be in a daze, she said softly, "You catching the killer will do us no good. Nothing will help. Nothing at all. She stared down at her feet again. "I told him to stop taking divorces and switch to another specialty, but he wouldn't have it. I think that he got a kick out of dealing with people's personal and intimate lives."

From a stooped position, she suddenly straightened herself up. "How did he die and when? Was he shot?"

Hawk and Nora exchanged glances. They knew it would further devastate her if they described the details of the murder scene, and they wanted to obtain more information from her before she lost it. Besides, the information about how the bodies were found needed to be withheld for use in interviews of suspects. Only the killer should know the coital position of the victims. But they had to inform the wife that her husband's associate was also murdered in the office.

Nora asked, "When was the last time you communicated with your husband?"

"He called me about five o'clock yesterday to tell me that he's swamped and needs peace and quiet to work on preparing for trial. That he'll be home late and not to wait up for him."

"And you haven't heard from him since then?"

"Yes, I just told you how I tried to call him." She glanced at the three detectives with sad eyes. "I've been going through hell since then."

From behind the sofa, the standing Mortimer, who remained quiet so far, suddenly blurted out, "Your husband and his associate were shot together in his office. As a matter of fact, they were found—"

Nora interrupted Mortimer before he gave away information that Angie's husband was found on top of the woman. She quickly said, "Yes, Mrs. Visser, unfortunately, both your husband and Elizabeth Durand were together in your husband's office when they were shot."

"What?! Why? Why would Elizabeth be shot as well? And what was she doing in the building that late, especially on a Friday night?"

Mortimer grunted and blew out a deep breath showing his displeasure with Nora interrupting him. He let out three booming sneezes and cleared his throat by coughing a few times.

"Is he all right?" Angie asked, concerned. "Sir, would you like some water?"

"Oh, no, thank you. I'm fine. But I do have a question for you." Both Hawk and Nora held their breaths, not knowing what he would come up with. He craned his long neck downward as he glared at the distraught widow. "You knew that he was having an affair with his associate, didn't you?"

Her eyes flew open, and her hand trembled, "What?! That's impossible. My husband loved me and only me. I know it. What you're insinuating is vile. Are you trying to put me in my grave with such garbage? Please leave!" That is exactly what Hawk and Nora feared. Antagonizing the witness so early prevented them from asking further questions.

Hawk said, "Mrs. Visser, Detective Holliday was only following procedure. The question is one that needed to be discussed since it appears that they were, in fact, having an affair."

"I simply can't believe it. You're lying. If you think that I killed them because I knew of the affair, then you're full of shit. I was with my girlfriend having dinner last night and didn't come home till 9:30." She exhaled in disgust. "What time were they killed, anyway?"

"The Medical Examiner believes it was between five and seven."

"Well, I was at the Country Club until 4:00 o'clock. Then I drove straight home, took a shower, dressed, and, fighting the busy Friday traffic, met up with my friend, Goldie Hendrix, at a restaurant. I was at the restaurant at about 5:30. Goldie came a few minutes later because she said that she ran into the same awful traffic."

"Where did you go?"

"Uno Mas Taqueria Mexican restaurant. So, if you think that I could've killed my husband, I couldn't have done it. So don't blame me." Angie turned her head away from the eyes of the detectives. Then she turned back to them and said, "I loved my husband and would never, ever kill him."

Nora continued, "You didn't expect your husband to be home for dinner last night?"

"No, he usually comes home late on Fridays. Many times, he sleeps in his office when he's too busy. Besides, he called me and told me not to expect him home for supper."

Mortimer asked, "And you didn't think that that was suspicious? You didn't think that he might be having an affair behind your back? Surely, you can't be that naive?"

"Sir, I told you before. I was not aware or suspected that he was two-timing me. I still can't believe that. He loved me very much. He always paid a lot of attention to me."

"Mrs. Visser," Hawk spoke up in a soothing voice as opposed to Mortimer's gruffness. "Please understand that we're not accusing you of anything. We need your help with the reports, filling in lots of blanks. As you know, spouses need to be eliminated as suspects quickly so that we can move on. I know it's annoying, but that's something that needs to be done. Please bear with us for a few more minutes. Would that be all right?"

Angie looked at Hawk and forced a smile. "Okay. I'll answer what I can."

"What time did you arrive at the Country Club?"

"You mean yesterday?"

"Yes."

"We practiced our tennis game to prepare for today's tournament. I believe I arrived about two."

"Who was there with you?"

"Jen Steinburg, Melanie Johnson, and Adriana Pennington."

"And you were with them until you left the Club?"

"Yes. And as I said, I came straight home and then met up with Goldie."

"I've been to Uno Mas Taqueria and enjoyed it. Isn't it just a few blocks from your husband's law office?"

"Yes. Is that all, now? I'm not physically able to answer any more questions.".

Nora asked, "Just a couple more questions, please. You mentioned that you have been trying to reach your husband since breakfast. Didn't you miss him before that?"

In an angry, raspy tone, her round jaw tightened, she cocked her head to the side and said, "My faithful husband is… oh God…was a terribly busy attorney who spent a lot of time in trial. He had to constantly prepare, and there were quite a few times that he simply slept overnight on his couch in the office, as I told you before. He has a cabinet with sheets, pillows, and a blanket for just such occasions. He has a change of clothes at the office, and his private bathroom has a shower."

Nora continued, "Thank you for your answer. I assume that you didn't call him during the evening to see how he was doing?"

"Oh, I usually don't. He always became upset when I did…he said I was interrupting his concentration. Now, I am through. I can't go on. I need time to take all this in and prepare what I tell the kids. Will you leave now?"

Hawk said, "Yes, of course. Thank you so much for your time, and we are sorry for your loss. Here's my card and please call me if you need anything from us or if you think of anything that we need to know. At some point, we need to talk to you about what you remember your husband might have told you about the men who threatened him."

"I doubt whether I can help you there. He was careful not to use the names of clients or names of spouses. He would just tell me of some crazed drywaller out to get him or a rancher from Burlington that threatened him. Stuff like that."

"That's exactly what we need. Would you be so kind as to write down what you remember of him telling you about these people and e-mail me ? Or we'll be happy to come by and get the information from you verbally. Also, please include the addresses and phone numbers of your friend, Goldie, and your tennis partners. My e-mail is on the card."

With teary eyes, Angie showed them to the door and quickly shut it as they stepped out. In the Jeep, Nora asked Hawk to drop her off at her house since it was nearby. Mortimer wanted to return to Orlinski's house so that he could pick up his vintage Oldsmobile. They sat in silence for a few minutes. Hawk was about to ask Nora if she'd join him for dinner but decided against it—Mortimer was bound to ask if he could come along, and besides, he heard Nora make arrangements with Morgan. He hated the thought of those two together.

On the way to her home, Nora asked, "Well? What do you think of Mrs. Visser? Or are the two of you too tired to talk about it?"

Mortimer said, "I didn't like her. She's lying."

"Oh, why's that?"

"Nora, there's just something about her that I don't trust. She was too melodramatic and fake in her responses. I don't know why you cut me off, but I really wanted to pin her down that she knew or suspected her husband of an affair."

"That was not the time to accuse her of anything, Mortimer. For God's sake, she just heard that her husband was killed."

"Yeah, I guess you're right. Josephine also tells me that I'm not very sensitive to other people's feelings. But then, I really don't think she is either."

Nora said, "But I agree with you that Angie Visser is lying, not knowing about the affair, and maybe lying about everything else. Her alibi seems weak."

CHAPTER 9

AFTER HAWK dropped Nora off at her house, a sense of gloom gripped him. He watched Nora as she strolled up the walk. He waited until she reached the porch, and when she did, she turned around and waved. He really wanted to be with her tonight, and he felt that that was what she wanted as well. They needed to talk. As he drove away, he suddenly thought of Marcie out of the blue. *The hell with Marcie. Why is she so often in my thoughts? Nora is here, not in California, but here, and I should be so lucky that such a beautiful and sexy woman wants me. She's right. It is time for me to settle down. Wow! What am I thinking? Am I thinkin' marriage? No, no, not yet. How can I be sure that Nora is the right one for me and live with her for the rest of my life?*

After exchanging goodbyes with Mortimer, Hawk stopped on his way home and got a couple of fish tacos for himself and three beef tacos for Stella, his blonde Labrador mix. He was ready to relax and be greeted with the enthusiasm and excitement with which his dog greeted him each time he came home. She was especially wound up after spending the afternoon at Mrs. Lucero's house, the neighbor next door. Mrs. Lucero is kind enough to keep Stella while Hawk is away, sometimes for hours at a time. The only problem with that arrangement is that Hawk provided her with a large bag of organic dog food for Stella, and she tended to be overly generous and overfeed the now slightly overweight five-year-old dog.

After both he and Stella devoured the tacos and Hawk gave her a chewie, he collapsed on the sofa with Stella by his side next to the couch. As he lay there, first Nora crept into his mind and then Marcie. Both were attractive, about the same height of five-foot-seven, with amazing figures—Marcie was blonde with sparkling light blue eyes, whereas Nora was a brunette with radiant blue eyes. He first fell for Marcie, and then Nora came along with her charismatic and bubbling personality, confusing him as to whom he liked the most. He knew that if he were to get serious about Nora, he had to get Marcie out of his mind once and for all. But Marcie also wanted to get serious, and once women start pushing, he shies away, afraid of a life-altering commitment. Besides, he could not believe that just a few dates with Marcie would make her feel serious about him. So serious that she expected him to drop everything and move to California with her. He did not think that he ever led her astray or promised anything like that. It was more in her mind than in his.

Maybe I should call Marcie just to see what's up. See what vibes I get. Before he called, he went into the kitchen to get an oatmeal cookie from a Keebler bag sitting on the dark granite counter. He sat down at the island and began munching on the cookie. He found Marcie's number under "Contacts" and clicked on it. She answered on the first ring. "Oh my gosh! Clint, I was about to call you. I've been thinking about you."

"Me too. It's good to hear your voice. How's it going there in California?"

"California is California. How is it in Colorado?"

"Everything is just fine. Work keeps me busy. How are you enjoying engineering?"

"You know, I'm enjoying it more than I thought I would. My father was right after all by insisting that I work for his firm. He keeps telling me that it'll be all mine as soon as he retires in a few years."

"Sounds good. Any plans for visiting Denver soon?"

"Only if you'd invite me and tell me that you have agreed to quit the police force. You know how I feel about that. I told you before that I could never go through worrying about the danger you face every day. I'd be a nervous wreck wondering if you're in one piece."

"Oh, come on, Marcie! It's not every day that I face danger of any kind. I know that I was in some tight spots, but that happens rarely."

"Clint, I do miss you a lot, and I wish you'd reconsider. Dad had agreed to open a branch of our firm in Denver, so you don't even have to move to California. I'll manage it there." She hesitated. "I'd move to Denver in a heartbeat if you'd quit. I really see you having your own office as a psychologist since you're only maybe a year from a Ph.D. So, what do you think? Would you do it for me?"

Hawk had heard it all before, and he was getting fed up with her demands. He grabbed another cookie and slowly sauntered back into the great room with its cathedral ceiling. "Marcie, as I said, I like my job, and it really isn't that dangerous." He approached the unshaded window while listening to Marcie going on about how he was fooling himself. At the window, he grabbed the shade cord to pull down the shade when a piece of the cookie broke off, falling to the floor. Trying to beat Stella to the fallen piece, he quickly stooped to snatch it.

Suddenly, he heard a gunshot, and simultaneously, the window glass shattered as a slug whizzed over his head. It struck and shattered the large Navajo vase displayed prominently on the mantle of the fireplace along the opposite wall. Stella's incessant barking added to the confusion.

CHAPTER 10

"OH GOD! WHAT WAS THAT!?" Marcie screeched into the phone. "Clint, Clint, are you all right? Was that a gunshot? Say something. Are you all right?!"

"Marcie, I'm fine. I don't know who's shooting, but I need to go. I'll call you back later. Don't worry."

"That's exactly what I was saying and why you need to –"

Hawk cut her off and slipped into his sneakers. He clicked off, but before he did, he heard Marcie yelling that he better quit or she was not interested in a relationship. He shoved the phone into his pocket, grabbed his pistol lying on the coffee table, flew out of his townhouse and across the street to the vacant lot designated for more townhouses, Stella at his heels, barking. It was the same lot that he had a gunfight a few weeks ago with two hired killers in the previous major case. The lot took up a whole block, and as he sprinted, he spotted a hooded individual about to climb into a white Chrysler 300 parked on the parallel street behind the open lot. That person heard Stella and spotted Hawk and, with no hesitation, began firing. Luckily, the bullets landed in front of Hawk, one coming dangerously near him. Hawk dove onto the ground, and the gunshots stopped.

Still barking, Stella kept running toward the individual, paying no attention to Hawk's commands to stop. Afraid that she would be shot, he jumped to his feet and began firing his Sig Sauer. The person jumped into the car and, in a matter of seconds, took off, the tires screeching. Hawk tried to read the license plate, but the car was too far away by the time he got there. He did notice, though, that it was a red and white rental fleet plate.

Shaken to the core, Hawk petted Stella, and both returned to the townhome. The neighbors piled outside to see what was going on. He explained that he was all right and didn't know what that was about. "A drive-by shooting, no doubt, one of them said. Another neighbor, a board member of the homeowners' association, was more belligerent. "Mr. Hawk, this is the second time that someone has tried to shoot you in our peaceful neighborhood. You're endangering the neighborhood; do you realize that?"

"I'm sorry, ma'am. It's something that I certainly couldn't help. Two freak occurrences, but I'm sure it won't happen again."

"Well, it better not, or else I'll bring it up before the Board."

That hurt Hawk. He tried to be a good neighbor. *Surely, they can't make me move. This will be devastating and embarrassing.* The phone rang, and it was Marcie. "Marcie, I'm fine. We just must figure out what happened. Marcie, are you crying?"

"Well, yes, you fool. Of course. I don't want anything to happen to you. Please follow my advice or…you're not serious about Nora, are you?"

"Marcie, please. This is not the time for me to discuss anything. I need to call the patrol unit and deal with that. I have so much on my mind now that I think I'll explode. Let me sort some things out, and I'll give you a call in a couple of days."

"Hopefully, you'll get some sense and decide to change careers. I love you, Clint, and feel that you care for me the way you look at me.

I want us to be together, but the ball is in your court. Unless you get rid of that dangerous job, I don't think we'll make it."

"I understand. I'll call you as soon as my head clears a bit. Bye, Marcie." *Make it! Make it! Why is she so sure that I want to make it with her, anyway? I never promised or suggested anything like that to her—ever. She's a strange bird, that's for sure.*

He heard a siren in the near distance and assumed that one of the neighbors called the police. A moment later, a Ford Interceptor cruiser rolled up to his home. Hawk took out his badge, waiting to be questioned. After explaining what occurred, the officer took the report and called in the forensics team. He told Hawk not to disturb anything until they were done and that it would be better if he didn't enter his house until then.

Mrs. Lucero walked up to Hawk and gave him a bear hug. "I was so scared," she said in a gentle tone. "My husband works for a glass company, and he'll repair your window tomorrow."

"Thank you for that, but tomorrow is Sunday."

"That's no problem. He works every day if there's an emergency."

Even though Mrs. Lucero invited Hawk to come in and wait for the team to come, Hawk decided to sit on his porch bench instead. While he sat there, the forensics team arrived and began taking photographs, examining the shattered window and the glass bits and pieces on the floor and the couch. They searched for the bullet fragment and quickly found it embedded in a stud in the back of where the vase was positioned.

Watching them coming and going, Hawk's heart continued to pound a mile a minute as he tried to come up with a reason for the shooting. It was not a drive-by, he knew. The shooter specifically targeted him from across the street in the vacant lot. He would have been hit had it not been for stooping down to retrieve the cookie at the very precise moment that the bullet rocketed through. The last time someone tried to kill him and Nora was when a hitman was sent by one of five corrupt cops that he and Nora had put away. Their trials would be coming up soon and he and Nora would be prime witnesses against them. In addition, revenge is a great motivator, and one of them or all of them would want to get even. At that time, he and Nora barely escaped with their lives. *Oh shit! Is it possible that O'Leary or Bradford hired another hitman? Not again. Nora will be devastated.*

Oh God! Nora could be next! Man, I could be too late. I should have called her right away.

"Hello, Clint, what's up?"

"Oh, wow, I'm so happy to hear your voice."

"That's nice. What's going on?"

"I was just shot at, and you may be next. Better take precautions immediately. Stay away from any windows and have your gun nearby."

"Are you serious?" He heard the alarm in her voice.

"Nora, I'm dead serious. Be careful."

"Okay, okay, you got me all rattled now. Where did it happen, and where are you?"

"The shooter shot at me as I was standing by my window trying to draw the shade. The forensics team is at my house now. Now, please do as I say."

"All right, all right, I'll be careful. After that last incident with Finn O'Leary, my house is like Fort Knox."

"Good. Maybe O'Leary escaped again, but I don't think it was him. Whoever shot at me had a different MO."

"You think he's another hitman hired by O'Leary's cousin or maybe even Bradford? I wouldn't put it past them. Without our testimony, the DA doesn't have much of a case."

"Quite possibly…I just had an idea. Since the shooter had been here already, maybe you should stay here for the weekend until we figure out what's going on."

"You'd like that, wouldn't you? What? You need my bodyguard services?" She laughed.

"Yeah, you can put it that way. After all, you saved me several times already. You're the hero."

"Flattery will get you nowhere. I'll be fine. But thanks for making me a paranoid, nervous wreck."

"That's exactly why we need to be together. Please come by, or do you want me to join you?"

"Clint, I'm okay. I'll have to protect you another time." She giggled, but Hawk sensed nervousness in her laugh.

"Hey, I thought you had a date with Seth."

"I cancelled. Didn't feel like it." Clint smiled to himself.

CHAPTER 11

NORA WALKED into the Homicide Unit at 7:45 o'clock Monday morning. No one else was there yet. She sat at her desk, the one next to Hawk's—both situated in the back of the rectangular room—and began working on her incident report regarding the murders in the law office. A few minutes later, Stan Orlinski walked in. She thanked him for the nice party, hoping that he would not ask too many questions concerning the murders. He persisted, as he always seemed to, and she provided him with only the highlights. Afterward, Orlinski shuffled back to his desk located at the front of the room, by the door. He liked it that way because, as the Unit's gossip, he felt he would have a better handle on whatever juicy tidbits that fell his way.

Shortly before eight o'clock, Detectives Nancy Salazar and Harry Ling strolled in, laughing about something. At eight sharp, Hawk appeared. As usual, his clothes were impeccable, in the latest fashion sporting a dark gray suit, a slightly striped light-blue shirt, and a solid red tie. His light brown wing-tipped shoes and belt stood out, accenting his wardrobe. *How much does he spend on clothes,* Nora thought? *Probably more than I do. And I'm pretty bad.* She, like Hawk, took pride in dressing well. Nora usually wore high-quality ladies' business suits with colorful blouses that complimented her light-olive complexion, long dark hair, and dark-blue sapphire eyes.

They smiled at each other as Hawk approached his desk. "I see you made it out alive," Nora teased.

"I'm glad you did, too. Anything unusual?"

"No, not since you called early this morning…and several times yesterday…and before you finally fell asleep."

"Just worried about you, that's all.

"Thanks. I guess I like that. It looks like we have something else to worry about, don't we…or nothing at all?" Hawk grunted and sat down behind his dark-wood laminated desk.

At five after 8:00, Captain MacGregor and Lieutenant Perez walked out of their offices and called a Unit meeting. It was one of MacGregor's impromptu meetings for a status report after a new homicide case came in. She liked Perez's approach to solving cases with the detectives working as a team yet still assigning individuals to specific tasks.

Just as the detectives turned their attention onto the brass, the door flew open with a bang, slamming against the wall, startling everyone, particularly MacGregor who seemed to jump. "Oh, sorry," Mortimer said. "The door got away from me. I must've pushed it too hard."

Mortimer came in wearing clothing that they had not seen on him before. The brown pants were extra wide and too short, hanging above his ankle bone, exposing his socks. One was black, and the other one was dark blue. His striped beige jacket hung extra long and baggy, with the shoulder pads falling past his stooped shoulders. He wore his signature green suspenders and a matching bow tie over a white wide-collared shirt.

Iona MacGregor's wide mouth flew open as she appraised Mortimer with disgust. "Have you decided to join the circus, Holliday?"

Everyone laughed, but Mortimer was unable to understand the humor. "Oh, I wouldn't do that. I'm afraid of clowns." His clueless comment brought on more laughs and smiles.

"Oh, did I say something funny?"

"Your pants and jacket," MacGregor said, her voice raised. "Where in the hell did you get those clothes?"

"Josephine was delighted to find them at a thrift shop yesterday. Frankly, I wasn't sure that you would like the pants and the jacket, and I told her that. I told her that you wanted me to wear something that is appropriate for a Denver detective. She assured me that it was appropriate…that I look very dapper. Besides, she said she got a great bargain on them."

Nora felt bad for Mortimer to be singled out like that. Obviously, he and Josephine either have no sense of fashion, or Josephine is just too cheap to buy a suit in a department store.

"Detective Holliday, after we're through here, I want you to go home and change. I won't have one of my detectives walking around like that. And sometime this week, I'm ordering you to go to a men's shop or department store and get a modern suit that fits. Tell your Josephine, whoever the hell she is, to stop looking for your clothes in secondhand stores. Do you understand?"

"Oh, I do. I'll do as you say, but Josephine won't like that. She doesn't like spending more than absolutely necessary."

"It's necessary, Holliday. Now, since you're standing, give us a report regarding the murders of the two lawyers."

"Oh, okay." Mortimer took out a folded sheet of paper from the inside pocket of his criticized jacket and began reading from it. "Um…Nora, Clint, and I arrived at the law offices on Logan Street and were met by Corporal Jenkins, who, by the way, will be promoted to sergeant. He told us the two women who found the bodies of two deceased lawyers were waiting for us in a conference room. We first proceeded to lawyer Visser's office, where the victims were found, the male on top of the female, both shot in their foreheads, creating a bloody mess. The smell of blood and death was overwhelming. It was a disgusting sight, and Josephine was totally appalled by the immoral—."

Lieutenant Perez interrupted, "Holliday, can you just stick to the facts and your observations."

"Oh, yes, sir. As Nora and Clint were examining the bodies and talking to the medical examiner, I thought for modesty that I should stand away from the immoral scene and concentrate on a motive. So, as I stood slipping into a trance, which I often do, I concluded that by timing the shooting, the killer sent a message of jealousy and revenge at the precise moment that they were copulating. As such, I don't believe that it was one of the divorced husbands, as Mrs. Visser blamed when we interviewed her, but someone who had a romantic interest in one of the lawyers."

"That makes sense," MacGregor said. "After your interviews with the spouses, what's your take on them?"

"Oh, Um. Norman Durand admitted that he suspected his wife of having an affair. She had a history of that in their marriage. He really didn't seem to mind much. I don't think that he is the murderer. Besides, he might have a good alibi if he was working at the bar that he owned during the time of the murders. Of course, that will have to be verified.

"Now Angie Visser, to me, is not credible. I think that she lied about not knowing about the affair. How can she not suspect it if he was gone most Fridays and supposedly slept overnight in his office with the excuse of a heavy caseload? He didn't want her to call as it would interfere with his concentration while working. I find that it is unrealistic for the wife not to suspect something with that kind of behavior from the husband. Her alibi is that she was with her friend, Goldie Hendrix, all evening and couldn't have committed the murders."

"Maybe she's just plain dumb," Nancy Salazar said with a chuckle. "Or maybe she buried her head in the sand and didn't want to know. She was probably the happiest when he was gone, anyway, just as I wish my husband would be gone more often." Her chuckle was joined by most of the people in the room , except, of course, Mortimer.

Mortimer glanced at her. "Oh, I think she's smart enough to know what is going on."

MacGregor remained silent for a moment, as did everyone else. She did not take her eyes off Mortimer as she thought about the man. She could not understand exactly how it was that he was hired by the Denver Police Department. Rumor had it that he had some connections with the Chief—through Josephine. Or the Tampa Police Department had built him up to get rid of him. But, overall, his track record of closing cases had been better than average and even now, his analysis was not bad. It surprised the captain.

"Thank you, Holliday. Makes sense. Now, I want you to fill in the information you provided on the Department's form. And, please, leave Josephine's individual opinions out."

She craned her neck toward Nora, "Ricci, do you have anything to add, and do you agree with Holliday?"

"I like Mortimer's reasoning about someone sending a message, but there are a lot of people we need to interview before jumping to conclusions. Mortimer is already focusing on the widow, and he may be perfectly correct, but I'm not so sure. I agree with Nancy that she just did not want to know or think about it. She lives her happy Country Club life with rose-colored glasses and tries to keep it that way. Or she might just be one of those women who is clueless as to her husband's activities."

How about you, Hawk? What's your take on this?"

"I agree with Nora that it's too early to tell. But if she knew of the affair, that doesn't necessarily make her a murderess."

"All right, then, people. Lieutenant Perez will give you assignments." MacGregor stood, but before leaving, she mentioned the shooting that Hawk engaged in on Saturday night. The gossip mill had not caught up yet, and the detectives were surprised to hear the news. "To keep people in this Unit from bothering you with questions about the shooting, tell everyone now how it went down, but keep it short."

Everyone turned their attention to Hawk, and he felt very embarrassed. It seemed that only he and Nora were always targeted, and he was getting tired of it. He knew it was due to revenge from the corrupt cops for bringing them down. Only after he and Nora give their testimony at their trials and the criminals are put away at the penitentiary, perhaps, only then, would their lives return to normal.

Hawk looked around the room and forced a fake smile, "Well, someone took a potshot at me while I was closing a window shade in my house. If I hadn't stooped down to pick something up at that precise moment, the bullet would've struck me. I tried to chase the bastard, and he started shooting at me and my dog. To prevent my dog from getting shot, as she ran toward the gun, I shot back. The guy then jumped into his rented white Chrysler 300 and got away. No big deal, really." He chuckled.

No one else thought it was funny. Nancy gasped, placing her hand over her open mouth. Ling shook his head, thinking, *why is it that Hawk gets shot at more than all the detectives in Denver put together? One of these days, his luck will run out.* Orlinski exhaled deeply, then mumbled, "Geez Louise, not again." Mortimer finally sat down, closed his eyes as he lifted his head and remained silent for a second then sneezed three times. Nora, of course, knew exactly what transpired and did not react outwardly. A knot inside her stomach tightened at the terrifying thought that they may have another killer out to get them.

"Well, it is a very big deal, Hawk," MacGregor said. "Actually, I want to see you and Ricci in my office after Lieutenant Perez is through." She nodded to Perez, "Okay, it's all yours."

At that moment, Perez began barking out orders. "Orlinski, I want you to get on the social media sites. See what you can find related to the victims and their families. Maybe you'll figure out who else Visser or Durand were screwing. Hawk, you and Ricci take off for the Visser law offices and start interviewing people. Ling, I want you to go with them and help. Nancy, I have something else planned for you, so hang on. Now Mortimer—"

"Aren't I going with Clint and Nora?"

"No, I have another job for you. I'd like you to go to the jail and find out all you can of any persons who came to visit the jailed cops— Bradford, O'Leary, Jeffries, Murphy, and Williams. Anyone and everyone! That includes the names of lawyers, family members, girlfriends, you name it. The inmates should be separated from each other, but verify that and find out if they get together in common areas. Got that?"

"Oh, okay. What's this about, though? Does it have anything to do with this case, or does it have to do with Hawk being shot at?"

"Yes, it's about Hawk."

"Should I interview the inmates?"

"No, not at this time. But you might ask the deputies if they had seen those five individuals conversing during those yard breaks. But try to be as discreet as possible without mentioning your purpose. We don't want them to know that we may be onto them." He looked at Salazar and told her to check out all who rented a white Chrysler 300 in the past week.

Mortimer spoke up, "I have an old car, and Josephine doesn't like me driving it much. Are you going to give me a car to take to the jail?"

"Sorry. I don't have any now to give you. You'll need to use your own."

"And the Department will reimburse me for the gas?"

"Look, it's not far from here. Gas should be minimal, but yes, keep track of your mileage, and I'll see that you're paid."

"Does that mean that I'll get reimbursed for driving to my house to change clothes since I was ordered to do so and then from there to the jail?"

Perez looked hard at the man. He shook his head. "Holliday, just go. We can discuss your mileage later."

In MacGregor's office, Hawk and Nora were cautioned by her to watch their backs. She was not pleased that their lives may again be in jeopardy. She told them that she was close to ordering them to go into hiding until the trials of the cops were done—scheduled five weeks away. If so, they would be assigned to routine office-type work from that location. That idea did not sit well with either Hawk or Nora. They started to protest, but MacGregor held up her hand to stop them. She told them that she hoped it was just some strange, isolated incident and would never happen again. She said it, but she did not believe it herself. MacGregor also suggested that for their own safety, they should stay together, even at night, to cover each other. She will also assign an officer to guard the house they decide to stay in for at least a short time.

As they left the office, Nora's heart pounded, her breathing labored. A tension headache suddenly gripped Hawk. "I don't believe that it's just a freak occurrence, Nora told Hawk. "There's someone out there to get us. We just must find and get the asshole first." She then thought about what the captain said about staying together. She looked forward to that idea. She liked being with Hawk and perhaps the situation would bring them closer, especially now since their relationship appeared strained. "Clint, walk with me to an empty interrogation room. We need to talk."

After they sat down across from each other, Nora asked, "So, what do you think of MacGregor's suggestion that we stay together, even at night?"

Hawk thought about it briefly as well. It made sense to him. They could protect each other against the killer, and, more importantly, Hawk thought being with her for at least a few days would help him decide if he could live with Nora for the rest of his life. With a wide, happy smile on his face, he looked into Nora's eyes. He grabbed her hand that was extended on the table, squeezed it gently, and said, "I like it. I want to be with you."

Nora returned the smile. "Does that mean that we're no longer angry at each other? Do you forgive me for bringing Seth to the BBQ?"

Hawk squeezed her hand again, replying, "I can't stay mad at you very long."

CHAPTER 12

HARRY LING offered to drive. The vehicle issued to him and his usual partner, Nancy Salazar, was an older white Chevrolet Tahoe that had seen better days and had been driven by several detectives in different divisions over the years. Nora took the front passenger seat while Hawk sat in the back. Shifting the gear shift to "drive," Ling said. "You'll get used to the lingering tobacco smell. I tried to get rid of it, but nothing seems to work, but, hey, it's transportation, right?" He chuckled. "Perez promised me an upgrade, maybe a brand new one once the budget is approved."

Hawk said, "That'll be sweet. I hope you get it. Ours is also an old clunker." As he spoke, he studied the cars around him, including the vehicles behind them, as Harry left the police parking lot and turned onto Colfax. Since he had been followed, threatened, and shot at several times before, he tried to be even more aware of what was in front, back, and to the sides. It became almost a habit with him whether he drove or was a passenger. Nora, too, made a point of keeping an eagle eye on the vehicles to the front and to the back. She could not forget the frightening incidents where both of their lives were in danger from a psychotic killer or a crazed motorcyclist. Now, all white Chrysler 300s were particularly of interest, although both knew that after that incident with Hawk Saturday night, the killer must have gotten rid of it and is now in another vehicle. *I hope that Nancy finds who rented the Chrysler,* Nora thought.

She decided that a conversation with Ling would ease her tension. She asked him, "Harry, how long have you been a detective?" She had never worked with Ling before and wanted to know a little more about him.

"I've been at it almost thirteen years." There seemed to be a tinge of bitterness in his voice. "That makes me a senior detective to both of you." He let out a quick chuckle but then hesitated. "Nancy and I seem to get stuck on the same types of cases…mostly drive-by shootings. For instance, the case we should be working on today is one in LoDo—lower downtown—where a couple walking out of a bar was shot by someone from a passing car. The man died; the woman is in critical condition. We think that they were specifically targeted. Unfortunately, so far, we're not making any progress."

He took a quick look in Nora's direction. "So, Nancy and I are senior detectives, but it seems that you two are the ones that Perez assigns the more interesting and unusual cases."

That statement upset Nora, "Oh geez, Harry, we don't mean to step on any toes. We just do what we're told. Perez thinks that you two are extremely busy and since we hadn't been at it very long, we don't have as many cases to work on."

"Oh, I shouldn't have said anything. Nancy and I see how good you two are at bringing cases to a close. Perhaps you'll feel the same way in a few years, as Nancy and I do, that the cases start to become routine and unexciting. Don't mind me…the object is bringing the murderers to justice, and we all need to work together."

Hawk said, "You got that right, partner. Say, I met your wife at Orlinski's BBQ. A charming lady. Had you been married long?"

"Oh yes. Maybe too long." He laughed. "You know what I mean?"

"No, he doesn't," Nora said. "He's not married and probably never will be." She chuckled.

"Smart man," Ling said. Laughing. "No, actually, I'm very happily married. We have three smart boys. We're a very cute family, everyone says," laughing. "My wife's a chemist and makes twice as much as I do. I'm not sure, being the male, whether I'm really comfortable with that, but I like the income. So, I figure, let her work. What the hell?"

Nora's remark about him never marrying really got under Hawk's skin. *Geez, Nora, lay off. I've almost made up my mind.* He twisted his neck around again to take another glance at the traffic behind them as Harry was parking in front of the Visser law offices. He saw the same silver Toyota Corolla that had taken the same route was about to pass. It seemed to slow as it approached. *I'm probably paranoid, but why take chances?* "Nora, Harry, take shelter, now!"

Nora did so immediately, no questions asked. She knew the drill. Hawk took out his gun and squeezed himself toward the corner of the backseat. Slouching down low, he still would be able to shoot back if necessary. But Harry could not understand why and reacted slowly. The Toyota slowed a little more as it passed but then increased speed as it proceeded south on Logan Street. Hawk was only able to see the rental plate but no specific letters or numbers, nor was he able to get a look at the driver, who wore a Rockies' baseball cap pulled low over the face.

"What in the hell is that about?" Harry asked.

"I've been eyeing a car that has followed us since we left the station. Did you, by chance, catch a glimpse of the driver, Harry?"

"Well, no. I turned to see what the hell you were yelling about. Anyway, what car? There were several cars behind us. What's this about?"

"Sorry, Harry. It must've been a false alarm. I thought it might be the person who shot at me Saturday night."

"That's what I figured," Nora said. "Clint and I will be on edge until we know who that shooter is and why he tried to kill Clint."

"Geez. I don't get this kind of excitement driving around with Nancy."

"Let's hope you never do," Nora said. "Now, can we go in?"

As they walked up to the building, Harry asked, "How do you want to play this?" He looked at Nora, then Hawk.

Nora said, "Let's check out the crime scene first. Go through Visser's and Durand's desks, drawers, everything, just in case anything comes up."

They stopped at the reception desk, pointed to the badges on their belts, and explained that they would be spending some time in the building. With sad eyes, the young, attractive, red-headed woman mumbled that she understood. After that, the detectives proceeded to Visser's office and stooped under the crime scene tape to enter. An obnoxious odor still lingered in the room, and took a few moments to get used to.

At first, the search revealed nothing much of value until Hawk looked under the attorney's laptop and found a small three-by-five-inch note on light-pink paper. In fancy cursive writing, the note read, *"Will you be coming over tonight? I miss you, tiger."* There was no signature, no date, only a drawing of two hearts at the bottom.

Still wearing his nitrile gloves, Hawk stuck the note into a transparent plastic bag, one of many that he carried with him in his side coat pocket. He wondered how the note might have been delivered to Visser. *Did the woman bring it in personally? Was she another lover, or did the note come from Elizabeth Durand? And why would she leave a note rather than just asking him? And if it's another woman—.*

"Whatcha got there, Clint?" Standing beside him, Nora looked at the note through the plastic as Hawk held it up for her to read.

"Nora, I'm just wondering if this note is from Elizabeth Durand or from yet another lover. If so, how did it end up here? She must've slipped in while he was gone and left it on his desk. Or he brought it in with him."

Nora looked closer. "Nice writing. I wish I could write like that. It's almost artistic. It may be important, or it may mean nothing. Let's see if Chet's people can get fingerprints off it. I bet we'll find Durand's writing samples in her office."

Harry had already left them a few minutes earlier to inspect Durand's office. As they came in, they saw him studying all her diplomas, certificates, and awards from several organizations such as Kiwanis, Boys and Girls Club of Denver, and Assistance League. The frames were artfully arranged on the hunter-green wall behind her desk. "What a waste," he commented. "Looks like she was very active in the community and could've made a difference to society."

"That's for sure, Harry," Nora commented and headed for Durand's desk to search for handwritten material. In the meantime, Hawk rummaged through credenza drawers while Harry seemed fascinated by a laminated newspaper article about Elizabeth describing an award she received from United Way for her fund-raising efforts.

"When did she have the time to do all this and still see clients?" Harry mumbled to himself.

Hawk opened a drawer and rummaged through some personal notes and photographs. He studied one photo of Elizabeth Durand, Visser, and the profile of another woman sitting on a bench. What caught his eye in the photograph was the blonde who stared adoringly at Visser. She was a well-endowed woman and sat closely to him, her right hand on his, the other around his shoulder. They appeared more intimate than Durand and Visser. "Nora and Harry, how would you categorize the way that woman on the right is looking at Visser?"

Both Nora and Harry studied the photo carefully. Harry said that he did not see anything unusual, just that they were having a good time displaying their toothy smiles. Nora, though, seemed really focused on the faces of the three pictured. "Well, that woman certainly has an expressive face. Do you think that she's enamored with Visser? Is that why you ask?"

"I think so. I'd like to find her. Maybe she's the one that wrote the note I found."

Nora studied the photograph a little more critically. "Yeah, I definitely think that there's something there. And notice the sparkle in Visser's eyes. His head seems to lean a little toward hers. But why would Elizabeth keep that photo, I wonder? It's hard to find out now unless someone in the office recognizes her."

Harry chuckled, "Well, I'd sparkle too if I stood between those two women."

Nora grunted disgustingly as she picked up a yellow pad full of cursive writing to examine. It looked like legal citations and notes from cases. "This writing must be Durand's. She was researching the enforcement of a court order for child support in a different state and the conflict of laws between Colorado and Missouri. You can readily see that the writing is sloppy, even worse than mine, and leans toward the right, quite different from that in the note that you found."

"All right then," Hawk said. "We have a mystery person out there." He thought of the note and photo, "Maybe even two."

They were startled by a loud knock on the door. After opening it, they faced a tall and large-boned man with a significant beer belly, dressed in a dark blue suit, white shirt, and no tie. "My name is Winfred White. I'm a partner in this firm. I thought I'd introduce myself. I'm sure you'll have questions for me, but I have a deposition that I need to get to in fifteen minutes." He suddenly looked morose as though about to cry. "We're going to miss Baxter and Elizabeth. They were good people."

"I'm sure you will," Nora said. "Have you worked with them long?"

"Ever since we moved into this building about seven years ago. But we really didn't work together on cases. Visser had his family law cases, and neither I nor our other partner, Lorenzo Garza, wanted anything to do with them."

"So, what are you going to do now?" Hawk asked, knowing that as a partnership the surviving partners were still responsible for the divorce cases that Visser left behind.

"Yeah. Their deaths created a huge problem for us…threw us into turmoil, quite frankly. With Baxter and his only associate, Elizabeth, gone, there is no one here to take over. I and my associates don't know enough about that area of the law to continue with a tremendous caseload…and neither does Lorenzo."

Harry asked, "What is your area of specialty?"

"I only do personal injury cases. Hell, the last time I had any experience in family law was when I first started out and that was forty years ago. Everything had changed since then. Lorenzo, who only handles property and business cases, never had a divorce case and doesn't want them."

Hawk said, "I can see your predicament."

"Yeah. It's a hell of a jam. I suppose that for upcoming court hearings, my associates will have to beg for continuances until a qualified lawyer can take over. It's not that easy to get rid of divorce cases. They haunt you for years. We must find a firm that will take on almost a hundred cases that are still open in various stages of activity. Visser should've withdrawn from most of them after the final decree, but he left many open." He shook his head. "We're in a hell of a dilemma, sir."

"Ouch," Harry said. "Any idea who could've killed them?"

"Who else would have killed them but some disgruntled client? No, sir, we want nothing to do with divorces. Hopefully, some clients will seek their own attorneys to take over, and we don't have to burden ourselves with it."

Hawk asked, "Do you know who had a grudge or threatened either one of the deceased lawyers?'

"There's been a bunch over the years. You really need to talk to Ursula Hamlin, Baxter's long-time paralegal. She knows everything that's going on in this place." He glanced at his watch, "Geez, I'll be late. Got to go."

"One more routine question, please," Nora said. "Where were you Friday night?"

White stopped in his tracks and gave out a hearty laugh, "Are you kidding me? This is the worst thing that could happen to this firm. Neither Garza nor I would subject ourselves to this nightmare by killing those two. You think one of us could've done it?"

"Humor us, please. We need it for the report."

"Okay. Quickly." Beginning to speak rapidly, he said, "I was with my wife having dinner with our friends at their home. Their names are Ken and Dora Roundhead. We were there from 6:00 to eleven. Took us half an hour to drive home."

"Just one more question, Mr. White," Nora said, "Did you know that Visser and Elizabeth were

lovers?"

"Darlin,' everyone knew. I even think that their spouses knew but didn't give a shit."

"Thank you. We'll be in touch."

"Oh, I'm sure, young lady, I'm sure," he blurted out as he took the first step down.

Harry said, "He sure volunteered a lot of information."

"Maybe a little too much, as though he's covering something up," Nora said. "He certainly wanted to make sure that we knew that because of the mess that the murders put him in, he had no motive to kill them."

"I don't think so, Nora," Harry said. "He's simply in a hurry and is very efficient. I liked him. Do you want me to talk to Garza and the staff on this floor?"

"That'll be great, Harry, thanks," Nora said. "Clint, what if I take the receptionist, and you talk to the paralegal, Ursula?" Hawk nodded in agreement.

CHAPTER 13

BRITTANY LARSEN, the receptionist, smiled welcomely at Nora as she approached the reception desk. After noticing how beautiful the woman was, with her soft-looking long strawberry-blond hair, brilliant green eyes, and toothy smile, Nora was glad that she would be questioning Brittany rather than Hawk. She had previously caught the appraising look the well-dressed receptionist gave Hawk when they first entered. *This woman could knock Clint off his feet. Am I showing a bit of jealousy? I should be ashamed.* She chuckled to herself at the thought.

Nora introduced herself to the receptionist and asked if she could join her in one of the conference rooms for a few questions.

"Certainly, no problem. I'll just ask Melody to cover for me."

They proceeded down the wide hall to one of the conference rooms. In the long but narrow room, taken up mostly by the table and eight swivel chairs, Nora sat down across from the woman.

"You don't mind if we record this conversation, do you?"

Brittany laughed, "No, not at all. I'm an open book."

"Great, let's start with your name, address, and date of birth, please."

"Brittany Larson, but everyone calls me 'Brit.' My date of birth is May 18, 1991, and I live in the Highlands area on Tejon Steet. I'm renting a little guest house in the back of the owner's place. They are really sweet people and give me a reduced rate. I'm very lucky."

"That's wonderful to find a place like that. How long have you worked for the law firm?"

She blew out a breath, her cheeks puffing out as though she were a squirrel. "Let's see. It's been about five years as of last month."

"Did you know Baxter Visser or Elizabeth Durand very well?"

"Well, yeah. After five years, you get to know a little about everyone here."

"What did you think of Elizabeth?"

"Not much. I didn't like her. No one did except, of course, Mr. Visser."

"Oh, why's that?"

"She was so arrogant to the staff with the attitude of I'm somebody because I'm a lawyer and you're peons. Pushy, demanding. Do I need to go on?"

"I think I get the picture. Any of the staff that disliked her more than anyone else?"

"Probably, her paralegal, Melody Elmers." She hesitated. Nora could see her struggle whether to tell more.

Nora remained silent, looking intently at her. Brit again exhaled, "Well, I probably shouldn't say anything because that's just gossip among us chickens here, but we all believe that Melody has, oh, gosh, had a huge crush on Mr. Visser."

"Oh, did you notice anything between them yourself?"

"I only noticed her googly eyes whenever she spotted him…I think she kind of got riled up whenever Elizabeth and Mr. Visser spent too much time together."

"Do you believe that she was jealous enough to have killed the two lawyers?"

Brit chuckled, "No, I really doubt that she'd do anything like that. That takes a lot of guts, and she's more of a weakling who does her work quietly, keeping her annoyances with Elizabeth mostly to herself."

"I know how you felt about Elizabeth. You didn't like her." Nora looked right into Brit's eyes. "Would you have caused any harm to Elizabeth?"

Brit smiled. "For what? Because she was trying to show me how superior she is? Every office has someone like that. You just brush it off and say that it's her hang-up that eventually will burn her."

"What about Visser? How did you feel about him?"

She nodded and studied her long, manicured fingers. "Yes, I'm very sad that he's gone. I'll miss him a lot. He was a pleasure to work with." She looked into Nora's eyes. "I must admit that he swept me off my feet the first time I saw him. I'm a romantic, you see, and I imagined that he was the knight in shining armor that would carry me away. He was drawn to me, too. I even went out to dinner with him. He was a perfect gentleman; he brought me flowers, paid for dinner, and just as I wondered if I should invite him in, he kissed me on the cheek, said goodbye, and left. I was excited when he asked me out to dinner again. There, he mentioned something about his wife, and I freaked out. I didn't know he was married. He didn't wear a ring and acted as though he wasn't married. I mean, he never talked about her in the office. We never had seen his wife because she didn't come by until recently, and there are no pictures of her in his office."

Nora asked, "She never came by here to see her husband?"

"No, not for most of the years that I worked here. But then, she stormed in one day and asked me if her husband was in. I asked her which husband, and she replied, 'I'm Mrs. Visser, and I want—' She didn't finish her sentence and instead walked directly into Baxter's office. She came in later a few more times with no real purpose that I could see. The last time I heard them fighting. Baxter thinks that the door keeps his office out of earshot, but if voices are raised, I can hear some of the conversation."

"Did you hear what they were arguing about?"

"Not really. Their voices kind of overlapped each other."

"Back to your last dinner with Visser, it was important to you that he was married. You should be commended for that. I would assume that a lot of girls, if they really liked the guy and he was well off, would try to steal him away from the wife?"

"You see, I have my principles, and dating a married man is a no-no. I told him so at dinner and asked him to take me home right away. He did. Seemed a little miffed, and I figured that I'd be fired the next day."

"But you weren't fired?"

"No. He acted as if nothing had ever happened and continued to treat me with respect. Never a mention of our dates was ever made, nor have I told anyone about it."

"Brit, were you aware that Visser and Durand were seeing each other?"

"Well, sitting at the reception desk, so close to Mr. Visser's office, I could hear them carrying on at times. They spent a lot of time together, supposedly going over cases, but a lot of times, she'd walk out like the cat that swallowed the canary."

"Meaning?"

"She looked pleased and satisfied."

"You weren't jealous?"

"A little, I suppose. But having any kind of a romantic relationship with a married man leads to no good. At least, that's what my mama always said. And while you're doing that, you may miss meeting someone that is just right for you."

"Do you think that others in the building knew that the two of them had an affair?"

"Of course, the gossip grapevine is as good here as anywhere else."

"Look, Detective, how much longer ? I feel bad for Melody covering for me."

"I just have one more question, Brit."

"As the receptionist, you took the brunt of clients or their spouses calling or coming in threatening the lawyers. Do I have that right?"

"Oh yeah, almost daily someone is calling, bitching about something. But as far as actual physical threats, we only get them occasionally."

"Do you remember any?"

"Well, I do, but Ursula, Mr. Visser's paralegal, has kept an accurate track of all the threats. You need to ask her." She thought a moment, "The one that really sticks out in my mind is a guy who owned some construction company, I think drywalling, and he threatened to kill Mr. Visser. Said because of the divorce order, he'll have to sell and liquidate. That Mr. Visser ruined his life. Luckily, Baxter, I mean, Mr. Visser, was in court at the time. Otherwise, I think he was hot enough under the collar that he'd probably kill him. That night, our windows were shot out. I think the police talked to him, but he denied it, of course."

"How long ago was that?"

"Oh, not too long ago. I think maybe a few weeks ago."

"Well, I don't want the people covering for you to do so for too long. I think we're done here for now. Thank you. If I need more information, I'll contact you."

"Good." As she got up, Brit hesitated, then asked meekly, "By the way, is that good-looking detective married?"

Nora was taken aback. *That conniving bitch wants to put her claws into Clint. The gall of it all.*

"No, he's not, but he's in a relationship." *At least, I hope.*

CHAPTER 14

THE TALL, a shapely paralegal wearing black slacks, a turquoise blouse, and low-healed black alligator shoes, reluctantly accompanied Hawk to the conference room. What appeared to be her naturally light blonde hair was cut in a short bob, straight at the chin and curved at the tips. She appeared sad and, at the same time, nervous. She looked older than the rest of the staff. They exchanged introductions. She introduced herself as Ursula Hamlin. As she sat down across from him, Hawk noticed tiny beads of perspiration on her forehead and a slight quiver in her hands. She looked uncomfortable, fidgeting in the dark leather swivel chair.

Hawk smiled at her before he began questioning, but she did not return the smile. Her full lips remained downturned. She avoided Hawk's eyes as he asked, "If you don't mind, I'll record our conversation." He smiled again. "It'll make it easier to remember what we discussed when I write the report for the boss." She sternly nodded. *She's going to be a tough one.*

"Well, let's get on with it then," she said crisply.

"Quite right." Noticing her eyes focus on her fidgeting hands, he said, "I'm sorry that we need to do this, realizing how hard it must be for you. Losing your boss like that and finding out about it this morning must be devastating."

"Then don't ask any questions, and I can get back to dealing with Mr. Visser's clients."

"Unfortunately, I need to take a little bit of your time. Anything you tell me would certainly be extremely helpful in finding the killer."

"Well, I know nothing about that. You're wasting precious time with me. A time that you could be out there searching for whoever did this."

"You're absolutely right, except that we don't know who to search for yet, and we need your help."

"Okay, okay." She became more irritated, arching her eyebrows. Ask away then, for crying out loud, but make it quick. For me, this is a horrible day. I lost the best boss anyone could ever have. He was wonderful. The kind of person that you don't see very often. He was so considerate and—" She turned away and wiped her eyes. When she turned toward Hawk, he could see her blue clouded with tears. Then, a trickle ran down her high cheekbone and down her smooth, slightly flushed face. Abruptly grabbing a tissue out of the box on the table, she ruthlessly wiped the tears away. After sniffling a few times, she regained her composure. "Will you get on with it?"

"You cared deeply for Baxter Visser, didn't you?"

"Yes, of course. I can't stand this building any longer with him gone."

"I'm so sorry, Mrs. Hamlin."

"It's Ms., please. I'm divorced and don't like to be called missus."

"This is a very sensitive question, Ms. Hamlin, but did you and Visser have…ah…a relationship other than strictly as employer-employee?"

She widened her eyes, her eyebrows raised. "How can you think that? We were professional and best friends."

"He never invited you to lunch or dinner?"

"Well, of course, we had lunch together frequently. He wanted my opinion on a case, or he just wanted to confide in me. But never dinner, and we certainly didn't have any sexual relations."

"Did he confide in you regarding his wife or Elizabeth Durand?"

She stared at Hawk for a moment, then curtly said, "No."

"Never?"

"Never." Her eye twitched. Hawk knew that she was lying but decided not to push it at this time.

After obtaining her address and date of birth, Hawk asked her how long she had worked for Mr. Visser.

"Fifteen years. I was with him when he first opened his office. We were buddies. We could talk about everything, and I helped him with the practice. I remember there were months when I wasn't paid until funds came in. He felt bad about that, but I didn't mind. I wanted him to succeed."

"When did you move into this building?"

"When he got together with those two upstairs and formed a partnership." She frowned and shook her head.

"I take it you didn't approve?"

"I advised him not to do it, but he wanted to start a big firm with other specialties. He said that each attorney could refer to the others and get the clients in-house. Unfortunately, he didn't listen to me."

"There was a problem?"

"Yes. All they did was fight about money. At first, things ran smoothly since they all brought in about equal income into the firm. Then, Mr. White had some big settlements, and he really resented splitting his large fee with the others. He began harping that he was the one who brought in most of the income and wanted to amend their partnership agreement. The other two, particularly Baxter, objected, saying that he was lucky that year, but next year they may have to carry him."

"So, what was White's response?"

"He was adamant about breaking up the firm, getting rid of divorces, and keeping the building. Baxter and Lorenzo didn't go for it. So, they fought, and last week, I thought they'd come to blows. Baxter stormed out, and as he descended the stairs, he yelled back to White, 'Over my dead body.'"

"And White's reaction?"

"He yelled back, 'That can be arranged, you sonaofabich.' I really don't believe he would have killed Baxter, though. Those words were said in anger. Are you through yet? I've got work to do."

"Just a few more questions. It is obvious to me that you liked Mr. Visser very much."

"Yes, I did. He was terrific. Next question."

He was almost afraid to ask the next question but thought he'd like to see her reaction. "You were actually in love with him, weren't you?"

Her cheeks puffed out, her eyebrows raised, "Of course not. He was a married man."

"But you knew that he wasn't very faithful to his wife, so why did that stop you?"

"Mr. Hawk! This is something very personal between him and me." Hawk remained quiet, focusing on her eyes. "All right. I admit that I had feelings for him and wouldn't have minded marrying him. We went out to lunch quite often to talk about the cases, and I really looked forward to that."

"And it pained you to see him carrying on with Elizabeth and others?"

Ursula stared back at Hawk, her eyes fixed on him this time. She didn't say anything for at least thirty seconds. Hawk remained silent as well. She bit her lower lip and looked defeated. "Detective, you're right. It was hurtful, but not hurtful enough for me to kill them. Are you happy now with what I think is an inappropriate question?"

"Thank you for your candor. Unfortunately, it isn't inappropriate because of the way they were found murdered. You heard about that, I take it?"

She hesitated, lifted her head, and closed her eyes, her long lashes so prominent. She was an attractive lady, and Hawk wondered if Visser had made moves on her. She denied it, but knowing more about Visser, he pondered if, in fact, they had an affair. Or, maybe she was frustrated that he never hit on her. Maybe they really tried to keep it professional.

But why is she taking so long to answer the question of how the victims were found? Did she know, and if so, is she the one? Finally, she looked up at Hawk. "I don't really know how they died. All we were told by the police officer when we walked in was that both were killed in Visser's office."

"Yes, the officer was there to make sure no one entered the decedents' offices. I'm curious: why did it take you so long to answer that?"

"I don't know. I guess it's the thought of them dying in there. It's such a horrible, horrible shock to all of us."

"Do you know of anyone else that Baxter Visser had an affair with?"

"No. Next question." Hawk watched her face and saw her nose twitch along with the left eyebrow.

"We understand that there have been many threats against Baxter Visser. Can you shed any light on that?"

"Of course, I've been keeping track of it, and I have it all written down—names, addresses, types of threats, etc. So come to my desk, and I'll give you the list so you can see what threats the people made. I really don't have time to go into it. I've spent more than enough time with you, and I'm leaving."

"That's fine. I'll come by and get the list. I appreciate your time. Thank you."

With that, Ursula quickly rose from her chair and stomped out the door.

Hawk sat back in the chair and tried to let the interview sink in. *Is Ursula a suspect? She obviously was in love with him. It must've been difficult watching him carrying on with Elizabeth under her nose. She lied when she said that she didn't know of any more affairs. Maybe it was hers?*

Nora walked by the room and saw Clint by himself through the wide window. Upon entering, she smiled, "Taking a siesta, are we?"

"I wish. For the most part, the paralegal was rather uncooperative, and I'm just trying to digest it. I may bring her in for interrogation as I think she knows a lot more than she's telling. Are you through with the receptionist? Anything of interest with her?"

"Yeah, she wanted to know if you're married." Nora laughed. "I saved you. I told her you're in a relationship. I lied."

Hawk laughed. "Too bad, she's pretty hot. I always liked redheads."

Nora threw her notepad at him in jest.

CHAPTER 15

NORA VOLUNTEERED to question Melody Elmers. Hawk advised her that Ursula Hamlin told him that Melody was smitten by Visser. Melody hated the idea that he and Elizabeth, whom she disliked, were carrying on in Visser's office. Nora wanted to pursue this information with Melody. Hawk asked Ling to follow him into the basement. He wanted to study the area more closely and get Ling's take on whether he thought, as Hawk did, that the killer waited down there before coming up and shooting the lawyers. In the meantime, Nora called Melody to the conference room. In a shaky voice, Melody asked if she could come in a few minutes as she needed to finish something.

Nora settled in the room and waited. After five minutes, a timid-looking, petite woman with short hair topped her cute, pixy face, moused in. She looked extremely nervous as Nora motioned for her to sit down across from her.

"Good morning, Melody," Nora began. Looking at her watch, she smiled and said, "I guess it's still morning. My name is Detective Nora Ricci, and your full name?"

"Ah…it's…ah…Melody Joan Elmers. Just like the glue," she attempted to chuckle, but it sounded more like a sneeze.

"And your address and date of birth? By the way, you don't mind if we record our conversation?"

She saw the agonizing look on Melody's expressive face and said, "Oh, don't worry, it's just for my report. This way, I don't have to write everything down."

"Okay. It's okay. I moved in with my mother in Aurora to take care of her. She was severely injured in an auto accident and now can't function on her own. The house number is 4499 Haynes Street. I was born on September 30, 1993." Nora was surprised that she was thirty. She looked so much younger, maybe early twenties.

"I'm sorry to hear about your mother. I hope she'll get better soon." Melody mouthed a 'thank you.' But you, Melody, you look much younger than your stated age. What's your secret?" She asked, trying to get her to relax a little.

"Oh, you're so kind. I've always looked younger than my actual age. My mom is fifty-five, and people tell her she looks barely forty."

"Good genes. Good for you. I wish I had them. My parents look every bit their age." Melody gave a toothy smile, making her look even younger and cuter. "Melody, how long have you worked here?"

"About three years."

"I understand that you were Elizabeth Durand's paralegal. Is that correct?" Melody's fading smile had abruptly changed to a frown. Her eyes portrayed her dislike of the woman. Her face seemed to scrunch up. Nora had never seen such an expressive face.

"I take it by your vivid expression that you didn't like her."

Melody took time to answer. "I know it isn't very Christian of me, and I pray that God would forgive me, but you're right. I didn't like her."

"Why's that?"

Again, she hesitated, seemingly deep in thought. "First of all, she was not a kind person to me or to any staff person. She berated me when I made a simple mistake, rubbing it in, making sure I knew that she was superior. She was a hypocrite. She put on this fake façade when she dealt with clients and other lawyers in the building. And she really conned Mr. Visser."

"What do you mean by that?"

"She played up to him, trying to get him to divorce his wife."

"How do you know that?"

"It was obvious. She played up to him and seduced him."

"That bothered you?"

"Yes, very much so. I think that Mr. Visser was once a good person but fell into temptation. Both were married, and they violated the commandment, 'Thou shall not commit adultery.' They did so commit adultery, confirmed by the fact that I found out this morning that they were killed together in Mr. Visser's office."

"Do you know where the bodies were in that office?"

She hesitated. Nora could feel her brain cells working overtime. "No, not really. I assume that they were on the sofa committing sin. They were sinners, after all, and God punished them. He sent the angel of vengeance after them."

Nora leaned back in her chair. She was surprised by Melody's responses. *She's a religious fanatic. Who knows what she thinks God may tell her to do?* It was early in the interview, but she thought it might be appropriate to raise the question. "Melody, are you that angel of vengeance?"

Her eyes shot up toward her dark eyebrows. "Oh, sweet Jesus! You don't actually think that I'd do anything like that. That would be a grave violation of the commandment, 'Thou shall not kill.' That would mean that I would've committed a mortal sin. I would be damned to the eternal fires of hell." Her hazel eyes fell intently on Nora. "I'm a good Christian, as I told you. I would never violate God's commandments."

Nora didn't know where to go from here. She hesitated as she reviewed the few notes she had taken. "Melody, how did you feel about Baxter Visser?"

"At first, I thought he was amazing, and I admired him. I must admit that I sinned by dreaming of him. Then I found out that he was married. And when I saw him carry on with Elizabeth Durand, I quickly realized that he was nothing but a huge sinner and I started to resent them both. Which probably is a sin as well. A couple of months ago, I applied to other firms. But just last week, I was accepted to a large firm with an increase in pay. I was going to tell Mr. Visser about it today, as a matter of fact."

"Melody, if you had feelings for Mr. Visser, and you saw Durand spend so much time in his office, didn't that really make you angry?"

"Yes, probably, but not for what you think. I was angry that they blatantly violated God's laws."

Nora was at an impasse. At a time like this, she wished that Hawk was there just in case he would have a different twist on her statements. She felt that she did not cover everything she needed, but the religious angle threw her off. *She seems sincere, and I think she believes what she's telling me. On the other hand, she might be extremely smart and use religion as an excuse to show that she couldn't possibly have done it. Wow! This is a tough one. She's good. My mom always said, 'Watch out for the quiet ones.'*

CHAPTER 16

HAWK AND Ling left Nora to deal with Melody and headed for the basement, a cellar, really. They found the light switch and proceeded down the rickety wooden steps. On the way, Ling described his interviews with the lawyers and staff whose offices were upstairs. In his concise fashion when giving reports, he said, "I'll explain when we have a meeting with the brass, but all I can tell you now is that no one is too sad that they're dead, in my opinion."

At the bottom of the steps, Hawk asked, "Visser and Durand weren't too well-liked?"

"Especially that Durand woman. She rubbed everyone the wrong way. Not so much with Visser, but still, they're not shedding any tears over him. I don't think, though, that anyone disliked them enough to kill them. It's really a separate operation between Visser's group and White's and Garcia's. By the way, Hawk, what are we doing in this dungeon? That old furnace looks like an octopus with all its tentacles ready to strangle us." He chuckled.

Hawk laughed. "Good imagination, Harry. Those ducts sticking out of this ancient furnace do look like tentacles, don't they ? It's a wonder the furnace works at all. Anyway, I want to show you an imprint of what I believe is a butt that I think must've belonged to the killer as he or she waited for the right moment to strike."

Ling looked closely at the imprint. "Looks like a woman's butt to me…I'm no expert, though. It's really hard to tell. Every time I look at a woman's ass, my wife yells at me. So, I must do it furtively." Harry laughed, joined by Hawk. "All right, Hawk, why else are we down here?"

"When I first came down, I looked carefully for any footprints in the floor dust. But the concrete slab is so rough that it would be impossible to find. But what bothered me afterward was how the killer knew when to strike. Is Mortimer's reasoning right when he said, 'to send a message?' If that, in fact, was the purpose, sitting here in the basement wouldn't have helped. He or she had to know the precise moment when they were naked and on top of each other. It might be a coincidence, but I don't believe so. The person had to have heard Visser and Durand before rushing in and shooting them at the moment of passion." While Ling pondered what Hawk said, Hawk had an idea, "Harry, please do me a favor."

"Afraid to ask…what?"

"As far as I can figure, this basement is close to being underneath Visser's office, although a little off to the side. Perhaps the killer could hear from down here. Would you go into his office, shut the door, and say things out loud in a normal voice?"

"Like what things?"

"I don't care, recite the Gettysburg Address or look at your phone and read off Yahoo News."

"Okay, I'll do it. How long do you want me to talk?"

"How about five minutes."

"Roger that. Give me a couple of minutes to get there."

Hawk listened hard and did not hear a thing. Deciding that his idea was wrong, he started to head upstairs when he glanced at the chest once again. *I wonder if the crime lab people looked under the chest or the back of the chest.* He pushed it aside, lit the flashlight on his phone, and concentrated on the dusty floor between where the chest stood and the wall. He searched the floor and as his light shone on the metallic corner at the back of the chest, he noticed one blond hair that was wedged in the narrow crack between the wall of the chest and the loose metallic corner. *That's interesting. Could it possibly be the hair of the killer that fell out while he or she was sitting on the chest? Or, more likely, a student who used the chest in the dorm room in college. Better check it out.*

He slipped on his vitrine gloves, lifted the thread of hair, and placed it into an evidence bag that he had in the side coat pocket. Then, remembering Harry, he rushed upstairs. As he passed the reception desk, Brittany Larsen smiled at him. He smiled back. Before he rounded the desk and headed to Visser's office door, Brittany stopped him and, in a silky tone of voice, said, "Detective, my name is Brit Larsen," she brushed her fluffy hair with her hand as she tilted her head slightly. "I wonder if I could have one of your cards…you know…just in case I think of something that might help in your investigation." Hawk didn't fail to notice the pouted lips as she talked.

"Sure." Hawk reached into his side pocket and pulled out a card.

"Pleased to meet you, Detective Clint Hawk," Brit read his name off the card. "I'll be in touch if I think of anything."

"Thank you, that would be very helpful." She continued with her beaming smile.

"By the way, is there anything wrong with that detective, the Asian guy? The one's in Mr. Visser's office?"

"No, why?"

"Well, he's strange, a little off. He just walked into the room, shut the door, and began to talk to himself in a loud voice. At first, I thought he was on the phone, but I moved closer to the door, and it sounded like he was reading the news or something. He's kind of crazy, isn't he?"

Hawk exploded into a hearty laugh. "No, Detective Ling is not crazy. I asked him to read something out as an experiment."

"Oh, that explains it. Sorry that I snooped, but that was odd." She leaned toward Hawk, tilting her head again as she gently bit her lip. "My parents said that I'm just too curious for my own good," she giggled. "All my life, I heard the corny saying that 'curiosity killed the cat.' I think I have cat's eyes, anyway, don't you think." She batted her bright green eyes at him, her long black eyelashes fluttering.

"I don't think so; you have perfect human eyes." He was still laughing when a thought struck him. "Brit, you can hear what's said in Visser's office?"

"Not really if the conversation is normal, but if voices are raised, I usually can." She had a sneaky smile when she added, "I have to get closer to the door, then I can hear much better. I don't think that Mr. Visser ever realized that the room was not very soundproof. It's that old, paneled door. I think that single thin layer of wood is so dry that sound filters through it."

"You never warned him?"

She giggled once again. "And spoil my fun?"

"Then you must've heard Visser and Durand talking and carrying on with each other?"

"Yes, if I made a point of it." She smiled mischievously when she added, "And it made me hot and bothered when they were at it. You know what I mean?"

Hawk's smile faded as he decided to change the subject. "Brit, please do me a favor."

"Anything."

"Come with me to join Detective Ling…oh, he's just coming out. Harry, I'd like you and Miss Larsen to go back in. Sit behind the desk." He looked from Ling to Brit. "And Brit, would you sit at the chair across? Talk normally for a few minutes, but not as loud as Harry did before. I want to know if I can hear anything."

They closed the door, and from the reception desk, he heard only low, muffled conversation emanating from the office. He then moved toward the door, and when he came within four feet, he heard them speaking. He did not understand what they were saying, but putting his ear to the door, he caught Brit asking Harry what Hawk was like. Harry laughed and said, "He's okay for a detective, and his partner, Nora Ricci, is also good. They make a good team. Actually, she saved his hide a couple of times." Hawk smiled as he listened.

"Oh, I'd like to hear all about that. Maybe I'll get a chance to talk to Detective Hawk about that sometime."

At that point, Hawk pushed the door open and walked in. "Thank you, both. I now think I have a theory that I need to run past the team." He did not want to say any more with Brit in the room, a possible suspect. "Well, that's all I have at this time, Harry. As soon as Nora is through with her witness, I think we can take off. And thank you for your help again, Brittany."

She smiled sweetly. At that moment, Nora spied the three of them at the reception desk as she and Melody walked out of the conference room. They heard Nora thank the witness, and as Melody went back to her workstation, Nora approached the reception desk. She noticed that Clint was in no hurry to leave Brit's company, and she did not like it at all.

"Okay, Nora," Hawk said. "Are you ready to go?"

She did not want to wait a minute longer with Brit, but she thought of some more questions to ask her that slipped her mind before. "In a minute, guys, I have just a few questions for Brittany."

"Yes, if it'll help," she replied, wiping the smile from her oval face.

"Do you know of anyone else that Visser had an affair with besides Durand?"

"No, not really. I mean, there were all these divorced women that tried to make a go with him, but he really was very ethical. I noticed their flirting, but he wouldn't think of sleeping with his client and violating ethics."

"How about anyone else? Not a client. A friend?"

"No, I can't think of anyone right now. I'll call if I do. I have Detective Hawk's card." *Oh, you do, do you? How convenient. She never asked me for a card.*

"That's fine, but have you seen anyone bring a note to give to Mr. Visser?"

"You mean, just a piece of paper?"

"Yes, it would probably be in an envelope." She shook her head.

Nora took out her notepad, tore off a blank sheet, and asked Brit to write a couple sentences for her in cursive.

"Oh wow, I seldom write anything anymore. I use the computer for everything. I hadn't written in cursive since college, so it may not be very good. What shall I write?"

"Write your name and write down the following: dogs like to eat and bark. I like cats more."

The result was more scribbling than writing. Nora showed it to Hawk and Harry, and all three realized that she would not be the one who wrote the beautiful note that Hawk found under the keyboard. She had also asked Melody to do the same when she interviewed her, and her writing didn't match either. Hawk asked for a sample of Ursula's writing when he passed her desk earlier in the morning. Also, not a match. They realized, though, that that did not really mean anything. Whoever killed the lawyers would be smart enough to mask their writing when asked for a sample.

Nora asked one more question after pulling out the photograph of Visser and Durand and the unknown woman. "Brit, do you, by chance, recognize the woman in this picture?"

"Yes, that's Theresa Martinez. I haven't seen her in years. She was Baxter's computer tech. He always called her because he wasn't good at technology, and he needed her to help him out. In fact, she was good friends with Elizabeth. It was she that got Elizabeth the job with Baxter after she graduated from law school."

"Do you know where she is now?" Hawk asked, hoping that they could locate her,

"Not really. Last I heard, she moved away to South Carolina. I haven't seen or heard about her for at least three years."

"Back to square one," Nora said as they walked out of the building.

"Not necessarily. I might've found some evidence of the killer, Hawk replied."

CHAPTER 17

JOSEPHINE WAS livid when Mortimer came home early in the morning to change his suit. She could not believe the gall of that nasty captain. "How does she have the right to order you to change his suit and buy a new one? It's none of her damn business!" It pained her to take more money out of Mortimer's account just for clothes that she didn't think he needed. "I told you, Mortimer, that you dress just fine. You always look nice, and your Captain is an idiot."

"Oh, I don't think I'll tell her that, though."

"You better not. I know what a blabbermouth you can be."

"Oh well, I better buy you a friggin suit, and a suit jacket and couple pairs of pants. I'll take you to the store this Saturday. I'll see who has the cheapest suits in your tall size. Shit!"

Mortimer came out of his bedroom wearing a little more modern chalk-striped-style suit circa 1990's. At least these pants were long enough, and the jacket did not hang. "Okay, Josephine, I must go to the jail and get some information. Don't know how long it will be, so don't wait for me for lunch."

"What?" You had better come home to eat. I don't want you spending good money on unhealthy food in some expensive restaurant, understand? I'm making spinach and cucumber sandwiches on a bed of homemade hummus. They're nutritious and will fill you up. And make sure that they'll reimburse you for the gas you use and the wear and tear on that old heap of yours." Mortimer nodded. "Make sure you tell them."

Glad to get out of the house, Mortimer scrambled into his Oldsmobile and slowly drove away. His flip-top cell phone did not have any map apps, so he studied a paper map before he left for the jail. When he finally arrived, he was upset that he had to pay for parking.

At the jail, he asked for the deputy sheriff in charge. After showing his ID and leaving it, along with his Glock 19 pistol and cell phone, in a basket, he was shown to the office. A female assistant sat in a small cubicle, one of several, and asked what he needed. After he introduced himself, he told her he would like to talk to someone about seeing what visitors or cards, gifts, letters, or anything that inmates Kent Bradford, Devon O'Leary, Westly Williams, Wally Murphy, and David Jeffries might have had in the last month or so.

The dark, short-haired, rotund woman said, "I can help you with that, Detective. It'll take a few minutes to bring up everyone you need on the computer." Mortimer continued to stand. "Please sit down on this chair here," pointing to a wooden chair.

"I'd rather stand."

"No, you don't. You sit. I don't like anyone hovering over me." Mortimer complied and sneezed.

"Bless you," the woman said as her nimble fingers banged away on the keyboard.

After she brought up information on Bradford, she asked if he wanted copies of all visitors, gifts, and correspondence that each received. Mortimer replied, "Isn't that what I asked for?"

Looking aggravated, the woman said, "No, you didn't ask for copies. You wanted to see the information."

"Wouldn't it be logical to give me the copies even though I didn't specifically say copies?"

"All right, all right. I'll get them. But first, I need a pick-me-up. You want a cup of coffee?"

"That sounds good. I'll go with you."

Mortimer followed her down a hall to the staff's breakroom. His sharp eye immediately homed in on a couple of boxes from Crispy Crème Donuts sitting on the counter. While the woman was pouring the coffee, he quickly snarfed down two donuts, powdery sugar sprinkling on his dark jacket, and was about to reach for a third when the woman slapped him on his hand. "Detective, these donuts are for the staff. Everyone here chips in."

"Oh, sorry. I'll keep that in mind."

"You know you're a big pain in the ass. Anyone tell you that before?"

"Yes, sometimes Josephine tells me that…well, there have been other people as well."

"Josephine, your wife?"

"Fiancé."

"Poor woman doesn't know what she's getting into, does she?" The woman laughed.

Mortimer, of course, did not laugh. "Oh, you said something funny. I didn't follow."

"Geez, man, you're somethin' else."

"Thank you."

"That was not a compliment, but I must admit that you livened up my boring day. You're a funny guy." She laughed again. "Okay, let's get back to my computer, and I'll whip those reports out for you."

"Oh, by the way, I'd like to see videos that you may have of any visitors for those men."

"Oh, for crying out loud. Why didn't you say that before?"

It took her a few minutes, and she brought up the videos of specific visitors seeing the five men in question. She sat Mortimer at one of the spare computers and told him, "Have at it."

Mortimer saw some woman visiting Williams every week. He assumed it was his wife. She walked out crying every time. Bradford, Murphy, and Jeffries had no visitors, but O'Leary was visited by two different women. *It must be his wife and a girlfriend, maybe.* In one segment, he saw O'Leary put up his palms toward the glass as the woman carefully studied his hands. *Must have a message written on his hands.*

He asked the sheriff's assistant if she would be able to cut a CD for the videos. She grumbled but complied. He thanked her, and ten minutes later, he was in his car on the way back to the station. But first, he thought he should stop at home, make Josephine happy, and have some lunch.

CHAPTER 18

THEY STEPPED out of the law office building and carefully scanned the surroundings. Since the attempt on Hawk, the thought of upcoming danger never quite left their minds. Hawk and Nora had hoped that it was just a one-time event, but deep down in their guts, they knew that O'Leary or Bradford had hired yet another hitman to do away with them. Out of habit from his days as an officer, when he felt impending danger, Hawk unsnapped his holster, resting his hand on the handle of his SIG Sauer pistol. Fortunately, they saw nothing out of the ordinary, and Nora, Hawk, and Ling made their way to the police vehicle. This time, Nora jumped in the back behind Ling, so Hawk took the front passenger seat.

After Ling made a left and then another left onto Clarkson Street, heading back to the station, he said. "If you want to talk about who we saw, I'd rather not. My brain is tired. MacGregor or Perez will be asking us about it soon enough."

"You're right," Nora said. "Might as well save our thoughts until then. As far as I'm concerned, the ladies working for Visser and Durand all had a motive."

"Agreed," Hawk said. He then turned toward Nora. He wanted to see how she was doing, plus he liked looking at her. The small-boned woman who could take down a bear with her Taekwondo moves was always nice to look at. He admired her strength and vitality. As the morning sun lit up her face, she looked stunning, and he wanted to gather her in his arms. He admitted to himself that her going out with Seth Morgan devastated him. He missed her, and it maddened him that it did. Because his days of being a carefree bachelor might be coming to an end soon. For a man with commitment issues, that was scary.

"What?"

"Nothing just wanted to look at you."

"Oh, you're comparing me to that tartof a receptionist with all that red hair, aren't you?"

"No. Not at all. There is no comparison; there's no one like you."

"Yeah, yeah. Okay, if this is an invitation for lunch, then okay." She smiled to herself as Hawk turned back to face the front. She liked that he was paying more attention to her since she said she wanted to break up, which she really did not.

"That's so sweet, Hawk," Ling said, chuckling. "Watch out. I was sweet to my wife once, and then I got married," still laughing as though he said the funniest thing ever.

"Yeah, watch out, Hawk," Nora said in amusement. "Could lead to something." She joined Ling in laughter. "Got that?"

"Geez, you both like to gang up on me. All I want is for Nora to join me for lunch if we have time."

Once at the Unit, Hawk hoped that he and Nora could sneak out for lunch, but Perez showed up for an update. "Captain MacGregor wants these cases solved fast. She expects much publicity because two lawyers were murdered while carrying on an affair, and neither she nor our Chief wants to answer questions that they don't have answers to. I know it's lunchtime, but this shouldn't take us long. Ling, I'll start with you."

Ling flipped open his notepad, cleared his throat, and said, "I don't have anything earth-shattering—nothing that solves these cases. I talked to a couple of lawyers, Lorenzo Garcia, one of the partners, and Jonnie Chin, an associate of Winfred White. My take was that they didn't like Elizabeth Durand at all. Baxter Visser was okay, but they wanted both of them out of the building. They need to expand and take over Visser's space. Chin was angry that White assigned her to go to court and get continuances for Visser's upcoming court actions.

"The two paralegals told me that they were sad that the Visser and Durand were killed, but they really didn't have much to do with them. They had their own work and kept their noses to the grindstone, so to speak. They knew that Visser and Durand were having an affair from the gossip in the building. They didn't know of anyone else that Visser was having an affair with. I don't believe that anyone I interviewed would've had a strong enough motive to kill the vics."

After Ling, Nora gave her report. She summarized the conversation with the receptionist, Brittany Larsen, and Durand's paralegal, Melody Elmers. "I wouldn't rule them out. They each had a motive to kill the lovers. I felt that Larsen hid her true feelings about Visser. She used the excuse that she wouldn't date a married man, but was that the real reason? I don't think that. Visser might've spurned her and yet carried on with Durand. She tried to deflect from herself by pointing the finger at Elmer's. Elmers might've tried to hide her true feelings for Baxter by pretending to be a religious fanatic who would never commit murder. And from what I've heard, I wouldn't rule Mrs. Visser out either. We need to talk to her alibi, Goldie Hendrix, right away."

After Hawk summarized his conversation with Ursula Hamlin, Visser's paralegal, he opined that Ursula also had a strong motive to kill the lovers out of frustration or revenge. "Sounds like she carried him in the early days, has helped him for years, and, in my opinion, fell in love with him. Although, she denied that. But if she did, it must've been very painful to see them carry on right under her nose."

Hawk added that he suspected that someone who knew the building hid in the basement until an opportune time to strike. He opined that after everyone, other than the victims left the building, the killer made his or her way to Visser's office, knowing that he or she could hear what was going on inside through a porous door and was able to strike at the precise moment that he or she intended.

"Oh yes," Hawk said, looking at Nora since he had not had a chance to tell her. "I don't know if it's anything, but I found a hair attached to a metal bracket of the chest in the basement. I'll take it to Chet to do a DNA test, just in case. I know it's a long shot."

"Your theory of someone waiting in the basement may be a stretch, Hawk," Perez said. "But work that angle for a while. And the hair is a long shot; it could be anyone's. And yes," turning his attention to Nora, "You and Hawk talk to that Hendrix woman."

Hawk added, "Also, I wouldn't rule out the partner, Winfred White. He had a strong financial motive to get rid of Visser. Let's just see where the evidence leads with so many possible suspects."

"Now, let's talk about a possible hitman out there," Perez said. "I certainly wouldn't put it past O'Leary or Bradford. Nancy, what did you find out from the car rental places?"

Nancy brought up the screen where she had notes saved. "I was getting a big goose egg until I called Dasher Car Rentals. They were the only ones who rented three white Chrysler 300s in the last two weeks. And after Hawk called me to check out a silver Toyota Corolla, I called them back and they told me that they rented both vehicles to the same woman. She brought the Chrysler back, saying she didn't like driving it, and then rented the Toyota. They gave me the name of Darcy Smith from Lometa, Texas. I'm waiting for a fax with a copy of her driver's license. They also assured me that they'd find the video feed of customers during that time frame and email it to me. They took a credit card for possible damages but did not run it through because she paid in cash." Nancy glanced at her watch, "I should've had the stuff by now. I'll call them again. Renting a car to do a hit on someone is plain dumb unless everything about the woman is fake."

Ling asked, "Wouldn't the clerk know that the photo is fake?"

"Harry, I don't think they look at the picture that closely. And if they did, driver's license pictures are notoriously bad. And if the person on the other side of the counter has dark glasses, a big hat, or some other kind of disguise, the clerk can't tell, especially if the person somewhat resembles the photo."

"Okay, Nancy," Perez said. "Yeah, call them again for that information. Tell them it's a rush on the video as people's lives are at stake. And as soon as you receive it, bring it to me." He looked at Mortimer, who seemed to be in a daze, staring up at the ceiling. "Holliday, what did you find out at the jail?"

Mortimer sneezed three times, then coughed before he began speaking. "Well, I have a CD of the visitors that the inmates in question saw during the last two weeks. I have copies of their correspondence and a list of visitors. Josephine and I reviewed the CD over lunch carefully, and we decided that one segment was suspicious. Devon O'Leary's girlfriend, Marla Smith, according to the witness list, intently studied O'Leary's hands as he placed his palms low against the glass. Then, that woman slides her chair back and hurriedly gets up and leaves. He must have sent a message to her that way."

Perez couldn't help but chuckle, along with everyone else, "I'm glad that Josephine agrees with you."

"Oh yes, she's sure about that." Everyone laughed, making Mortimer confused as to why.

Perez decided to tease him a little more by saying, "I hope you had a good early lunch, Holliday."

"Oh, not really. Josephine made these boiled spinach and fresh cucumber sandwiches using two slices of some awful stale garlic bread.

The boiled spinach was soggy, and the combination almost made me throw up. I ate them to make her happy, but they were really bad. I feel kind of sick to my stomach."

The laughter continued. Mortimer said, "I must have said something very funny. I don't understand."

"Never mind," Perez said, "We're just being silly trying to lighten up what we do here." He asked Mortimer to bring the CD up. He and the rest of the detectives gathered around Mortimer's screen and watched. Afterward, Perez said, "O'Leary used the same MO to hire his cousin, Finn, to kill Ricci and Hawk. We never could find that woman. She used a fake ID and disappeared. Now she has resurfaced, and we'll try again, but I'm not optimistic. I can't believe the jail people didn't spot her. Her picture should've been plastered all over the place."

"Holliday, I want you and Orlinski to follow up on this, Marla Smith. Maybe the FBI facial recognition would help. We must find her…okay, Orlinski, what did you find out on social media?"

"Angie Visser has tons of images on both Facebook and Instagram. We know that the Vissers liked to party and travel. She plays tennis and golf. Aside from her kids, she's often pictured with someone called Goldie. As is Baxter Visser. He's seen quite a few times with Goldie and Angie at social events. After I heard Nora mention the name of Goldie Hendrix, I looked up Goldie Hendrix and she has a ton of photos as well. Most of them depict her with trophies as a sharpshooter or receiving pistol awards. There is one image of Baxter, Angie, and her standing next to each other. Visser has his arms around both. Pretty chummy, I'd say. As far as Elizabeth Durand, she wasn't much of a presence on social media sites. Just a few here and there."

Perez said, "Okay, people, get some lunch. Ricci and Hawk, I'd like you to talk to Goldie Hendrix as soon as you can. The fact that she's good with guns intrigues me."

CHAPTER 19

AT A QUIET "ma and pa" Greek restaurant on Sixth Avenue, Hawk and Ricci were seated at a corner table. The talkative young brown-haired waitress, who they later learned was a newcomer to the area from Virginia, handed them the menu. The eatery was Nora's suggestion since, lately, she had an appetite for Mediterranean cuisine. Hawk liked to eat, and he did not really care what he ate.

Nora ordered the eggplant salad with a side of pita bread and hummus, while Hawk ordered a gyros sandwich plate. After the server took their orders, Hawk said, "I feel bad for telling Mortimer that he couldn't go with us. He wanted to so badly."

"Yeah, he looked rather sad. I even thought he'd cry. But you managed it well telling him that we have something to discuss just between the two of us. Do we have anything to discuss? I really don't want to talk about the murders."

Hawk laughed, "Ricci, we always have something important to discuss."

"Oh, yeah, like what?"

"Like…um…like…that I didn't like it at all when you showed up with that sleazy Morgan character."

Nora laughed. "You idiot, I was trying to make you jealous. Looks like it worked." She continued to chuckle in merriment.

"Geez, Nora, you really play hardball, don't you?"

"Well, you know how I feel about you." She grabbed his hand and squeezed it. "I don't want to lose you. But, as you know, I want something more serious."

Hawk looked away for a moment. He sat up in his chair. Nora could see how hard he found it to answer her and decided that it probably was of no use. *He really has a real psychological problem with committing himself.* She released his hand and heaved a sigh as she was about to tell him to "Just forget it!"

Suddenly, Hawk looked at her straight in her eyes. Reaching out, he took her hands into his. "Nora, I don't want to lose you either. I'm going to say three words that I've never said to any other woman except, of course, to my family…I love you. I have been going crazy since Saturday realizing that I really do love you. When I'm not with you, I miss you."

Nora's eyes went wide in astonishment as Hawk continued, "You're right, baby. It's time for me to settle down. *Oh my God! Is he going to propose to me here, now?*

But Hawk did not propose. Instead, he said, "Um…let's commit to each other and see how it goes." *See how it goes? See how it goes? What does he mean by that…On the other hand, it's a start, I guess.*

"Clint, I love you too, but then you know that. I became infatuated with you from the moment I saw you. So certainly, I'll commit to a serious relationship."

Hawk stood up and leaned over her, raising her chin towards him. He gave her a hard kiss on her red lips. At that moment, the waitress came up to them, holding their orders. "Wow! How romantic. I wish my boyfriend would do that to me just out of the blue like that."

Clint and Nora giggled like two teenagers. They continued to act like that, passionately kissing, once they were in their police vehicle.

Afterward, Hawk backed out, and they made their way to question Angie Visser's alibi witness. Hawk felt good. It was easier than he thought to express his feelings. Nora felt tingles up and down her spine, replaying in her mind every bit that Clint said. Her hopes were up that it would, indeed, lead to marriage and children. She could not help smiling every so often, almost forgetting that there may be a hitman out there to get them. But she did not forget. She craned her neck about, eyeing the area around them just in case the killer was out there, watching them. Hawk, though, had his mind on something completely different. He caught Nora's attention by pointing to the back seat with his eyes.

"Oh no! We can't! I know exactly what you're thinking. Can you imagine the repercussions if someone caught us back there? Especially the killer that may be out to get us. Wouldn't that be ironic if he were to shoot us while we're romping around in the back ?"

Nodding in agreement, Hawk reluctantly said, "You're absolutely right. We must make sure that we keep it strictly professional at work. Otherwise, they'll separate us."

"You got that right, Buster. Let's get down to business and see what Goldie Hendrix will tell us about the Vissers."

CHAPTER 20

ANGIE'S FRIEND lived on the seventh floor of a newly constructed condominium complex on Clayton Steet in the Cherry Creek area. Nora and Hawk discussed how much the area had changed in just a few years from small quaint shops and cafes in two three-story buildings to skyscrapers resembling another downtown area, only very ritzy. "Looks like Goldie has a few bucks," Hawk said.

"Yeah, to live here, she has to."

In the locked foyer, they called Goldie through the intercom and explained why they were there. "Yes, yes, come on up."

They were not disappointed in what they expected of a luxury condominium—parquet floors, Persian carpets, ultra-contemporary colorful furniture, tall ceilings, and unusual modern light fixtures hanging from beautifully carved medallions that matched the wide crown moldings. After the introductions were made, Goldie asked them to sit and offered a cup of tea. They both accepted.

While Goldie hummed and fussed in the open kitchen, separated only by an island with a nearly pink quartz countertop, Hawk and Nora admired the original artwork, whose brilliant colors stood out even more on the dark mauve walls. Hawk thought that one of the paintings was like the style of the Chinese artist, Lui Wei, depicting a city scene.

He thought of getting up and glancing at the name of the artist to see if he was right but decided that he had better stay put. Their attention also fell on contemporary bronze statues sitting on elaborate lighted glass stands.

A few minutes later, Goldie approached them sporting a wide smile as she held a tray with an English Chintz teapot, three matching porcelain cups and saucers, and an assortment of butter cookies. After pouring them each a cup, she sat down across from the detectives. "Please help yourselves to the delicious German cookies, my favorite," speaking in a noticeable southern accent. Still smiling pleasantly, she extended her arm and insisted again that they try the cookies. Her hand had rings on most of her fingers. The largest was an emerald set in a diamond cluster.

The detectives lifted the saucers and took a sip of the tea from the cup. Hawk tried a cookie, complimenting the hostess on how good it tasted. She clasped her hands together, brought them up to her mouth, and said with sincerity, "I hope you like the tea. It's also one of my favorites. I import it directly from Turkey. It's a little pricey, but the flavor is terrific."

"Thank you so much," Nora said, smiling. "You shouldn't have gone to all this trouble."

She waved her hand in a dismissive manner, "Trouble. Do you think it's trouble? No, it's a pleasure, dear. Now, what can I help you with?" She suddenly looked attentive, as though she really wanted to help. "I know you're here to talk to me about the Vissers. It's a horrible, horrible tragedy what happened to Baxter… and, of course, his associate." Having said that, she gave the detectives an appraising look.

Nora and Hawk had been doing their own evaluation of the woman. She was an extremely beautiful woman, perhaps exotic looking with her long black curly hair framing her smooth oval face with large dark brown eyes and a straight nose with narrow nostrils.

The light application of makeup and the bright red lipstick on her olive skin added to her striking appearance. She did not appear at all nervous about being questioned by detectives.

She was maybe a year or two older than Nora, perhaps thirty-five, and Nora could imagine that men would be attracted to her like flies to honey. She took a quick glance at Hawk, who, she thought, might be admiring the woman. She was so completely opposite in appearance from her friend, Angie Visser. Nora's impression of Angie was that she was rather plain, unexciting, and not overly attractive. As she studied Goldie, she thought *there might've been a fling between her and Baxter, knowing what a womanizer he was.*

"Mrs. Hendrix, thank you for seeing us."

"Honey, call me Goldie. Everyone does. I lost my husband, Edgar, about two years ago. He was murdered right on the back porch of our old house in the Hilltop area by someone who shot him from the alley. And I don't want to be reminded of the incident by being called Mrs. Hendrix. That's my overbearing and meddling mother-in-law." She chuckled.

"We're so sorry for your loss," Hawk said. "That was certainly quite a tragedy that is hard to forget, I'm sure. Did they ever catch who did it?"

"Sweety, what do you think? Lieutenant Carpenter assures me that they're still investigating, but unless the murderer just comes into the station and gives himself up, they'll never catch the bastard. Excuse my French." She smiled wide, her perfect white teeth glowing. "Now, detectives, you have questions for me about the Vissers? Although, you'll probably have just as much luck in finding the culprit as Carpenter has had in catching my husband's killer."

Nora took a sip of the herbal tea and asked, "How long have you been friends with the Vissers?"

"Oh, ever since they joined the Country Club. My husband was still alive, so probably six or seven years now. My husband and Baxter became friends after he handled his divorce. Evidently, he did a hell of a good job. Edgar sponsored the Vissers for admission to the club. They seemed ecstatic to belong, but I believe that Baxter had a tough time coming up with the high admission fee to the Club at the time, so Edgar paid it for them."

"Sounds like you were on very friendly terms with the Vissers," Hawk said.

"Honey, we got to be very good friends. They were both very amiable and fun to be with…of course, I saw Angie much more often." Hawk noticed a slight twitch of her eye.

Nora asked, "What did you think of Baxter Visser, other than him being fun?"

"Oh dear! Well, he was incredibly good-looking and charismatic." She looked at Hawk and patted his leg. "Just as I imagine Detective Hawk is, am I right?" Looking at Nora, she laughed. Nora did not respond. "Anyway, he just drew people to him. The women thought he was adorable. They loved him."

"Did you feel the same way?"

After two quick coughs, she said with a laugh. "Did I love him? Well, I wouldn't even think of going there. After all, he was my friend's husband. I admit that I liked being around him, but that's as far as I would dare to go."

"How often did you see Angie Visser?" Hawk asked.

"I saw her at least twice a week for tennis and swimming. She usually had her kids there and let them do their thing as we sometimes played cards, had a drink, and stuff like that."

Hawk asked, "I'm curious. How did you meet your husband?"

With a wide smile, she said, "I was an actress off-Broadway in the Big Apple. He came to a couple of performances, and then I came back to my dressing room, and there he was. Sitting there with a great big bouquet of red roses. Even though he was fourteen years older, he swept me off my feet and brought me back with him to Denver."

"Interesting. What was your stage name?"

"My maiden name and my stage name were Goldie Stern, honey."

Nora said, "Last Friday night, Mr. Visser and Elizabeth Durand were killed in his office. Where were you between five and seven?"

Goldie smiled and swallowed hard. "I was with Angie."

"All that time between five and seven?"

"Actually, I was in traffic for part of that time trying to get to the restaurant to meet Angie. The traffic was absolutely horrible. It took forever, it seemed, to get to the place. I thought that I'd be late for our 5:30 meeting, but once I got there, I was the first to arrive. Angie came a few minutes later. She also had traffic problems. Friday traffic, you know."

"Are you sure that you came before Angie to the restaurant?" Nora asked, remembering that Angie said that she had to wait for Goldie.

"Why, yes, I'm sure. I wondered where she was since I was running late also."

"What restaurant did you go to?" Hawk asked.

"We went to a Mexican place by the name of Uno Mas Taqueria.

Hawk asked, "What time did you arrive at the restaurant?"

"Honey, I can't remember the exact time. I think it was closer to six. Surely, Angie isn't a suspect in the murder of her husband, is she, honey?"

Hawk said, "Please don't call me that. Whose idea was it to meet at that restaurant?"

"Sorry. I'm just used to calling people dear or honey, that's all. Going there was my idea because both Angie and I really felt like Mexican food, and we loved the enchiladas there. They are absolutely scrumptious."

Nora commented, "Not too far from Visser's office, is it."

"I guess not. Never thought of that."

"Were you ever in the law office building?"

She hesitated as though thinking hard, "I was. Angie and Baxter gave me a full tour of the building on the way to a Country Club event a few months ago. I was anxious to see it because of its beautiful history. Too bad that they turned that wonderful mansion into mundane offices."

Nora said, "Thank you so much for cooperating with us. And thank you for the delicious tea and cookies."

They said their goodbyes, and once Hawk and Nora were in the elevator, Hawk asked, "Your thoughts?"

"I'm thinkin' that we may yet have another woman with the hots for lover-boy Baxter. And I'm thinkin' that both Angie and Goldie have terrible alibis. Oh, darn, I forgot to get a sample of her writing."

"That's okay," Hawk said. "We'll get it another time."

As they were walking out of the building, Perez called.

CHAPTER 21

LIEUTENANT PEREZ commanded Hawk and Ricci to return to the station ASAP. Captain MacGregor had called for a meeting to discuss Orlinski's latest information on the possible hitman. With her body tensing up, Nora replied that they'd just finished with Goldie Hendrix and would be on their way.

"What do you think, Clint? Sounds ominous, doesn't it?"

"Could be, I wonder what Orlinski found out? Whatever it is, it doesn't sound good at all."

After they scrambled into the new vehicle issued for their use, a Ford Interceptor, Hawk drove off, scrutinizing the vehicles and pedestrians in the street. Once again, their insides felt tight, as though a python was squeezing their innards. Neither said another word for several minutes, deep in similar, frightening doomsday thoughts. Shaking her head and rubbing her forehead, Nora wondered when it would all end—this constant fear that their days were numbered. *Or will it ever end if those corrupt cops are alive? I don't know how much more I can take of constant worry—constant fear—constant stress. It's not right that we are singled out like this, doing our jobs. They have money stashed where they can hire hitmen.*

Hawk glanced toward her and forced a grin as her eyes met his. Her usual, vibrant, uplifting smile was gone.

"Clint, baby, what are we going to do?"

"Well, first, let's find out what Orlinski has, then we'll figure it out and deal with it. I hope he has enough on the hitman so that we know who we're dealing with. But remember that shot at me might not mean that there is anyone out to kill us. It might just have been a fluke, and we're stressing over nothing."

Nora finally chuckled. "Do you really believe that Clint? Or are you just trying to make me feel better?"

"I guess I'm trying to make me feel better too."

MacGregor, Perez, and the others gathered around as Orlinski told them what he'd discovered from the FBI database. "To put it bluntly, nobody knows who she is." Both Nora and Hawk exchanged glances, surprised that the killer was a woman. "They call her the "ghost" because she's like a spook—gets in and out of houses as though she walks through walls. She uses different aliases, never leaves fingerprints or DNA behind, and has a variety of disguises. I'll bring up what she looks like."

With an inappropriate chuckle, Orlinski showed images of eleven women. "That's her."

"Which one is she?" MacGregor asked, looking confused.

"She's all of them, Captain."

"What are you talking about, Orlinski? Those are eleven different women, all from young to old."

"Yes. The FBI thinks that she could've been a makeup artist for a movie studio and knows how to disguise herself professionally. She may even use rubber face masks."

"Well, I'll be damned," MacGregor commented. "Any pics that show what she really looks like?"

"Nope. They don't have a clue."

Hawk asked, "Anything about this woman renting cars?"

"Yeah, for sure. She rents an ordinary, common car, changes license plates with one she steals from a similar car, and then, when she turns the car in, she replaces the rental fleet plates and throws away the stolen ones. All done with latex gloves so as not to leave fingerprints. And she rarely uses a gun to kill her mark." Everyone again appeared surprised.

"How's that?" Nancy asked.

"There was a notation in the FBI file that most of her victims were killed after she was long gone. They believe that she figures that she has less chance of being caught that way. She arranges boobytraps like a bomb going off when you open the door, an explosive device when you pick something up, but mostly, she's best with poisons. Evidently, she's very good with both explosives and poisons."

"Oh, I know about poisons myself," Mortimer said. "I've studied and experimented with deadly poisonous plants. If you know what you're doing, you can make lethal poison very easily. The plants that are the most dangerous are sometimes the prettiest, like water hemlock or the nightshade. You can even extract cyanide out of lima beans or almonds."

"That's just it, Mortimer," Orlinski said. "She seems to know how to do it."

Nora asked, "So how does she poison her victims? Doesn't she have to target an individual, and to do that, she has to be in proximity?"

"Well, according to the FBI, she enters the house and finds ordinary items that you consume, and then she laces them with a poisonous substance. For example, you don't want to use any tea or water left in pitchers, or water left over in coffee makers or teapots, or drink wine with corks or any left-over sauces. For instance, there may be an open bottle of some juice that she can throw some poison in."

"If you have a whole household of people, that's mass murder," Nora said.

"So far, she's only used poison targeting individuals that live alone."

"Holy mackerel," Hawk said. "I have milk and both orange and cranberry juices in the fridge all the time, all been opened. I have a wine rack with corked bottles, I leave the water in my expresso machine. Boy, she can drive someone absolutely bonkers if you know what she's up to." He heard Nora let out a deep sigh.

Orlinski said, "Yeah, but you now have an advantage in that you know what to watch for. For example, in wine bottles, look carefully for any needle marks where she might've used a hypodermic needle to insert the poison. Get rid of all those open liquids you got lying around."

"But both Clint and I have good security systems with cameras. We should be okay there."

"Well, hate to break it to you, Nora," Perez said. "After Orlinski showed me what he found out, I called a buddy of mine in the FBI. I asked him to give me more information on that "ghost" person. He called me back a few minutes ago and basically reiterated what we had heard so far. He added that she or someone she works with is skilled in hacking wireless systems and cameras. Since most systems are now wireless, she knows how to disarm them."

"But whoever it was took a shot at me," Hawk said, "Doesn't sound like the MO that you described."

"I said that she rarely uses guns, but she does when necessary or when she thinks it's safe to do so. She was staking out your place and saw an opportunity to get you when you were at the window closing your shade."

"Thanks, Orlinski," Hawk said. "That's not what I wanted to hear."

"Okay, enough," MacGregor said, "Clint and Nora, I suggest you get more cameras in your homes using different security codes. And resort to the old-fashioned method of checking if anyone has entered your home by placing a small piece of transparent tape, like Scotch Tape, on the very bottom or very top of the door and frame and do the same with your windows. Walk around the house and check them carefully to see if they were disturbed before you enter. And my suggestion that you stay in one house for protection still goes. I'll have it watched 24-7."

Hawk looked at Nora and sidled closer to her. He wanted to take her in his arms and make her feel better. Her expression was one of shock, her mouth open, her sad eyes wide.

MacGregor continued, "We'll discuss your list of suspects in the lawyers' murders tomorrow morning. I want Hawk and Ricci to go home now, figure out where they're going to stay, and check everything out, even before entering your houses. So, you two take off."

As they walked out of the building, Hawk asked Nora. "How do you feel about us staying under the same roof for a few days?"

"Actually, I think it's a good idea. That way, I can earn my keep as your bodyguard." She forced a laugh, which Hawk unenthusiastically returned.

After Hawk and Nora left, Perez called Mortimer and Orlinski to his office. Pointing at the side chairs for them to sit, he said, "How's it coming with finding the woman who visited O'Leary?"

"Oh, I haven't worked on that aspect yet," Mortimer said. "But I do think that she may show up to visit O'Leary again. I alerted the Sheriff to make sure his deputies watch for her and detain her this time."

"Well, that's a start," Perez said. "Orlinski, how has your facial recognition search been going?"

"I'm going through the FBI database on that. So far, there hasn't been a match. We don't have a really good image of her from the jail video, so it's taking a while. I had the same problem with that when Devon O'Leary used her to hire his cousin, Finn O'Leary, to eliminate

Hawk and Ricci. For some reason, her face just doesn't pop up in the system."

"That's strange, all right," Perez said. "Maybe you should just use old detective work and check videos in surrounding buildings and see where she went. Maybe some camera picked her up."

Mortimer said, "The jail parking lot camera showed nothing?"

"Yeah," Perez said. "She must've walked, and there's gotta be some video of her somewhere. We got to find her. She knows how to contact contract killers. So, Orlinski, while your computer searches for faces, I want you and Mortimer to hit the streets bordering the jail, show her image around, and look through security camera videos."

CHAPTER 22

WITH HEAVY hearts weighing them down, Hawk and Ricci scanned the vehicles parked along the street and in the surrounding parking lots. Once in the car, both were tense as Hawk's Jeep made its way toward Nora's house to pack up her toiletries and a change of clothes for at least a couple of days. The plan was to hole up in Hawk's townhouse and try to concentrate on the lawyers' murders. However, they were not sure how much they would accomplish because of the overwhelming stress of knowing that the "ghost" was out there. Her unorthodox method of eliminating her targets greatly disturbed them.

Hawk was angry at himself for being such a wuss and for allowing his hand to tremble while he inserted his key into the car door back in the parking lot. He feared that the ghost had already placed some sort of incendiary device hidden within the car, and it would go off as soon as he opened the door. *What a way to live—afraid to get in—afraid that any container in my house is poisoned. We must find that bitch before she drives us bonkers, not knowing how and when she'll kill us.*

On the way, they sat in silence, both wondering what lay ahead. As they approached Nora's house, Nora was about to pull out her extra garage door opener from her purse when Hawk warned, "Wait!

The signal from that device might set off a bomb." Nora sighed as she put it away.

"Gads, this is driving me freakin' crazy. I'd rather have some shooter out there than all this intrigue with explosives, poisons, maybe even deadly snakes." She shook her head back and forth in total disgust. "Okay, hot shot, what are we going to do?"

"Let's check out the perimeter first."

They walked around the house, checking all the windows and the back door. Everything looked in order. By the door leading from the garage to the backyard, Clint concentrated on a footprint in the wet soil. "What is it?" Nora asked as she hustled up to him. "Oh, my God! It's a print of a woman's sneaker, and it isn't mine. It's at least one size smaller, perhaps a seven and a half."

Nora stepped back, still staring at the footprint. "She was running out of the house. Wasn't careful and stepped off the sidewalk, and I bet she leaped onto the grass and took off for the back fence and out to the alley." Without hesitating, Nora ran toward the alley and looked down at it in both directions. She didn't see anyone, not even any of the neighbors.

Hawk waited for her to return before he said, "She was obviously in your house. We really must be careful. I'll call Chet from the crime lab. We need to make a mold of that print, and his team needs to scour your place."

"Great, now they'll see my underwear." She tried to laugh and make a joke out of it, but she could not make the sound. She stepped back from the door and slowly twisted the brass doorknob. Nothing. But they really did not expect any bombs to go off at this door since it wasn't the one they would've ordinarily used to enter the house. The most logical one would have been the side garage door or, less likely, the front door.

The front door looked untouched, still locked, with no evidence that anyone had entered through it. Nora inserted her key into the lock, and both she and Hawk held their breaths as they opened the door. "Shouldn't we wait for Chet and his crew first?" Nora asked, her heart racing.

"Smart thing to do, but I can't wait. Let's at least take a quick look. We don't want Chet and his crew to be blown up if we find an obvious booby trap."

"What if we triggered a bomb to go off with a delay once the door is opened?"

"Well then," Hawk forced a chuckle, "It was great knowing you."

Nora hit him in jest across his shoulder, "That is so mean, Clint."

The door opened into the living room. After carefully examining each room, including the basement, Nora determined that nothing seemed out of place. While in the kitchen, Hawk slid into a pair of nitrile gloves and picked up a red electric tea kettle. It was half full of water. He took a deep whiff, and his mouth flew open.

"Nora, come and smell this."

Nora put on her gloves. "Oh no. I hope it's not what I think."

She took the kettle from him and smelled the inside. "Smells kinda weird, doesn't it?"

"What does it smell like to you?"

"Clint, I don't know exactly. You're the one that can sniff things out just like a dog." She chuckled nervously.

Hawk smirked, "Thanks a lot. Woof, woof."

"All right, so what do you think?"

"I'm pretty sure that the water is laced with cyanide. To me, it has the faint smell of almonds. I bet she laced several items in here. What open containers do you have in the fridge?"

Nora opened the refrigerator door. Prominent on the shelf was an opened half-full bottle of orange juice along with a bottle of apple juice, a pickle jar, a half-gallon of milk, and embarrassedly for her, a bottle of prune juice.

"All of these could be poisoned," Nora said. "Let's not touch anything and let Chet analyze everything in the fridge. If we had stayed here tonight, we would've had some tea perhaps, maybe even a glass of juice either tonight or in the morning. I know that I would've had a glass of milk before bed to help me sleep. This is awful, Clint. They could've found us dead in the morning."

"Well, thank God for Orlinski and Perez. They saved our lives with that meeting when they described her methods of murder."

"Boy, that's for sure," Nora agreed but looked so discouraged and frightened. He totally understood. Her house was violated by the "ghost." Hawk noticed Nora shiver, so he pulled her toward him, kissed her on the cheek, and held her in his arms for a long minute. By then, Chet Watkins and his crew had arrived. They came in a big white Ford van with the words "Crime Scene Investigations" plastered all over it. Nora felt even more embarrassed at the notoriety she had caused when she saw her curious neighbors crawl out of their homes.

"So, you're at it again," Chet said, shaking his head. "I can't remember anyone having as many death threats against them as you two."

"It's more than just a threat, Chet," Nora said. "First, let me show you the footprint. The killer was inside my house. My house! Then, I'd like to see if you can pick up anything at all that might identify her. Hopefully, there is loose hair of hers lying around. Then, we suspect that the tea kettle and the items in the fridge are laced with poison. All are waiting patiently for us to drink from them."

"Okay, okay, I get the message. Show me the print."

Hawk said, "I bet you'll be able to tell us the brand of the shoe just by the sole."

Hawkins smiled, "I bet I can and tell you the size."

As he saw the shoeprint, Chet studied it carefully. It's unusual, all right. I hadn't seen too many before, but if I had to guess, I'd say it's a size seven and…" He lifted his cap and, with the thumb, scratched his head. "This really is a tough one, and I'll have to verify it, of course, but I'd guess that it's from a Sher sneaker."

"Never heard of them," Nora said.

"Like I said, you don't see too many of them, but, hey, if you can find a woman wearing one, she might be the killer. You can look online and see what styles they have."

"I knew you'd know," Hawk said.

"Whoa, hold on. I still must verify what I'm thinking."

Nora quickly packed a few things, and they left Chet and his crew to continue their investigation at her house.

On the way to his townhouse, Hawk wondered what surprises there may be in store for them. Nora sat silently, staring out of the window.

"How are you feeling?"

"Terrible, Clint."

"Well, look at it this way, Nora, we're still alive, and I feel much better now that we have an idea of what to watch out for. That's a huge advantage. We just have to be really vigilant."

"You're right. We should consider ourselves fortunate. You know, I think that she never expected us to leave work early, and we scared her off before she could cause any more havoc. I think that when we walked up to the house, she spotted us and took off. That's why she was sloppy and left a print of her shoe…she was in a hurry to get out of there."

"Makes sense. But she could've shot us as we entered."

"Maybe she didn't want to get trapped in the house. Maybe she thought that she could get only one shot off before we fired back. It doesn't sound like she wants to take any chances. So, Clint, what are your plans once we get to your house?"

"First, we'll walk the perimeter. Check for anything that seems out of place or tampered with, and then we slowly proceed into the house. And we're almost here."

Nora felt sick to her stomach, worrying about what lay ahead.

CHAPTER 23

HAWK'S NEIGHBOR, Rose Lucero, while walking Hawk's dog, Stella, flagged down the detectives as they pulled up to the townhome. She rushed toward the car and, in an agitated voice, said, "I just saw a strange woman stroll out of your garage, Clint. She had a garage door opener, and she closed it afterward as though she owned the place."

Both detectives slid out of the vehicle. Stella was excited to see them, especially Nora, who she took a big liking to. "What did she look like?" Hawk asked quickly, his heart racing.

"See for yourself, she didn't get far." Pointing her out, she said, "That's her in that black gym suit." They spotted the woman less than a block away, walking at a leisurely pace as though she had not a care in the world and seemingly enjoying the wonderful, cloudless, sunny afternoon.

Without saying a word, both Hawk and Nora took off after the woman. Stella broke loose from Lucero's grip on the leash and shot out like a rocket toward the woman as though the dog understood that was what Hawk wanted. The woman glanced back and saw them chasing her, so she bolted toward her car parked around the corner. She was fast, but Stella was faster. As she pulled open the door to her car, the big yellow dog leaped onto the small woman, knocking her to the street. Showing her teeth with her upper lip curled back, Stella growled, not letting the woman up. The woman went for her pistol, but Stella latched onto her hand, preventing her from moving it. By that time, Hawk caught up with the dog with Nora at his heels. "Good girl. Let go, Stella," Hawk commanded as he twisted the micro compact nine-millimeter Smith and Wesson pistol from the woman's grasp and threw it several feet away.

Stella kept growling, and Hawk was totally in shock at her behavior. Even though he trained her, he had never seen his dog show any aggression toward anyone before. *Ahh, she remembers her. She was the one shooting at us, aiming for Stella.* Nora rolled the silent woman onto her stomach, pulled her arms back, and tried to cuff her. While Nora was bending over, the seemingly subdued woman suddenly came to life, like Lazarus from the dead, and rolled hard into Nora, flinging her elbow into her chest, knocking the wind out of Nora as she fell backward. The woman sprang up as though she was on springs and threw a hard kick at Hawk's abdomen as he came to Nora's aid. She twirled around and in one smooth motion, kicked Hawk again and almost kicked Nora again. Nora flinched and, with her Taekwondo moves, went on the attack. Both women jumped, twirled, and twisted, each trying to subdue the other. A real kicking brawl ensued for a minute. The woman was good, obviously schooled and seasoned in Judo, but Nora was faster and, after a few powerful kicks with her longer legs, was able to knock the woman down to the ground.

Before the woman was able to spring up again, Hawk grabbed her arms, turned her over, and, with his knee on her shoulders, managed to hold her down. She squirmed like a feral cat trying to break loose, but with Nora's help, Hawk was finally able to subdue her well enough for Nora to place her in handcuffs.

When they searched her large pockets in her jogging jacket, they found a generic-looking garage door opener, a pair of needle-nose pliers, and a small roll of very thin wire with just a few strands remaining. The wallet had an ID with the name of Thelma Manheim from Arlington, Texas, and, to their shock, pictures of both Nora and Hawk, their addresses written on the back.

After calling Lieutenant Perez and explaining what had just transpired, Hawk and Nora waited about ten minutes before a patrol car arrived and placed her in the cruiser. Perez told Hawk not to have them take her away until he got there. While in the back of the police car, Nora placed her under arrest, recited the Miranda rights, and asked if she understood. With her cold gray, piercing eyes staring out into space, the woman remained expressionless, not uttering a word. Nora almost broke out in laughter when she noticed that the corner of one of the woman's fake eyebags began to slide down her face, loosened in the fight.

Both Hawk and Nora were in pain, especially Nora, who took some hard hits. When Perez arrived, he offered to call an ambulance to have them checked out, but both refused. "We'll be all right. Just a little rest is all we need," Nora said.

"All right, then. So, you sure this is the "ghost" that no one could catch before?"

"We're sure," Hawk said. "The woman's face was heavy with makeup—her nose, cheekbones, bags under her eyes, and a layer of something or other under her chin. And then, her shoes matched the footprint pattern we saw by Nora's back door. And she had photos of both Nora and me in her wallet."

"Okay, then, good job. Are you sure you're all right? Both of you look like shit."

Hawk chuckled. "We'll be fine. My house is just a block away. We'll drag ourselves there and crash for a couple of hours."

"But Clint," Nora said, her face scrunched from pain. "What about your house? She was in it. We don't know what evil she left there."

Perez said, "I'll come with you. Here, get into my car, and I'll drive you back. I don't think you're in any shape to walk."

Before he climbed into Perez's Interceptor, Hawk explained to Rose Lucero and the many neighbors who witnessed the ordeal that she was a wanted, dangerous fugitive, and they were lucky to get her. He thanked Mrs. Lucero for her sharp eyes and mentioned that there might be a reward for her.

"That would be great," Rose said. "Here, let us take Stella back to my house so that you can rest."

During the short ride back to Hawk's place, Nora sat deflated in the back seat, bearing her pain and praying that this nightmare would soon be over.

CHAPTER 24

PEREZ PULLED up next to Hawk's garage, and the three detectives walked up to the double door. Hawk pressed the open button on the garage door opener found on the "ghost," and a series of lights went off. "It's searching for a signal," Hawk said. A few seconds later, the door began to lift.

Perez headed for the inside of the garage with Hawk a step back when Nora yelled out, "Stop! Don't move!"

Perez and Hawk came to a sudden halt. Perez looked at Nora, "What the hell? What is it?"

"A tripwire! Just a few inches away from your foot!"

Perez stepped back. "I don't see anything."

"It's hard to see. From where I'm standing, the western sun illuminates it. See." She pointed to the thin, gauged, almost transparent wire strung across the garage floor. "If Hawk had driven his vehicle inside as he planned, the wire would've been tripped, and the bomb would've gone off."

"Oh God! That was close. Thanks, Ricci," Perez said, shaken by the thought of how close he came to being blown up.

Hawk stepped over the wire and entered his garage. On one side of the double garage, he had a couple of kayaks, a bicycle, and a jet ski stored. The other side was meant for his Jeep. Perez and Nora remained out. He followed the wire and immediately saw a homemade explosive attached to the wall. "Here it is. I'll try to disconnect the tripwire, at least."

"No! Don't touch anything," Perez said. "Let the bomb squad handle this. Get back here."

"I want to check out the house first."

"Detective, let the bomb squad do that. Let's wait for them. That's an order."

The three piled back into Perez's vehicle to wait. Hawk sat down in the back, and Nora took the front passenger seat. She leaned her pounding head back and, without addressing either Hawk or Perez, said philosophically, "You know, we really don't have much control whether we live or die. It's all up to fate or God and our angels. We've been just so damn lucky so far. Think of it! If we had come any later and the "ghost" didn't have to rush out of my house and leave a footprint, we might have been blown up. If you, Lieutenant, hadn't told us about the poison, we would've chucked down some juice and had coffee that was laced with cyanide. The footprint alerted us to a possible danger. Then, here, if Clint's wonderful neighbor hadn't told us about the woman exiting the garage, I know, Clint, that you would've pulled the Jeep into the garage, and we would've been blown up. If she hadn't pointed her out, we wouldn't have caught her. Of course, it was Stella, the awesome dog, that chased her down. If Stella hadn't, we wouldn't have caught up to her in time. She would've been gone by the time we got there. Isn't that fate?"

The two men sat silent for a minute, mulling over her words until Hawk said, "You're absolutely correct. We are not meant to die just yet. You should be relieved."

"You bet I am, but she was able to plant some heavy-duty kicks on me, and I really do need to find a couch and stretch out and then take a hot bath to relax my muscles."

"Look, Ricci, let me call an ambulance. You may have some internal bleeding."

"No, I'll be all right with some aspirin and rest. Where is that bomb squad, anyway? It's been a while, hasn't it?"

"No, it's only been ten minutes. They should be here any time now."

A few minutes later, a big bruiser of an armored van pulled up behind them. A policeman jumped out of the van and ordered everyone in the vicinity to evacuate the area for at least three hundred feet. Then, a policewoman from the bomb squad donned a heavily protected suit and gingerly entered the garage after being advised of the tripwire. She came back within five minutes holding the explosive device, about the size of a small paperback book and placed the device in a special, lined box in the back of the truck. Then, with a bomb-sniffing dog, she made her way into the townhouse and, after ten minutes, came back with another incendiary device, which she also placed in the same lined box.

Hawk saw the second bomb, and his heart sank. He really did not expect that there'd be another. He could have been blown up walking in or around the house. *Thank God Perez kept me from going in.* After shedding the heavy protective gear, the friendly, sturdy-looking policewoman came up to Hawk, Perez, and Ricci. "You're lucky, folks," she explained. "It could've been bad. It took Melvin, our bomb-sniffing dog, and me a while to find the second bomb. I've never seen anything like this before. The device was planted behind your living room couch. The tripwire was under your cushions. Once you sat down on the couch, that'd be it—you'd be gone," she chuckled. "Wasn't your time to die today ? Anyway, it's all clear now, and you can go in."

"There you go," Perez said. "You must really feel relieved now that the killer is captured."

"Yes, yes, yes!" Nora shouted out. "I just hope she's the last one."

"That's why Orlinski and Holliday need to keep looking for that woman who seems to be the go-between the inmates and the hitmen. By the way, get rid of all your open liquids and food just in case the "ghost" got to them with her poison."

CHAPTER 25

ORLINSKI AND Holliday had spent the morning searching for cameras on nearby buildings in the hope that one would have captured an image of the mystery woman that visited O'Leary in jail. Finally, a little before noon, the owner of an old building across from the sheriff's office allowed them to look at his videos. Orlinski was elated when, on one of the tapes, he spotted the woman walking on Delaware Street, then stopping at the light to cross Colfax. Once she crossed onto Tremont Place, she walked out of the range of the camera. Orlinski was anxious to search the buildings there and told Mortimer to follow him across Colfax. Mortimer had other immediate plans. He told Orlinski that he was starving and running out of energy. "We've walked miles, and I'm just not used to this high altitude yet. Could we take a break? I need sustenance."

"Doesn't Josephine feed you enough for breakfast?" Orlinski chuckled.

"Oh, she is incredibly careful with the portions. They are never enough, but she tells me it's for my own good."

"Geez. Okay, there's a Subway sandwich shop nearby."

"Oh, is it expensive? Josephine only gave me five dollars to keep in my wallet."

"Don't worry about it. I'll get lunch. You can get it next time."

"Oh…I'll have to ask Josephine about that, but I guess it'll be all right."

Orlinski shook his head and laughed. "Mortimer, don't worry about it. I'll survive."

"Oh, okay. Thank you."

At the sandwich shop, Mortimer ordered a twelve-inch meatball sandwich on white bread, two bags of potato chips, and a large Coke. Orlinski had a six-inch chicken sandwich on whole wheat and a glass of water. After Orlinski paid with a credit card and received their order, they sat down at a table next to the window. Before Orlinski was even able to unwrap his food, Mortimer was already chomping away with almost half of the big sandwich gone. He emptied one bag of chips as his partner took the first bite out of his sandwich. After guzzling down his drink, he sprang up and refilled his cup with more. Before Orlinski was half done with his food, Mortimer had devoured the rest of his sandwich and the second bag of chips. Orlinski could see him eyeing the chocolate chip cookies lying on the counter, but he did not offer to buy any. He could not believe how much and how fast Mortimer demolished the meal.

"Now, are you ready to go back to work?"

"Oh yeah. An afternoon nap would be great, but it never works out that way."

They walked back to the intersection that the woman had crossed, trying to follow her path. Once across Colfax, they came to a busy part of downtown. Orlinski spotted several cameras, and upon entering a business, they asked if they could view their security footage. After both provided the owner with their IDs and explained that they were searching for a dangerous woman, the owner quickly complied.

Both detectives were overjoyed when they spotted their target. The video showed her quickly removing her black-haired wig, which she furtively shoved into her bag, showing her natural hair color of light brown. She stood at the corner, apparently waiting for someone. A few minutes later, a Honda CRV pulled up, and she jumped into the car. Orlinski had a view of the Colorado front license plate but could not read anything off it.

"Is there a way to enlarge the picture?" He asked the woman. She shook her head and told him that she couldn't. "May I borrow this tape then? I bet with our equipment, we'll be able to read the plate numbers and letters."

She agreed after they promised to bring it back and provided her with a receipt on a scratch pad.

"Okay, Mortimer. We need to get back to the station and work on this tape. This may be a terrific lead."

"Good. I would sure like to nail her. Actually, when you said that she's a dangerous person, I felt that she might even be able to pull off a hit on Nora and Clint if the hired killer, the "ghost", didn't work out."

CHAPTER 26

THE COUCH, the one that was booby-trapped by that despicable killer, felt heavenly to Nora as she stretched out on it. She did not even want to think about the fact that if she had laid down before the bomb was removed, she would be dead. Instead, the pain and soreness occupied her mind. Hawk felt the same but wanted to make sure that Nora was comfortable. He ran upstairs and brought down a pillow and a blanket. He gave her a couple of Advils, brought her water, and told her to try to get some sleep. "Just think, we captured the killer, and we can really relax now."

Nora smiled as she opened her eyes and looked at Clint. "It does feel good to think that we don't have to worry about it any longer. You don't mind if I stay over tonight? I really don't want to go home and be by myself."

"Of course, of course. I like having you around. I'll prepare some coffee, and I have a tiramisu cake from Trader Joe's in the freezer. It's a small box, and it shouldn't take too long to thaw. We can have a little pick-me-up before dinner. For supper, I'll prepare some chops, baked potatoes, and a salad."

"You're kidding. You're going to do all that? I didn't know you could cook."

"What I'm going to do is really not cooking. No special talent for that."

Nora tried to laugh, but as she did, a stabbing pain struck her. She tried to sleep, being so exhausted, but the pain prevented it. Finally, it subsided, and she fell asleep. Meanwhile, Hawk took the cake out of the freezer along with a package of pork chops to thaw and looked in the pantry to make sure he had the potatoes he needed. When he returned, Nora was fast asleep. Hawk pulled a blanket over her and felt that he needed to stretch out himself. He went upstairs to his room and set the alarm on his phone to be awakened in ninety minutes so that he could start preparing dinner.

Ninety minutes later, Hawk jumped out of bed and made his way into the kitchen. As he started grilling a couple of pork chops on his back patio, Nora joined him. "Boy, you're really going at it. Are you doing okay?" She came over and rubbed his back.

He turned toward her and gave her a quick kiss. "Just a little sore, but overall, I'm okay. How about you?"

"I feel much better. Miraculously, a lot of the pain is gone. I knew that all I needed was just some rest." With her fingers, she gently squeezed the muscles around his neck. "It was so sweet of you to cover me up with a blanket. Did you get a snooze yourself?"

"Yeah. I conked out. Thanks for the massage. It felt wonderful. I needed that. Now I'm ready to fight crime again."

"That's somethin' that never ends. Do you think we'll be fighting it for the rest of our lives? Wouldn't that be exciting ?" She laughed, and Hawk detected the sarcasm in her voice.

He returned the laugh, "You bet. Don't you just love it?"

She chuckled, "Oh yeah. I just love it when my life is threatened not with only bullets but bombs and poison. Anyway, let's get off the subject. What can I do to help with dinner? I'll tell you what, I'll make a salad. I hope you have the lettuce in a sealed bag, though."

"Yeah. I threw away everything that was suspicious, including all the open containers. The cucumber is wrapped in plastic, and the shredded carrots haven't been opened yet. Unfortunately, I threw out the tomatoes. Just in case she injected the poison into them. Is that crazy or what?"

Nora said, "What," and laughed.

They sat down at the dinette table in the corner of the kitchen. The aroma of the chops with Hawk's special BBQ sauce from Texas filled the kitchen. Nora realized how hungry she now was. Her salad turned out all right, though a little skimpy with limited ingredients, and the baked potatoes were hot from the microwave. Hawk had a fresh, unopened container of sour cream, and they both dabbed a large portion of it on the potatoes.

Before Hawk joined Nora at the table, he pulled out a bottle of Merlot and began carefully checking for any puncture marks in the cork. He even found his magnifying glass to make sure he saw no needle marks. It looked fine. After opening the bottle, he poured a little into his glass and took several sniffs to determine if it smelled differently. He then took a sip and swirled it around his mouth. It tasted fine. So, he poured a glass for Nora and filled the rest of his glass. They toasted each other for surviving the day, but he noticed that Nora barely took a sip. Hawk also felt squeamish about taking a big gulp. "Okay, that's it. Let's not take any chances. I'll take it in for Chet to analyze it. How about plain water?"

"That's great with me. I mostly drink water with my meals, anyway."

They looked at each other and began to laugh hysterically at their paranoia. Finally, Nora commented, "This is sheer insanity. What had that nasty woman done to us?"

"I'm glad we caught her, that's for sure. But she was relying on those bombs to kill us. I don't think she bothered with the poison at my place. After all, we didn't find any indications in her pockets that she brought poison along."

"All right, then, Clint. Bring back that bottle of wine, and let's celebrate." They toasted to each other again and dug into the meals. Suddenly, their serene dinner was interrupted by the doorbell.

"I wonder who that might be?" Hawk asked.

Nora looked concerned. "Clint, don't open the door. I have a bad feeling."

CHAPTER 27

ONCE ENLARGED, the video revealed the license plate numbers and letters from the Honda CRV. The car was registered to Joseph Coretta in Arvada, Colorado, a northwestern suburb of Denver. With that information, Orlinski and Mortimer headed for the address shown in the DMV records. Their route took them to I-25, then west on I-70, and finally to the northbound Wadsworth Boulevard exit. Mortimer did not say much during the ride but looked worried.

"Something troubling you, Mortimer?"

"Oh. I'm concerned that it's getting late, and Josephine will be upset with me for coming home late for dinner."

"Doesn't she understand that duty calls and our job is not strictly nine to five, but however long it takes?"

"Yeah, she probably does, but I've determined that she is a very jealous person, and she may be concerned that I may be with another woman."

Orlinski almost laughed out loud but suppressed it. "Really?" *I can't imagine another woman would latch onto Mortimer, of all people.* "Why do you think that?"

"Well, I told her that I met this woman at the jail and that I thought that she was flirting with me. And she didn't like it and said that I must have come on to her and to cut that out if I know what's good for me."

"Wow. You really think that woman was flirting with you?"

"Well, she turned out to be very friendly after a bit and laughed at something I said. I didn't think it was funny, but evidently, she did."

Orlinski shook his head and rolled his eyes. *He doesn't know what flirting is.* "Well, maybe you should call Josephine and tell her that you're hot on a case in Arvada and may be late."

"Oh. I never thought of that. I'll do it." He pulled his flip-top phone from his pocket and punched in the numbers. Josephine answered on the first ring.

The speaker was inadvertently on, and Orlinski heard her raspy voice for the first time as she said, "This better be important. I'm reading a recipe for a vegan shepherd's pie, and I need to concentrate. Oh crap! I don't have any vegan Worcestershire sauce. Anyway, what do you want?"

"Oh, sorry. Just want to call you and let you know that I'm on a case with Stan Orlinski in a town called Arvada, and I'll be home late."

"It's Orlinski's fault, isn't it, dragging you out all over Colorado. What's so important in Arvada that you had to go? You and Orlinski are just goofing off, right?"

"No, Josephine. It's all work. We have a lead on the dangerous woman we're looking for." He noticed the old Main Street of Arvada as Orlinski turned onto Old Wadsworth Road. "Oh, we're in what looks like a charming downtown area of Arvada, and I have to go. I'll see you soon." He flipped closed his phone and cut Josephine off.

Orlinski said, "Wow. that Josephine of yours now blames me for your downfall," laughing so hard that he almost choked.

"I don't think that is funny at all. You heard?'

"Yeah, you had the speaker on."

"Sorry. She likes to blame everyone else. At least I don't get blamed all the time."

Orlinski laughed again and then said, "Coretta doesn't live far from the downtown area. The GPS shows him about four blocks away."

"I wouldn't mind walking around here a little. What do you know of the history of Arvada?"

Orlinski chuckled, "Nothing at all."

"Well, Nora knows the history of all these towns in Colorado. I think I'll ask her about Arvada when I see her."

"You do that. It's been a while since I've been here. I think I'll bring Sandy and have a tall glass of beer and a brat with sauerkraut at that German pub I saw on the way here. Maybe this Saturday."

Mortimer sat in silence after Orlinski's statement, deep in thought. Then he said, his tone suggesting envy, "It's nice that your wife would agree to come out and visit Arvada. Josephine would never do it. She'll say it's too far…will cost too much gas."

"You sure you know what you're getting into? It's not too late. You can still get out of marrying her."

"Oh. I committed myself. She wants to get married around Christmas. Originally, she told me it would be the summer of next year."

"Huh. Does that surprise you?"

"Yes, a little."

Orlinski parked on the street in front of a small wooden framed faded-yellow house with a brown door in the center and two windows on each side, also trimmed with brown paint.

They heard a dog bark inside as they stepped on a small concrete slab in front of the door. Before they had a chance to ring the doorbell, an unshaven man with a beer belly covered by a white T-shirt and wearing red shorts pulled the door open. A black and white mutt made its escape and took off down the street, but the man did not seem concerned.

"What do you want?"

The two detectives showed him their IDs and asked to see the woman that he picked up a few days ago at Tremont Place and Colfax. "Oh, geez, what did Adele do?"

Orlinski said, "We just need to talk to her about a case we're working on."

"Sorry, bub, but she took off in my car. I had my key on the coffee table. She grabbed it and told me that she was taking it. I didn't like it."

"Didn't you stop her?" Orlinski asked.

"No way, bub. She looked wild-eyed and determined to take my car."

"Any idea where she went?"

"Nope. Said she had some business to deal with in Denver. I asked what was so important, and she told me that it was none of my business. I'm hoping that I'll see my car again. She is dangerous, isn't she? That's why you're here?"

Mortimer said, "She could be."

"Well, I only met her about ten days ago at a bar. She came onto me, so I brought her here for the night. But now I can't get rid of her. I wish I never met her at all. She thinks I'm her servant. I'm not surprised that the police are looking for her because she's kinda of a mystery."

Mortimer asked, "Oh, what do you mean?"

"Well, for one, she told me she needed a place to stay, but I think that she has money. Her handbag and clothes all look like designer stuff. And she keeps getting all these phone calls as though she's a 911 operator or something.' But she tells me that she lost her job and can't find work. Do you think that she's just hiding out? I don't think that she's from this area."

"Could be," Orlinski said. "What's her name, anyway, and where's she from?"

"Detective, I swear that I don't know anything about her. She shuts me up if I ask any questions. She told me her name was Adele Smith, but I don't believe it's her real name. She's pretty suspicious and, quite frankly, a little scary."

"Why do you say that she's suspicious?"

"The way she acts…very secretive…always on the phone arranging things. But once it slipped out of her tight mouth that she had a boyfriend wrongfully accused in jail. And that she's going to do something about it."

"What did she mean by that?"

"Hell, if I know."

"Can we look at her room?" Mortimer asked, hoping that there would be clues as to her identity and where she might have gone.

"Yeah, no problem."

There wasn't much in the room—just a bed, nightstand, lamp, and a dresser. The small closet had a few of her clothes. Some underwear, a few T-shirts, and pajama bottoms were found in a dresser drawer. Orlinski looked under the bed and noticed a scrap piece of paper. He reached for it and pulled it toward him. The paper had some very sloppy handwriting. But Orlinski was able to decipher the chicken scratch to read, "Devon at 11:00 Thursday." He assumed that she meant Devon O'Leary, the inmate at the jail.

"Say, Mortimer, look at this note. This confirms it. She's the one who met with O'Leary. Probably the one that called the hitwoman to kill Clint and Nora." Orlinski bagged the note and crammed it into his pocket.

They shuffled back into the tiny living room and asked Joseph if he could remember anything else that she might've said before she left.

"No, I told you everything. Wait. She received a phone call that really freaked her out. I heard her say, 'What! Arrested! You idiot. I'll just take care of it myself.'"

"When did she receive that call?" Mortimer asked, expressing rare concern on his long face.

"About an hour ago. I guess she left right after that."

They thanked the man and ran back to the old, over-used Ford Crown Victoria police vehicle. Orlinski quickly dialed Hawk's number. Hawk didn't answer. He called Nora's cell next and had no response either. "Oh God! They may be dead already." His hand trembled as he called Lieutenant Perez and, in a nervous, fast voice, explained the phone call the woman had received. "I'm positive that she is out to get Hawk and Ricci. Can you send a cruiser to Hawk's house?"

Perez was sprinting down the stairs, two steps at a time, and out of the building while Orlinski was still talking. "I'm on my way, and I'll bring backup."

Mortimer said to Orlinski, "Put the lights and siren on and drive like the wind. I don't want anything to happen to Clint and Nora." Orlinski looked at him, and surprisingly, he thought he noticed his eyes well up. It seemed so unusual for Mortimer, who had never expressed any emotion.

As Orlinski dashed toward downtown Denver, Mortimer kept calling Hawk's phone numbers, then Nora's. He fidgeted in his seat, breathing slowly but hard, worrying what might have happened to them. Both he and Orlinski, and it seemed everyone in Division Six, had heard about the capture of the "ghost." But this woman, Adele, was a total surprise, and both Orlinski and Mortimer knew that Clint and Nora would never expect an ambush from her.

CHAPTER 28

THE DOORBELL chimed again as Hawk pulled his phone out of his pants pocket and clicked on the Ring door application. The screen showed an image of a blonde-haired woman who appeared anxious. He thought that she needed help, so he rose from the table to find out what the woman wanted.

"Who is it?" Nora asked, still suspicious of everyone, particularly some stranger at the door. Hawk showed the image to Nora and looked at the picture again more carefully. Suddenly, she seemed vaguely familiar. "Wait," Nora said, raising her voice. "Let me look at that image again."

Both Nora and Hawk studied it closely, and then it struck them at the same time that the woman was the one with O'Leary at the jail. What threw them off at first was that the woman had changed her hair color from black to blonde. "I think she's out to kill us for O'Leary," Nora said. "She must've had a message from the "ghost" that she was arrested."

Hawk agreed. They had to act quickly and come up with a plan. It turned dark while they were dining, and the only light in the house was a five-bulb chandelier over the table. Seeing the spooled wire, the "ghost" used for a trip wire that he left at a corner of the kitchen counter, he had an idea. "Hurry, Nora," he whispered, "grab your gun and hide in the pantry while I'll hide in the hall closet next to the entry. Before that, I'll run a taut wire from the leg of the couch across to the leg of the side chest in the foyer. Hopefully, she won't see it, and when she trips, you and I scurry out and grab her."

"All right," Nora said. "Might work. Oh, let's shut off the phones so they won't go off, and I'll turn off the kitchen light. Oh God, she's picking the lock. Hurry!"

Under the cover of darkness, Hawk ran the wire across as planned. Both the couch and the decorative chest were heavy and would hold the wire tightly. *I bet she thinks that we're out and will wait for us to return. Not on my watch, you won't, bitch.* As he heard the lock click and the door handle turn, he rushed and slipped into the closet, leaving a small gap open in the door.

A second or two later, he heard a footstep, then nothing. Then the woman took another step and waited again, listening intently to whether anyone was home. Then, she took the third and fourth steps and did the same. Hawk saw that she had not turned on a flashlight to guide her but relied on the light coming through the windows from a street lamp.

After waiting patiently for a few seconds, she decided that there indeed was no one home and she quickened her pace as if looking for a place to hide and to wait for Hawk to come home. She felt emboldened as she quickened her pace when her foot caught the wire. The chest moved as it scraped the floor, and at the same time, the woman swore as she stumbled but did not fall but remained off-balanced. Hawk did not wait. Flying out of the hall closet, he dove at the woman, tackling her. Her gun flew out of her hand as her head and shoulder hit the ceramic tile floor of the entryway. Nora was there in a flash, and together, they turned her over and used Hawk's cuffs. Still attached to his belt to secure her.

The shocked woman screamed and cussed as they stood her upright. Nora pushed her against the wall as she tried to kick the detectives. After the lights were switched on, Hawk undid the wire, and Nora searched the pockets in the woman's pants and secured her phone. There was nothing else to indicate who she was. The woman finally calmed down, and Hawk reached for his phone to call for a cruiser to take her away. He forgot that it was turned off, and while waiting for the phone to reboot itself, the front door tore open with the full force of a powerful kick. To Hawk's and Nora's surprise, Perez and two uniformed officers rushed in, their weapons drawn.

Perez studied the scene for a second and took a long look at the woman still being held by Nora. Perez blew out a deep breath, shook his head, and said, "Thank God that you're both alive! Even captured the suspect! That's O'Leary's girlfriend? Who is she, anyway?"

Nora said, "Yeah, the one from the jail visit. She clammed up but first said that she wouldn't talk without a lawyer. We'll interrogate her tomorrow."

"No, I want Orlinski and Holliday to handle this one."

"How in the hell did you know to come, anyway?" Hawk asked, still surprised that Perez showed up.

"You need to thank Orlinski and Holliday for that. They figured out that she was on her way to kill you. I must say, I never had heard of Orlinski being so concerned and frightened for your safety. We all tried to call you numerous times, but there was no answer, and that added to our anxiety that she got to you." He turned to the officers and ordered for the woman to be removed to jail.

Hawk's phone rang, and it was Mortimer. "We're all right, buddy," Hawk said. Thanks for your worry."

"Oh, you're welcome." And at that point, Mortimer said something that was so uncharacteristic of him. "Yeah, I didn't want anything to happen to you two. I need Nora or you to tell me the history of Arvada."

Hawk laughed. "Mortimer, that's a great joke."

"Oh, did I make a joke? I didn't think so."

After he hung up, Nora asked, "Surely, he was joking, right? That can't be the only reason he was worried about us?"

"Of course, it must've been his way of humor. But I must say, that was so unusual for Mortimer. Maybe it's all an act that he can't understand humor."

"Okay, now," Perez said, "Try to get some rest if you can. Your adrenaline must be way up there. Capturing two wanted criminals in one day is quite a feat. Take tomorrow off, and I'll see you the next day. I'm sure Captain MacGregor will want an update on the Visser and Durand cases."

CHAPTER 29

THEY SNUGGLED up on Hawk's sofa, their heads touching, their hands clasped as they wound down from the events of the day. "There can't be anyone else out to kill us today," Nora commented. "Can there?"

Hawk chuckled, "No way. I think we're safe. Not only did we capture the hitwoman, but we also snagged the messenger. Hopefully, O'Leary or Bradford will run out of people willing to get rid of us."

"Okay, then. Your words made me feel better. But I'm totally beat. I got to get to bed."

"I'll prepare the guest room for you. It'll only take a second."

"Actually, Clint…I don't think I can sleep alone tonight. My insides are still rattled from barely surviving. You know that if it wasn't for lucky breaks…we would have been killed. You don't mind if I join you in bed, do you?"

Surprised at her request, he was elated. No matter how many times in the past he had suggested to sleep together before, she wouldn't hear of it. This was quite an about-face, and he was all for it. "Of course, of course. Since you're my bodyguard, that's the best protection anyone could get."

"No hanky-panky, though," Nora laughed. "I just want you near me."

"No problem. We'll see how that goes."

Unfortunately for Hawk, by the time he laid down in bed, Nora was fast asleep. Her head was on the pillow, rolled over onto her side with her back to him. He had an overwhelming desire to touch her. Snuggling up, he gently positioned his arm, embracing her hip. She did not wake up. As he lay just inches away, he smelled the tinge of vanilla in the fragrance of her perfume, one that he had become so accustomed to. He liked having her in his bed. A moment later, overpowered by fatigue, he turned to his side of the bed, and he was out for the night.

In the morning, when Hawk awakened, he sniffed the wonderful aroma of coffee and heard Nora fiddling around in the kitchen. When he came down, dressed casually, Nora, dressed in navy blue slacks and a peach shirt, was already frying eggs for breakfast. "Sleepyhead, you're finally down. I hope you feel like eggs this morning with toast and marmalade?"

"Good morning to you as well," Hawk laughed. "I'm hungry enough to eat anything right now."

"Great. I thought that after breakfast, even though we have the day off, we should discuss who we think killed the lawyers. What do you say?"

"No problem. I'd like to get that case out of the way, that's for sure."

After breakfast, Nora asked Hawk for a couple of sheets of paper. Once he brought them, she wrote down the names of the potential suspects in the case. She began with Angie Visser and scribbled a box around the name. She did the same for Norman Durand, Winfred White, Lorenzo Garza, Ursula Hamlin, Brittany Larsen, and Melody Elmers. "Can you think of anyone else, Clint?"

"Yeah, I'd add Goldie Hendrix."

"Okay. But why Goldie Hendrix?"

"I'm not sure. It's just a gut feeling. We need to find out more about her husband's murder. And to do that, we should talk to the investigating detective, Carpenter. I'd like to know where the bullet struck him and from what distance the shooting took place."

"Surely, you don't think that there's a connection?"

"There might be. After all, Goldie is supposed to be good with guns."

"Interesting. Okay, let's place her on the list. So, what's your gut tell you about Angie?"

"I have mixed feelings about her, Nora. We know she lied about not knowing about her husband's affairs. She has a weak alibi that supposedly she was stuck in traffic at about the time of the murders. What do you think?"

"Angie would be the one with the best reason to kill Visser if she was aware of his philandering. And she knows the building. But I don't think she has it within her to take someone else's life. She strikes me as being soft. Besides, she has a great lifestyle—country club life—and why would she want to jeopardize that?"

"Well, I heard someone once say that everyone could kill if pushed far enough. But you may be right. Do you want to take her off the list?"

Nora said, "Not at all. I'd like to see if she has a nine-millimeter pistol registered to her or to Visser. I also think that we need to talk to her tennis friends and get the scoop on her from them."

"So, who's next on your list? Oh, yeah, Norman Durand. What do you think of him?"

"Well, Clint. I think we had written him off because of his alibi and the fact that he knew Elizabeth was messing around and didn't care. But maybe we need to check out that alibi at the bar. I have a gut feeling that it really bothered him that she messed around. He seems aggressive enough to do them both in."

"All right, let's make a trip to the bar. Maybe this afternoon for a cocktail."

"Ooh, I could use a margarita."

"Okay, it's a date."

At that moment, the doorbell rang, and both detectives jumped in their seats, afraid that it might be someone else after them. Clint looked at his phone and smiled, "It's Mrs. Lucero bringing Stella back. It was so nice of her to watch her all night. I would've been too tired to deal with the dog."

"Hello, my two heroes," Hawk said. "You two were absolutely marvelous." Stella jumped up on Hawk, then on Nora. Both showered the dog with hugs and scratches around the soft ears.

"Mrs. Lucero, please join us for lunch today. We'll go to your favorite restaurant."

"Oh, thank you, but you don't have to do anything like that. I didn't do anything extraordinary, just thought that woman looked suspicious, that's all. Besides, I have a few errands to run. But thank you. Next time."

After she left, Hawk addressed his dog, "Stella, you deserve a steak, and that will be your treat."

Upon hearing the word "treat," Stella ran to the pantry where the Milk Bones were kept, wagging her tail, ready to crunch down on two or three. Both Hawk and Nora laughed as Hawk said, "Well, I didn't mean those as a treat…okay, here you go." Stella couldn't wait as she lifted herself on her hind legs and greedily grabbed the treats.

She then laid down between Nora and Hawk, who sat behind the kitchen table, continuing their analysis of the case.

"So, Clint, where we at? You want to talk about the staff, Brittany Larsen, Melody Elmers, and Ursula Hamlin?"

"Sure. You go first."

"I don't think that Brittany is the killer. She admitted liking Visser, but since he was married and unavailable, that turned her off."

"Yeah, and I think she enjoyed vicariously listening to them make out in the office through a porous door."

"Yuck! You're kidding."

"No, she actually insinuated to me that it kind of turned her on."

"Okay, okay. Then there's Melody, who Brittany said had a crush on Visser, and every time he and Elizabeth got together, she really looked upset. She told me that she didn't like what they were doing because of her religious beliefs—they broke the Commandment against adultery. She said she could never kill anyone because that would be a violation of the Commandment against killing."

"So, what do you think, Clint?"

"Frankly, I don't think either one was the killer based on that butt imprint in the basement. Brittany's is too small, and Melody's is bigger than the imprint."

"Oh, you checked that out, did you?"

"Of course. It's all part of good detective work." Both laughed.

"Well, if that's your criteria, then what about Angie and that Goldie that you seemed to take a liking to.?"

"Liking to? You're hilarious, Nora." He laughed, and she joined in. "But to answer your question, and of course, I'd have to measure carefully, I believe that both Angie and Goldie would've fit the criteria." He chuckled. "I think I should go and check the women out."

Nora slapped him across his arm, chortling, "You'd like that, wouldn't you?"

Hawk was still laughing when he received a phone call from an unknown Denver area number. Accepting the call, he heard a sweet voice say, "Hello, Detective Hawk, this is Brittany Larsen from the law offices. I hope you don't mind me bothering you, but you asked me if Mr. Visser might've had any other affairs besides with Elizabeth."

"Yes, do you think he had?"

"It occurred to me that there was someone that came to see Mr. Visser without an appointment a few times. She wasn't a client or anything like that. But each time she came, Mr. Visser seemed to get rid of his appointment rapidly and almost ran out to see this woman."

"Do you know who she is?"

"No, he kept her name a secret from me and Ursula."

"Can you describe her, Brittany?"

"Um…I was just wondering if we could meet up in person, perhaps over a cup of coffee?"

"That won't be necessary. What if Detective Ricci and I come by later this afternoon?"

Sounding disappointed, she said, "Um…I guess that's all right. I really didn't want the other girls in the office to see me talking to the police again. They may think that I'm telling stuff about them or something."

"I see. Well, perhaps we could meet at Hudson's Hill on East Thirteenth Street at around four this afternoon."

"I'll see you then. I know the place."

Nora didn't look pleased listening to the conversation over the speaker. "Here we go again, another Tina Dionisio who wouldn't give up her information unless you had dinner with her. I'm coming with you this time for sure. She has a flimsy excuse as to why she and you need to meet in person."

Hawk chuckled, "Oh, Nora, you always exaggerate everything when you think some woman is out to get me. I'm not that easy to get. Besides, when someone calls like that, trying to be too cooperative, my suspicions as to motive are raised."

"What do you mean?"

"It's just that when a witness that's a possible suspect appears too cooperative and helpful, I sometimes wonder if they are covering up their own crime and pointing the finger at someone else. Think of it,

Nora, didn't you tell me that she was quick to pin the murders on Melody Elmers?"

"Yes, she did. And her not dating married men could be just a bunch of bunk. From what you told me, she listened to the two lawyers making out. I think she cared for Visser, and their screwing each other must really have driven her crazy. Crazy enough to sit in the basement and wait for the right moment to get her revenge." She nodded her head, "Hmm. You might have something there, Clint. Let's see what she says. I'll bet she'll try to pin it on some mysterious person."

Content with that analysis, Nora asked, "You interviewed Ursula Hamlin, Visser's long-time paralegal. What do you think of her?"

"I wouldn't write her off. She wouldn't admit it, but she carried a flame for her boss. She was with him when he first began practicing. She helped him get started, accepted late pay when he had cashflow problems and enjoyed having lunches with him. And just as we assume with Brit, it must've really hurt to see him carry on with other women. And yet, she denied that he ever made a pass at her. She might've flipped and couldn't take it any longer and shot them out of deep frustration and revenge."

"We're not eliminating anyone, it seems. What about the two partners?"

"Both had a strong motive to break up the partnership. But, to arrange the killings at the precise moment when they were making love doesn't make sense. It was a partnership disagreement, a business matter. I wouldn't think that they'd go to the trouble of shooting them in their own building."

"Unless White wanted to throw us off and make it look like a jilted lover getting his or her revenge."

"Geez, Nora, you're just complicating everything. You may be right on point. But I really don't think they'd kill Visser because he didn't want to move out. They're lawyers. They would've gone to court. What about Lorenzo Garza? We hadn't talked to him, but Harry can't see him killing anyone…what about a disgruntled client?"

"Nancy and Harry are working on that angle. Let's see what they come up with, but I don't buy it. Let's go get some lunch."

"Let's call Perez and tell him what we're doing and what we plan to do. Let's head out to Parker and have lunch and a cocktail at Durand's place."

<h1 style="text-align:center">CHAPTER 30</h1>

THE DUROS bar, owned by Norman Durand, was a free-standing building a block west of busy Highway 83 on the outskirts of Parker, Colorado. The interior walls were lined with empty beer, liquor, and wine bottles of every brand and variety, making the place interesting from that perspective. The food menu was limited, but not the liquor selections. Also limited was the number of tables, which happened to be occupied. Nora and Hawk decided to wait a few minutes for one to open. They looked around to see if Norman Durand was in the place but didn't see him.

Nora had an idea, "Clint, wait here for a table. I'd like to ask that bartender some questions." She walked over to the long bar and called out to the balding, round-faced, round-bellied man who then ambled over to what she needed. "We're looking for Mr. Durand. Is he available?"

"Lady, he's seldom here. He's the boss and just checks in once in a while."

"He's not here full-time on weekends or on Fridays?"

"Especially, then. He likes his boating and skiing." Suddenly, the man hesitated and winced, his face showing concern. With a sharpening of his voice, he said, "Come to think of it, he was here all afternoon last Friday until closing." Taking a few steps away, he threw out over his shoulder that he had drinks to get out.

Before he went too far, Nora asked, "One more question: what do you suggest on the menu to eat?"

He stopped, turned around to face Nora, and smiled for the first time, a tooth missing from his upper jaw. "I'd go somewhere else. The food here is not great."

Nora laughed along with his chuckle. "Thanks for the tip. Do you know when Mr. Durand will be in?"

"Nope. He just comes and goes." The man walked to the other end of the bar and grabbed a couple of beers for the waitress to serve.

"What did he say?" Hawk asked, knowing what Nora was up to.

"He said that we should go someplace else to eat since the food sucks." She laughed.

"No, didn't you ask him if Durand was working Friday afternoon and evening?"

"Yes, of course. At first, he said that Durand comes and goes, especially on Fridays and weekends. But then, as though he remembered what he was supposed to say, he said, 'Oh, I forgot. Yes, the boss was in all day Friday.' It was obvious that he was coached. The guy is a bad liar. If pressed, he'll tell the truth."

"So, it looks like Durand's alibi may not be all that solid." Hawk glanced around the place again, then asked, "Do you want to go somewhere else to eat?"

"No, I think we should try their fantastic food," Nora laughed heartily. "Perhaps Durand will grace us with his appearance. Also, I'd like to see what the waitress says."

A corner table opened, and the detectives grabbed it. Menus were stacked behind the napkin holder, and they began perusing the list. "What looks good to you?" Hawk asked.

"Nothing, but I'll try the smothered burrito, and you?"

"I'll stick to the hamburger."

They waited at least fifteen minutes before the ample-proportioned, ash-blonde waitress sauntered over. She looked like she worked out and could easily bench press three hundred pounds. She was the only server and appeared worn out. Nora thought her to be younger than she looked, maybe in her early forties, although she could have easily passed for fifty. Her bulging arm muscles were decorated with colorful, undeterminable tattoos. The width of her short neck was almost as wide as her head. The name tag on her full chest showed the name "Shirl."

Voraciously chewing gum, she asked Hawk and Nora what they wanted to drink. After both told her they just wanted water, she stopped writing on a pad and said in a gruff voice, "You gotta be kidding me? You come into a bar that serves liquor and only want water!" She shook her head.

"Nora said, "We came to eat, and we know what we want."

"Okay, it's your funeral. So, what do you want?"

"I'll have a hamburger with fries," Hawk said.

"Ain't got no fries. You want chips?"

"Sure, why not." She rolled her large green eyes as she turned her attention to Nora.

"Any chance that your cook can make a grilled cheese sandwich?" Nora asked meekly.

The waitress sighed, "This ain't a five-star restaurant. We only serve what's on the menu."

"In that case, I'll have the smothered burrito. By the way, is Norman Durand here?"

"He comes and goes. Chances are he won't be around, so if you want to complain about me, you're out of luck. Besides, I don't give a shit what happens." She swallowed hard with a belligerent expression on her oval face.

Surprised at her attitude, Nora said, "No, I don't want to complain about you. I think you're very efficient."

"Well, I ain't hearing that from nobody that much." She forced a subdued grin, showing her yellowed teeth.

"Surely, Norman is here on Friday evenings when you're real busy?"

"Ahh, you and Norman. What's this about Norman anyway? I told you that he ain't here much. That's all right by me. When he does show up, all he does is bitch that we're not selling enough booze."

"So, he wasn't in last Friday evening or night until closing?"

The woman suddenly became suspicious. She appraised both Nora and Hawk carefully. "Are you cops or somethin'?"

"Yes," Nora said, "we're just trying to find out if your boss was on Friday night. Sounds to me that he wasn't. Am I correct?"

"Look, I'll get you the grub, but no more information." She walked away in a huff. Hawk watched her as she moved away, noticing the back of her maroon T-shirt with the name Duros Bar emblazed on it and tan loose-fitting pants covering her rather narrow hips. Her wide black sneakers squeaked on the painted gray cement floor.

"She's a strange one. I can't figure out if that went well or not," Hawk said with a chuckle.

"I think it did. Both the bartender and Shirl said that Durand doesn't come in very often. So, as far as I'm concerned, Durand lied about being here from four o'clock to closing. We need to focus on him more. Ask him some more questions. But, boy, judging by her aggressive but hangdog expression, that waitress seems to have her own set of problems, don't you think?"

"Yeah, she has issues, all right. We do need to talk to Norman Durand again. This time, though, we need to get him into the station."

The patrons of the bar were an interesting bunch for the detectives to observe. Several motorcycles were parked in an orderly row outside the place as they drove up. Over half of the customers present were older motorcycle riders with tattoos, leather vests, and boots. Many were accompanied by their "motorcycle mamas," who were also dressed for the part; some were scantily clad. The rest of the crowd seemed to be blue-collar types there for lunch. Everyone knew everyone else, and laughter flowed easily. The music was loud, and a rerun of some baseball game was on the hanging television to the side of the bar. The beer flowed freely.

"A fun place," Hawk said.

"Yeah, if you like that kind of a place."

About twenty minutes after they ordered, Shirl showed up and plopped the platters down in front of them. A slew of chips flew off Hawk's plate. She left, but then a second later she made an about-face and came back to the detectives' table. Without asking, she grabbed an empty chair from the adjacent table and sat down with Hawk and Nora, elbows on the table.

"Since you're here asking about my boss, it's about them two lawyers that were shot, right?"

Nora said, "Yes, that's correct. Do you know anything about that?"

"Nope. But I do know that if anyone had a reason to kill, it sure would've been Norman. The way his wife treated him, always two-timing him and taunting him about her screwing that prick Visser. Carrying on in his office after hours, butt naked."

Nora and Hawk exchanged glances. "How do you know that?" Hawk asked, surprised that she knew about the affair and, more importantly, about them being naked.

"Norman told me about his whoring wife. Ain't got a notion how he could stand it for so long."

"You said they were naked in Visser's office?" Nora asked, her ears perked up.

"Dah. Of course, they were butt naked. How else do you screw on a regular basis as they did ? It wasn't a quicky, I bet. There was no one else in the building, right?"

"I'm surprised Norman told you all of this," Hawk said. "He actually told you that they were naked when they were killed?"

"Sure. When he's in the mood, he tells me a lot of stuff…mostly how horrible his wife is…was."

"Do you believe that he killed the two lawyers?" Nora asked, thinking that perhaps she knew.

"Kill? This is the deal here. Anybody can kill if they have to. It's how much they're shit on." She looked away, toward the entrance door, then twisted her neck back to the detectives. She looked at them, then abruptly stood, pushed the chair back, and before she shuffled off, spit out, "Figure it out, hotshots. If my wife were screwing her boss on a regular basis, I'd certainly kill them both."

The hamburger was thin. Hawk lifted the top bun and saw a thin piece of prefabricated meat, a pickle, and a piece of lettuce topped with mustard and catsup. Nora's smothered burrito, though, looked good. Nora took a bite or two of her food, and her eyes flew open. "Oh my gosh," she said. "I've had spicy before, but nothing like this. Must be a Carolina Reaper or something like that." She grabbed her water and flushed her throat with it. "I can't eat this fire."

Hawk took a bite out of his hamburger. It was dry and tasteless, like a piece of shoe leather. They glanced at each other and laughed. "Let's find a McDonalds," Hawk said. Nora nodded, and they got up. As Hawk did, he happened to glance at the kitchen door, which was just a few feet from the edge of the bar. He caught someone watching them through the dirty glass of the swinging door. As soon as their eyes met, the face disappeared. From what he could see, it seemed to him that it was Durand. They paid at the bar before they left, including a twenty percent tip for the waitress.

As they drove away from Duros Bar and headed out, neither one noticed that they were being followed. Finding the fast-food place, they turned into the drive-thru. Nora said, "I don't think I would've enjoyed a drink in that place. No wonder Durand is worried about his business. But then, supposedly, he's never there, and that's what happens when the boss is absent. There's probably a lot of theft—a lot of free booze for friends."

"If Durand is having financial troubles, it wouldn't be a bad idea to check on life insurance policies for Elizabeth, and while we're at it, check what Visser had," Hawk said. "It could be that Elizabeth was heavily insured."

On the way back to Denver, Hawk glanced in the rearview mirror. His eyes shot open wide with alarm as he saw a heavy-duty pickup equipped with a grille guard approaching them at a high rate of speed. They were on a two-lane road with heavy construction adding lanes as they headed back to I-25 from Parker. Oncoming traffic was heavy on Hawk's left, and a low-profile concrete barrier was on his right. There was nowhere to turn to escape the approaching truck that seemed determined to cause an accident. "Nora, brace yourself, quick! We're about to be hit."

<h1 style="text-align:center">CHAPTER 31</h1>

ONLY ABOUT one hundred feet separated Hawk's Jeep from the vehicle in front. He did not have the distance to outrun the truck, even if he could. Nevertheless, Hawk shoved the accelerator pedal to the floor. The engine whined, but Hawk was able to get some distance from the oncoming truck. He knew that whoever the driver was meant to do harm. The truck sped up. He could see it in the rearview mirrors. Nora could see it, too, as she turned her head and looked out the back window. "Oh geez," she shouted. "He's out to get us."

The truck struck the rear bumper of Hawk's Jeep, causing him to fishtail and almost lose control. He fought to stabilize the vehicle. Searching for any pullouts or driveways in which he could escape, but did not see any. His palms sweat as he notices the truck is about to strike them again, this time with greater force. Suddenly, it slowed, and Hawk gained some distance. But the driver had no intention of giving up. Instead, he floored the accelerator pedal. The distance helped build up the torque, and the truck shot out like a rocket toward the Jeep, bearing down on the smaller vehicle.

Hawk had to think fast. As with Moses in the parting of the sea, there suddenly was a break in the oncoming traffic, allowing him to escape into the oncoming lane, hoping to jump back into his lane as the truck passed, but the truck slowed and drove parallel to the Jeep not allowing him to get back into his lane before the oncoming traffic hit him. Hawk began to panic. The oncoming traffic was approaching fast. By some miracle, he spotted someone's narrow dirt road in the field just one hundred feet away. He slowed as much as he dared and abruptly yanked on the wheel to escape onto the dirt road. The tires squealed, Nora screamed, and they braced for the Jeep to roll. The passenger side wheels lifted off the ground, but not enough to flip the Jeep, and Hawk made it to the safety of the dirt road.

They sat silently, trying to settle their nerves from the traumatic event. Nora had her eyes closed while Hawk stared at the overcast sky through the windshield. His breathing was hard and rapid. Nora grabbed his hand. "Oh God! That was close." Her chest heaved as she tried to get her breath back. "Great job of driving, Clint. You're my hero." She squeezed his hand again. "Well, you certainly know how to entertain a girl," Nora said, a lame attempt to make a joke of the situation even though her insides still rattled. "What was that about? The guy was insane. If he had caused an accident, he would've been right in the thick of it. He had no escape either. I tried to get a glimpse of the driver through the windshield. Couldn't tell from the side since he had tinted windows, but it looked to me that it was Durand. Do you think it was just road rage or something more?"

"Hell, if I know. It was a man driving, and I can't say for sure, but you're right. It did look somewhat like Norman Durand. But I didn't think that Durand was such an idiot. Whoever that was was not the sharpest tool in the shed, that's for sure. A real dumb asshole."

"How can that be? How could he just happen to be behind us? And how did he know we were in your private car?"

"It must've been Durand, though. He saw us leave his place. I thought I saw him watching us from the kitchen door. And when we left the parking lot, I saw a black Ram 2500 truck parked on the side of the building. And it was a black Ram truck that was after us. He might've gotten pissed off that we were asking questions about him. I'm sure the bartender and the waitress told him."

"That's bizarre. What did he think he would accomplish by that stunt? That's just plain idiocy."

"I think he lost it. He must have a hell of a temper and can't control himself. That's what happens in all these road rage incidents. People just simply lose control of themselves and forget about the consequences. Like in this case, as you said, how would he have been able to escape from an accident that he caused?"

Nora said, "Maybe the idiot if he had a brain at all, thought that he could escape after causing the accident and find his way across the highway and take off through the field."

As they talked and tried to settle their nerves, a car pulled up behind them. "Now what?" Hawk said as he exited the Jeep, followed by Nora.

An elderly man and woman also exited their Honda Accord. "Are you folks all right?" The white-haired woman asked.

"Yes, thank you ," Nora said. "It's so nice of you to check up on us."

"Well, from what we witnessed, he really tried to do damage to you," the heavy-set man, with a full head of white hair and a nicely trimmed mustache and beard, said. "If you or he had lost control of your vehicles, who knows how many other people would've been hurt, or worse yet, killed. We felt that we had to find a way to turn around and see if you were all right or needed some help."

"You know, we saw what that nasty man was doing," the woman said. "Such awful road rage. Anger is an epidemic these days."

"Seems to be," Hawk said. "Were you behind him?"

"Yes," the man said. "I was a little nervous myself. I didn't know what he'd do."

"I think that was just criminal," the woman concurred. "But if it will be helpful to you, I did get part of his license plate number from that black truck, which we think was a Dodge. The first three numbers are 874, but we couldn't get the rest."

After introducing themselves, the detectives obtained their names and addresses. The older couple were shocked to see that they were police officers. "Do you think that he knew you were police and he targeted you?" The woman asked, looking bewildered.

Nora said, "Perhaps, but we can't figure out how the driver of the truck would know since we were in a private car."

As everyone was ready to leave, the parties shook hands, and Nora again thanked the man and woman for taking the time and effort to check up on them.

Back on the road, Nora patted Hawk's hand as he held the wheel. "I simply can't understand that if it were Durand, why did he do that? I mean, knowing that we're investigating him, why draw more attention to himself?"

"It is baffling. We were just trying to verify his alibi."

"Can someone become so angry as to lose control of his senses and pull a stunt like that? You're a psychology major. What do you think?"

"It happens. I tend to remember studying the phenomena. Intermittent Explosive Disorder is the name for someone who has an episode of impulsive anger that's out of proportion to whatever set the guy off. Usually triggered by financial problems, which Durand evidently has, and it may even be his way of grieving for his wife."

"Sounds like you're defending the creep," Nora said with disgust. "I feel no sympathy for him since he tried to kill us. His bizarre, stupid behavior and what Shirl said about him make him our prime suspect for the murders. He could've lost it and killed the two lawyers out of built-up rage like he exhibited with us."

"I'm not defending him. What he did was wrong. I'm just trying to explain why some people lose it and lash out in rage. I've been thinking about whether he killed the lawyers in a fit of anger. It seems to me that what he did today was an impulsive act that was beyond his control. Whoever had murdered, the lawyers had planned the killings. He or she had the patience to wait it out in the basement for the precise moment when the two were screwing. It still might've been Durand, but at the time, he had control over himself and knew exactly what he was doing."

Nora took another deep breath. She rubbed her neck. Looking at Hawk, who was examining his Jeep for damage, she said, "Now that I've settled down a bit, we're assuming that the driver was Durand. It's just pure conjecture on our parts based on a similar black Ram truck that you saw in the Duros parking lot. We better not jump to conclusions. We have a partial plate number, and we better check it out first. Don't you think?"

"You bet."

"Okay then, Clint. We have a couple of hours before the meeting with Brittany. Should we talk to Detective Carpenter regarding the murder of Goldie Hendrix's husband, or do you want to talk to Angie's tennis partners?"

"Actually, Nora, the stress of avoiding a major accident wore me out. My mind is shot right now. Since we're supposed to have the day off, what do you say if we go back to my place and hang loose till we meet with Brittany later."

"That sounds so good right now. I think, though, that I'll call Perez and tell him what we've been up to." She chuckled, "Some day off we're having."

CHAPTER 32

PEREZ COULDN'T believe what he heard from Nora. He was not at all pleased with them for not following his advice to relax before coming back to work. "I gave you a day off for you to calm your nerves from almost being blown up by one woman and then almost shot by another. And what do you do? Go out and almost get injured or killed again."

"Sorry, Lieutenant," Nora said. "Both Clint and I are anxious to wrap this case up. There's still a lot of work to be done. Anyway, we're anxious to solve it. We're too pumped simply to do nothing."

"I don't get it. I know if I had a paid day off, I'd find a ton of things to do besides work. All right, have a good interview with Brittany Larsen, and I'll see you in the morning."

Brittany Larsen looked disappointed when she saw Nora enter the coffee shop with Hawk. She hoped to get to know him better and vice versa. She hoped that, by chance, they'd hit it off. He appeared to be a decent man, unmarried. She found it difficult to find someone she'd like to be with. *All the ones I meet are creeps who think too much of themselves. All they're interested in is to get me into bed.* She was lonely and wanted to be with a companion that she liked.

She gave Hawk a wide smile and forced a smile at Nora. Brittany wore a sleeveless, low-cut yellow dress, her red hair flowing over one shoulder. Her make-up was light but blended well with her milky-white skin. She had a few freckles visible below her bright green eyes. She looked stunning, and Nora noticed the admiration in Hawk's face. *I'm glad I came. Without me here, she'd be all over Clint. I bet she really doesn't have any good information to give us anyway. This is just her ruse to see him.*

"Hello, detectives," Brittany said, "May I get you some coffee or something else?" They both declined. "I hope I won't be wasting your time with what I remembered. I also want to apologize for not seeing you in the office, but I thought it was best to talk without prying eyes, especially those belonging to Ursula. She watches everything that goes on in the building and will wonder why you came to see me again."

"We understand," Nora said, wanting to steer the conversation to be more between herself and Brittany rather than between the woman and Clint. "No problem, this place is fine. So, what do you have for us?"

"Well, Clint, I mean Detective Hawk, asked me if I knew of any other affairs that Mr. Visser was having besides with Elizabeth. I remembered that there was a woman about Mrs. Visser's age who came in about a week ago asking if Baxter was in. She had a southern drawl. I told her that he was with a client and asked if she had an appointment. She laughed and said, 'Oh honey, I don't need an appointment with Baxy. He's always happy to see me.' Then she sat down and waited for the client to leave."

"What did she look like?" Hawk asked.

"Rich. She had black curly hair and lots of makeup and wore fancy, expensive clothes."

Hawk went to his phone, clicked on Facebook, and searched for Goldie Hendrix. He thought that she would be on it, and sure enough, he found her image."

"Brit, would this be her by chance?"

She studied the picture carefully. "Looks like her, but I'm not quite sure."

"Thank you. Did she get to see Baxter, or as she called him, Baxy?" Hawk asked.

"Oh yes, Clint. As soon as Mr. Visser showed the client out, she strode toward him. He had a great big smile as he invited her in." Hawk did not like her calling him by his first name but decided to let it go this time. Nora did not like it at all and felt like punching the brash woman.

"Miss Larsen," Nora said. "What did you make of that? You think that they were lovers?"

"Could very well have been, Detective Ricci. They were speaking in hushed tones, but they seemed friendly enough. Actually, at one point, I heard them giggle like two high school kids in the back seat of a Buick." She chuckled at her own humor.

"Did you hear anything that was said?" Hawk asked.

"Some of it. As she was leaving, I did hear her say that she brought him something to remind him to call her later."

"Did you know what that something was?"

"No, Clint, I don't."

"Brittany, please call me Detective Hawk to keep this interview strictly professional."

"Oh, of course, sorry."

Finally, he said something. Nora was pleased that he put Brittany in her place. "Miss Larsen, do you have anything else to tell us?" Nora asked.

"No, not really."

"Did anyone else see the woman? She had to go past Ursula, wouldn't she?"

"She must've been away; otherwise, she'd be drilling me about that woman. Ursula is always so curious about what Baxter was doing, and if she saw him smile at the woman as he did, she'd really be upset."

"Why do you say that?" Hawk asked.

"Well, Detective Hawk, she seems to care who Mr. Visser saw, especially Elizabeth. On several occasions, she'd drop by my desk and decide to talk about the weather or something like that. But I know that she was listening to what was going on in Visser's office. Then she'd walk up closer to the door and pretend that she was looking for a file in the row of filing cabinets next to it. I knew what she was up to." Brit laughed heartedly. "I've done that myself."

"What was her reaction when Elizabeth was with Baxter?"

"She became agitated. Her face would turn red, and she would stomp back to her desk. Are you sure that you don't want any coffee? I'm buying."

Hawk laughed, "No, we're good. We really want to thank you for your information. It might be helpful."

"Please call me anytime if you think I can help. I love watching mystery movies and reading mystery books. And I sometimes fantasize about solving a murder. I even plan to write a novel. Say, Detective Hawk, I have an idea. Perhaps you can give me some pointers."

Yeah, that'll really go over well with Nora. Otherwise, it'll be fun. "I believe that I'll be too busy to help you much…sorry."

Looking disappointed, Brittany said, "I understand. But you have my number in case I can be of any help to you."

Nora shook her head as they left the coffee shop and rolled her eyes as Hawk looked at her. "She's a little aggressive, don't you think?"

"Yes. But no problem. I can handle it. After all, I have you." They both laughed as they got into the Jeep. "Now, my partner, let's find a nice, quiet restaurant where we can enjoy some fine food, drink a glass of wine, and chill."

"That's the best offer I heard all day." They both laughed. Before she belted herself in, she leaned over, pulled his face toward hers, and gave him a sensual kiss.

<h1 style="text-align:center">CHAPTER 33</h1>

FOLLOWING CONGRATULATIONS from fellow detectives for surviving the attacks, Hawk and Nora were ushered into Captain MacGregor's office by Lieutenant Perez. She seemed rather cold as she told them to sit. "I'm becoming very concerned about you two." Her grey eyes met Hawk's, then shifted to Nora's. "I believe you're acting irresponsibly when it comes to your own safety. You should be aware that O'Leary and Bradford still are somehow able to procure hitmen to kill you both so that you won't be around to testify. This incident with the pickup truck makes me wonder if that was someone else out to get you."

"We haven't thought of that," Nora said. "We think that it was the husband of the murdered lawyer."

"Why would he want to cause you harm?"

"He has a vicious temper and must've lost it when he found out that we were questioning his staff, particularly the waitress, who had a lot to say about him. I'm anxious to check out the three numbers off the license plate that a kind witness gave us."

Perez said, "Actually, I'd like Orlinski to search title registrations for the truck. Ricci gave him a full description of the truck and the three numbers on the plate. I want you and Hawk to concentrate on the murder cases."

"If it turns out that it was the husband," MacGregor said, her voice seemed more toned down, "then we'll contact the right authority to follow through on that. But if it wasn't him, then we should assume that there is someone else out there looking to prevent you from testifying. I really should order you to a safe house for your protection."

"Yes, ma'am," Hawk said. "It isn't necessary. It's most likely someone who didn't like my driving and went into an uncontrollable rage. Captain, we should've been more careful, but we were in a state of euphoria after the two hitwomen were captured, and we survived. I guess we let our guard down a bit. We will be more vigilant."

"You better." She finally took her piercing stare off Hawk and turned toward Perez. "Okay, Lieutenant, please gather the detectives. I want an update regarding the two slain lawyers. I'll be out in a few minutes."

Shortly before the meeting with the brass began, Mortimer ambled in, wearing a new dark blue suit and sporting a canary yellow bow tie with matching suspenders. He looked good and, in Nora's opinion, maybe even distinguished if that was possible. *Wow, clothes do make a difference.* With his typical serious face, his mouth down-turned even more so than usual, Mortimer nodded to both Hawk and Nora before he sat down at his desk and exchanged a greeting with Orlinski, his desk neighbor.

MacGregor entered the room like a windstorm. "Okay, people," MacGregor said, "Gather around. I want an update on the lawyers' murders." The detectives rolled their chairs closer to the big whiteboard. "Detective Ricci, please give us an update on where we're at with this case."

A little surprised that she was singled out first, Nora walked up to the board and proceeded to write the names of the two killed lawyers. Underneath, she listed all the suspects as she and Hawk had discussed yesterday morning. She began with the spouses, followed by the workers in the law offices, and, after catching Hawk's eye, listed Goldie Hendrix. Under each name, she scribbled a reason or reasons why they were a suspect." MacGregor and Perez interrupted quite often asking pertinent questions about each, as did Orlinski and Nancy Salazar. The discussion was remarkably like the one she and Hawk had yesterday, and Nora was thankful for that because it prepared her for the onslaught of questions.

"Detective Hawk," MacGregor said, turning abruptly to the man. "What is your personal read on Mrs. Visser and Mr. Durand."

Hawk cleared his throat. "Both are liars. Neither one of them has a solid alibi, and each one could've very well pulled the trigger. Durand most likely wasn't where he said he was, and Angie's alibi was her best friend, Goldie. Both used almost the same verbiage when questioned. I find that suspicious. And based on what the waitress at Duros Bar had said about Durand, basically fingering him for the murders, we need to interrogate him as soon as we can."

He looked at the other detectives. "No doubt you've heard of the truck that followed us onto a two-lane road and tried to force us into oncoming traffic or into a concrete wall or ram us into the car in front. Both Nora and I believe that it was Norman Durand. At least, the man looked like him from the brief glimpse we had. If it was him, we assume that he fell into an uncontrollable rage after he saw us in the bar questioning his staff and alibi. I remember seeing a similar truck to the one that chased us, in the parking lot of the bar as we were leaving."

"Does that mean that he's the killer?" Nancy asked.

Hawk mulled this question for a moment. "Nancy, I think that if someone has such a temper whose rage lasts for such a length of time as to wait for Nora and me to order, then go through a drive-thru in a restaurant, get our food, and then follow us to Denver, he is certainly capable of killing."

"Well, he's probably the one if he chased you."

"I'm not sure. In my opinion, the killer did not kill the lawyers in a state of rage. He had to plan the crime in some detail and execute it at the exact moment to catch the lawyers in a compromising position. That took a lot of patience. Because of that, I don't see Durand being patient enough to carry that out. He would've simply barged in and shot them."

Harry said, "Um, maybe you're wrong, Hawk. It's your supposition that someone waited in the basement. Maybe that never happened."

"You might be perfectly right on that , especially after talking to a waitress at Durand's bar. Out of the blue, she sat down at our table and basically accused her boss. She said that Durand should've killed those lawyers because of the way his wife blatantly carried on with Visser. We assume that Durand complained to her about it. Nora and I don't know what to think about that."

MacGregor said, "And my gut feeling is that it wasn't Durand that tried to run you off the road. I also doubt that it was a random road rage incident. Most likely, somebody else again was hired by the inmates." She looked at Hawk and later Ricci. "Do you get my drift?"

Nora's hand trembled as she answered. "Yes, Captain, we will be extra careful."

"Okay then, carry on, Detective Hawk."

"As far as Angie Visser," Hawk addressed Harry Ling. "Harry, I know that you interviewed the tennis partners. Were they together when you asked them questions?"

"Um. They seemed to be inseparable."

"Do you think that if Nora and I interview them separately away from each other, we might get different answers?"

"Yeah, possibly. Go for it, I don't mind. I had a tough time getting them to open up to me. They were very loyal to Angie."

"That's what we'd like to do in the next few days. We also need to canvas the neighborhood for any security videos of last Friday. I doubt that the killer walked through the front door. He or she would've used the back door from the alley. Too bad that the law office building has no cameras. You'd think that with the threats they received, the whole place would be surrounded by them. We need to check that out pronto."

Perez said, "Okay, Orlinski and Holliday, I want you to drop everything and see if you can check all the buildings for cameras in the area. Question neighbors, workers, whatever, and request to see their closed-circuit feeds for Friday afternoon. By the way, Orlinski and Holliday, you did a great job in finding that second hitwoman. I know that we'd been focused on the hitwoman or rather hitwoman, but we need to get the lead out as far as these murders are concerned."

"Sorry about that," Nora said. "We really appreciate what each of you had done to catch those women."

"We were damn lucky," Perez said.

"Thank you for the recognition, Lieutenant," Mortimer said. "I'll tell Josephine that you gave me a compliment. She doesn't always believe that I do good work around here." He began to sneeze once, twice, and three times and wiped his nose with the back of his hand. "But I'd really want to work with Clint and Nora. I could help them analyze what the witnesses say." Nora gave a quick glance at Hawk and rolled her eyes. They didn't need Mortimer's help.

"Oh," Orlinski laughed. "You don't love me anymore. Now I'm really hurt." He continued to make a joke of it, but all along, he'd be much relieved if he didn't work with Mortimer. The man just slowed him down.

"Not this time, Holliday," Perez said. "I'll tell you when."

"By the way, Holliday," MacGregor said, "I like your new suit. It's modern, and it fits you."

"Thank you, Captain. I'm glad that I finally pleased you, although you should've heard Josephine carry on about how much it cost. We had to go to a tall and big men's store, and they're not cheap. Buying this suit really gave her a huge headache. Oh yes, I'm supposed to ask you if I could take several days off next month. Josephine thinks that we need to visit my sick aunt in Florida before she passes away."

That made Nora's skin crawl. *Can Mortimer be so naive as to not realize what Josephine is up to? For all I know, the woman might even quicken the poor aunt's demise to get her grubby hands on Mortimer's inheritance.* She decided to corner Mortimer someday and try again to explain why she was so concerned. *Maybe this time, it'll sink in.*

"Holliday, we'll talk about days off later," MacGregor said sharply. "Now, where were we?" She looked at Perez to run with the ball.

"Salazar and Ling," Perez began. "What did you come up with the threats made to the lawyers?"

Nancy said, "We interviewed everyone on the list provided. Neither Harry nor I can see any of them doing the killings. The one most likely is the owner of a construction company. The same man who threw a brick through the window of the law office building. He blames Visser for all his financial troubles since the divorce. Said that and I quote, 'I guess there is justice in this world after all. Too bad that he wasn't killed before my divorce.' He's still mad as hell, but he has a good alibi."

"Yeah," Harry decided to make himself relevant. His name is Tobias Sandstrom. Tobias was at a construction site in Colorado Springs all afternoon and late into the evening last Friday. His drywall subcontractor hadn't shown up, so he did the work himself. Supposedly, he had a deadline, and he had to finish the house before being charged late fees. He gave us a list of workers who helped him and the other subs who worked on the project at the same time. Nancy and I talked to every one of them, and they all confirmed that he was at the work site. We even talked to three of the neighbors, and they also confirmed that his truck was there and saw him walking around the place. One of the neighbors complained that the construction noise and the workmen's laughter interfered with a peaceful evening with the TV."

"So, it looks like the people who threatened the lawyers are out as suspects," MacGregor said. "Of course, that wouldn't include someone who was really upset with what the lawyers had done but didn't threaten but instead waited for the opportunity to take revenge. We would have no record of that, would we?"

"Yeah," Nancy said. "We thought of that. I called the paralegal and asked her if there were any clients who were visibly upset with a bad verdict and blamed the lawyers. She laughed and said, 'Is the pope Catholic?' I asked her if there was someone who really stood out. She said that she wouldn't know where to begin, but no one that she thought would kill the attorneys."

"All right, then," MacGregor continued, "And from what I gather, you don't seem to think that it was one of Visser's partners. So, we need to focus on the list that's up there on the board. Have we made progress yet? Not much, it seems. Come on, people! Start hustling." The captain rose quickly and marched back to her office without saying another word.

Hawk and Nora had to wait until the afternoon to try to catch Angie Visser's three tennis partners at the Country Club. At least, they hoped that they would be there that day. In the morning, they decided to meet up with Detective Carpenter regarding the death of Goldie Hendrix's husband a couple of years ago. While Hawk made a call to Carpenter to see if he'd be available to meet, Nora searched the DMV records for all black Ram trucks in Colorado with the license plate number 874, knowing that Orlinski was too busy to get to it any time soon.

Carpenter said he was in for the next hour and agreed to see them at his office in District 2 on Holly Street. Hawk rolled his chair closer to Nora as she carefully studied the computer monitor. "Are you making any progress?"

"Didn't realize how many black Rams or Dodge Rams are listed. So far, I don't see 874 in any of the plates…oh, wait. Here's one. She clicked on the line, and the name of the registered owner came up. It's titled to John Dickerson of Federal Heights."

"Great, give it to Orlinski, and let's go."

Nora said, "Okay, I'm ready. Clint, if it wasn't Durand, could it really be that someone else is after us?"

"Geez! Here we go again. We better not tell the captain right away."

"What are we going to do?"

"Do what we always do. Watch each other's backs and be extremely vigilant." He hesitated as he thought. "I don't think this guy is a professional hitman, though."

"Oh, why?"

"He was too sloppy. I bet he's just some ex-con that was offered a few bucks if he got rid of us."

"Maybe a cellmate that had been released. Is that what you're thinking?"

"Sure, why not? He might've been promised money by Bradford or O'Leary."

Nora forced a chuckle, "So we're looking for a sloppy killer."

"Maybe." Hawk did not return the laugh.

CHAPTER 34

DETECTIVE CARPENTER was an affable black man with a pronounced belly, a thick head of graying hair, and a double chin underlining his round face. He wore a button-downed striped green shirt and a solid green tie that hung loose around his neck. "Detective Carpenter," Nora said. "Thank you for taking time to talk to us."

"No problem, but call me Rick. And I'll call you Nora and Clint if you don't mind. I'm not big on formalities."

"Sure, Rick," Hawk said. "As I explained over the phone, we'd like to talk to you regarding the murder of Edgar Hendrix."

"No problem, Clint. Unfortunately, we haven't a clue as to who did it. We think the killer was standing inside the yard, near the gate to the alley. A shooting is unusual for that ritzy neighborhood, and the neighbors were overly concerned and cooperative. We checked out all the cameras in the back of the houses, and all we got was a figure of a person dressed in dark pants, a black hoodie, sprinting fast down the alley."

"Could you tell if it was a man or a woman?" Nora asked.

"No. Hard to tell. The two videos that captured the image are in the evidence box. I'm sure it'll be all right for you to sign them out for a few days."

"Did you find any spent shells?"

"Yes, Nora, there was one. Whoever shot the man was a good marksman. One shot, right in the forehead. Anyway, the shell is in the box, along with the slug that was removed from the victim. No prints on it."

Nora said, "As far as I understand, Edgar Hendrix walked out of the back door, descended a step, and that's when he was shot. Any idea why he came out at that moment?"

"According to his wife, Edgar was a man of routine. He had a schedule for everything, not necessarily on paper, but in his mind. He was extremely regular. 'You could set your clock by him,' his wife, Goldie, told me. And it was Monday night and he headed out at 8:00 o'clock to a card game at the Country Club. He had to walk from the house to the detached garage off the alley."

"So, it was someone, like his wife, who knew his schedule," Hawk said.

"Either that or someone had watched him."

"Any suspects?" Nora asked.

"Well, of course, the wife is one. But she has an alibi. She was at Cartier Jewelers in the mall buying a necklace at the time of the murder. She produced a receipt dated on the date of the murder, and the time showed it at 8:11."

"How do we know that Hendrix was shot at 8:00?"

"Well, Nora, the ME estimated that the murder took place around eight o'clock. And, get this: when Hendrix fell, he must've hit his wrist hard enough to smash the expensive Rolex. It stopped working at precisely 8:01."

"That's mighty convenient," Nora said. "Any other suspects?"

"We talked to the people at the Country Club, particularly his card and golf friends. We talked to neighbors. Everyone seemed to like him, and no one knew of anyone that would want to kill him. We also talked to some disgruntled clients, but no one would want to go so far as to do away with him. No, we have no suspects. Tell me, though, why the interest in this case?"

"It's just a hunch that I have," Hawk said. "The case we're working on now, the two lawyers were also shot in the forehead. I'd like to compare the slug from your case with ours. It might've come from the same gun."

"Yeah, I heard about those two lawyers that were shot while they were…in the act." He laughed. Neither Hawk nor Nora returned the laugh, only a forced slight grin.

"Well, have at it," Carpenter said, noticing that his laugh might not have been appropriate. "Maybe you two hotshots will solve my case for me…who knows."

"Thanks for your cooperation, Rick," Nora said. "If you think of anything else, please call us."

"Sure thing. Good luck. I'll go with you to the evidence room to make it easier for you to sign out the evidence box."

After obtaining the box and thanking Carpenter again, they headed back to their District 6 station. Nora turned her head towards Hawk. "Wouldn't it be somethin' if the slugs came from the same gun? Would that point a finger at Goldie?"

CHAPTER 35

ORLINSKI AND Holliday set out on their quest to search for cameras in the square block of the law office building. Ling and Salazar would canvas the adjacent streets. Orlinski did not mind the task. In fact, he enjoyed meeting residents and office workers. He talked freely with them as though he had known them for years. He was pleased to discuss sports, the weather, global warming, cars—anything. He enjoyed hearing gossip about the neighbors, even though he did not know any of them. With such a friendly attitude, he thought that more people were willing to allow him to enter their houses or businesses to view security camera videos should they have any.

Mortimer did not have that gift of gab. His conversation was always direct, with a specific purpose in mind. After watching Orlinski, Hawk and Nora with their seeming ease of conversing, he realized that their conversational methods, not accusatory, often made the witnesses or suspects less guarded. He began to feel inadequate that he did not possess such talent and made it a point to learn from them.

For the first time in years, Mortimer felt as though he had good friends. Clint and Nora treated him with respect, and he cherished that. Generally, he was accustomed to people insulting him to his face or looking at him as though he was a weirdo. Now, with his rather pleasant time with his new friends, he began to realize the insults bothered him once again, and he determined that he needed to change—wear nicer clothes, watch what he said, and learn to understand jokes. In other words, changed his personality and his lifestyle. *That's probably not possible at my age. But I can try. If only Josephine would let me do all the things I would like to do, I'd go out to restaurants, explore the metro area, spend time in the majestic mountains and travel the States.*

Reflecting on what formed his dour personality, he blamed it on the excessive teasing and bullying in school, starting with kindergarten. He had to develop a thick skin to survive. He learned to disregard people laughing at him or what people thought of him. It was then that he himself stopped laughing or smiling. He isolated himself from his peers early, became a loner and fell out of touch with society. That way, he could avoid the dreadful jokes and laughter at his expense. He knew that he was odd, strange, eccentric or even a zombie, as he had been called more than once. And he learned not to care. He was used to it. But his interaction with Nora and Clint changed all that and now he craved to be part of the group.

Being smart, Mortimer passed the tests at the police academy with flying colors. It took him several attempts to be accepted by the Tampa Police Department, and after being barely accepted, he surprised everyone by closing more murder cases than any other detective. Before that, he received high marks for his work as a patrol officer. He was determined to show everyone up and used what he genuinely believed was his psychic ability to feel what took place prior to the crime. If he concentrated hard, he could even sense deep down inside who could be the perpetrator. People laughed at his odd behavior, not only behind his back but to his face. It did not bother him since he honestly thought that he had that ability. And, in some cases, his visualization came true.

On the way to their assignment, Mortimer remained silent, deep in thought. Orlinski decided to engage him in small talk to get his partner to open up. "How did you sleep last night?"

"Well, Stan, not too well. Even though Josephine was in the next room and we both had our doors closed, she snored so loudly that it kept me awake. She complains about me, but as the expression goes, people in glass houses shouldn't throw stones."

Orlinski laughed. "I'm sorry to hear that. Sandy also snores at times, but it doesn't bother me. Did you get any sleep at all?"

"Oh. I guess. I got hungry in the middle of the night and went to the refrigerator to see what I could nibble on to help me fall asleep. In Tampa, I always had some cheese around that helped. But there was hardly anything there other than a bunch of spinach leaves, an eggplant, and a cucumber. Oh yes, there was some oat milk, but I can't drink it. It gives me too much gas. I looked in the cabinet for some rice crackers that Josephine keeps, but they were gone, too. So, I went back to bed, thinking how hungry I was. Josephine keeps the refrigerator and the cabinets bare."

"That's too bad, Mortimer. You need to talk to her about that. Maybe have some cookies around. Maybe next time you buy a box of cookies and keep it in your closet."

"Oh no, Josephine says there's too much sugar in them, and she'll be upset. And if I criticize her in any way, she yells."

"Well, my friend, I don't know what to tell you. It's none of my business, but you need to think hard and fast before you hitch up with a woman like that for the rest of your life."

"Oh…Clint and Nora feel the same way. Even if I wanted to get out of the relationship, I wouldn't know how. It would be such a nasty scene. I'll tell you something in confidence, Stan. I'm a little afraid of her. That's crazy, isn't it?"

"Wow, you better decide soon before your marriage. We'll all back you up and help you."

"Thank you." Mortimer became silent again as he mulled over his relationship with Josephine. It all started when his brother, Seymour, and his wife presented him with a seven-day cruise to the Caribbean. He remembered sitting by himself during dinner when Josephine sat down across from him. Both sat silently for some time reviewing the menu, only to be interrupted by the waiter. After the order was placed, Josephine introduced herself and asked where he was from. After that, she managed to join him wherever she could find him on the ship. Mortimer was surprised but extremely pleased that a younger, fairly attractive woman took such an interest in him. No woman had ever done that before. She asked about his brother and other relatives. He told her about his sick, wealthy aunt. She became extremely interested in her and wanted more details about her family.

Even now, he remembered her exact words as she said, "If she dies, then you'll inherit at least one-half of her estate. Good for you."

The next day, she came to him with a super-wide grin on her face. "Mortimer, honey, I'm a lonely woman who doesn't have anyone, and you don't have anyone either. I have a great idea. Move out to Denver, and we can get married. Don't worry about finances because I have a lot of money that I inherited, and we'll be well set. If you want to work, we could try to get you a job with the Denver Police Department with your experience as a detective. What do you say? We would have a great life together."

Mortimer was so thrilled that at this stage of life, in his early fifties, he found someone who wanted to marry him. He had hoped that such a person would come along, and now he had found her. However, he realized that he may have a tough time keeping her because of his outward lack of emotion. He would not be capable of expressing his love for her, that is, even if he knew what it meant to love.

Mortimer's thoughts were broken when Orlinski said, "Okay, buddy, here we are in front of the place. I propose that we start walking north along Logan, then over to the alley, down the alley and then go east to Pennsylvania Street and back. What do you say?"

"Oh, that's fine."

As the detectives exited the vehicle, Mortimer stiffened motionless as a statue standing in the grassy areas between the sidewalk and the street. With his eyes closed, he lifted his head up to the gray clouds that threatened rain. Orlinski did not know what to make of this bizarre behavior. Passersby stared at the man, even twisting around to get another look as he walked by.

"Mortimer, are you alright?"

With his partner not immediately answering, Orlinski became concerned. He grabbed the man's arm, at which point Mortimer snapped out of a trance. "Oh, I tried to sense the movements of the killer prior to the lawyers' murders by standing in front but a little away from the building. It gives me more of a perspective. We need to start with the alley. The person sneaked into the back door, walking there from the front north side of the building using the fence and the side of the building for cover. I sensed that it was a woman, and later, she came out the same way. There might be a camera that recorded her from the back. That's why we need to start with the alley."

"Are you serious, my friend, or are you bullshitting me?"

"That's the feeling I have."

"What, are you psychic or something?"

"Oh, I don't know for sure. Sometimes, I just sense things."

"Okay. It makes no difference to me. Let's start with the alley."

CHAPTER 36

HAWK ASKED Nora if she would mind going to the Hilltop area. He wanted to walk past the backyard of the house where Edgar Hendrix was shot, supposedly on the steps leading out of the door. He also thought that it might be helpful to walk down the alley, which he assumed the killer would have done. Nora did not see much merit in pursuing that cold case after two years had gone by. It was not their case, and any connection between the two seemed remote. But for some reason, Hawk insisted that there may be a link between Edgar Hendrix's murder and that of the two lawyers.

"Clint, do you really think that you would find some evidence by walking down that alley?"

"It's a long shot, but I'd like to try. There's got to be a video feed around."

"Clint, it's been two years." Nora could not believe that Hawk would even consider it a waste of time like that. *I didn't notice his stubborn streak before.*

"Nora, please humor me for about an hour. I realize that it's probably a waste of time, but I have this gut feeling that it could lead us to something."

Nora rolled her eyes and released a deep breath in disapproval but finally acquiesced. They parked their police Explorer Interceptor in the alley and walked to the back of the former house that had been occupied by the Hendrix. The backyard was smaller than they had imagined, and the distance from the gate to the steps was not that great. They assumed the killer had entered the yard, moved closer to the steps, and waited in the shadows for Edgar Hendrix to come out the door.

They noted the distance to be perhaps thirty feet, not a difficult shot for someone good with a gun. Next, they strolled down the alley, imagining the shooter running fast down the cement-paved backstreet. The Hendrix house was close to the intersection with Third Avenue, and as they reached the end of the alley, Nora asked. "The killer most likely left a car along the street, don't you think?"

Hawk took a long moment to observe a house across from them. "I agree…that house catty-corner from us has a camera in the back aimed toward the alley and the street. It would've had a view of the killer if he or she came this way."

"No one keeps a copy of a video for two years," Nora said, smirking. "Besides, wouldn't Carpenter have checked it out back then?"

"You would think. Let's talk to the people in the house anyway. Maybe someone is home and might remember seeing something. Who knows?"

"Okay, anything you want. I'll follow you; I'll follow your gut to wherever it'll lead us, through thick and thin, through rain or shine, through…" Nora giggled as she voiced an old song. Hawk chuckled.

"Okay, okay, that's enough. I appreciate it." He threw his arm around her shoulder and pulled her close.

A short bald man opened the door before Hawk and Nora stepped on the front porch. Wide, multi-colored suspenders held up his brown, paint-stained pants underneath his hanging belly, barely covered by a tight-fitting red and green lumberjack shirt.

"I saw you looking around and eyeing my home," he said, his voice high-pitched. "I have cameras everywhere. What do you want? I'm not buying, selling or want to convert to another religion."

"We're not here for any of that stuff," Hawk said. "We're from the police and need to ask you some questions."

The detectives introduced themselves, and when asked, he told them that his name was Sam Fairfield. Hawk asked him if he knew about the murder of Edgar Hendrix that occurred two years ago.

"Sure, I do. Everyone in the neighborhood knows. What's this about?"

Nora said, "We believe that the killer must've run down the alley toward Third Avenue since the Hendrix house was just a couple of houses down. We thought that you might've seen something."

"Nope. And that's what I told those detectives way back then."

"Did you have your cameras up then?" Hawk asked,

"Yup."

"Did those detectives ask you about them?"

"Yup, but I wasn't about to show them anything."

"Oh, why not?" Nora asked.

"I didn't like their attitude, that's why." He chuckled, his brown teeth showing. He gave Hawk and Nora an appraising look. "You seem to be all right. Mighty friendly with each other, though. I saw you hug the woman." He chuckled as he eyed Hawk. Both detectives felt embarrassed. *We'll have to tone it down in public,* Nora thought. *This is awful not professional at all.* "It's okay. I was young once. I don't blame you a bit, bud," addressing Hawk. "She's a good-looking woman, that's for sure," he cackled loudly. Hawk returned the laugh, noticing Nora blush.

Before either Hawk or Nora were able to ask a question, the old man said, "I suppose your next question is going to be whether I have videos of two years ago. Well, I do. I don't throw anything away. After those detectives left, I looked at the video of the day that Edgar was killed. I didn't see anything of consequence. If I did, I would've called those detectives."

Neither Hawk nor Nora could believe their luck that the man still had security videos of the night Hendrix was killed. They glanced at each other in amazement. "We don't want to bother you too much," Nora said. "But maybe with new eyes, we could see something that would help us catch the killer."

The man rolled his thumbs under his suspenders, cocked them forward and let them snap as he thought hard about whether to let them into his house. "Okay, if you promise not to move any of my stuff."

He opened the screen door to let them in. As they entered, Hawk and Nora were hit hard with the most pungent, unpleasant odor. Glancing around the room, they immediately understood that the man was a hoarder. They followed him down a narrow path between large appliance boxes with smaller boxes stacked on top. The foyer and living area were totally taken up with what looked like trash. There were even narrower winding passageways between the boxes. *How does he get his big stomach through there?* Nora thought as she kept eyeing the clutter. Hawk was doing the same, his mouth wide open. From what they could see, one of the large boxes was filled with old, yellowing newspapers and magazines. Another box overflowed with empty cereal, milk, cracker and cookie boxes and other similar items. Two or three containers were jammed with plastic bottles and jars, while yet another had glass bottles, glass jars and cans. *At least he seems to be organized as far as that goes,* Nora thought. In the corner of the large, what was supposed to be a living area was a pile of rugs and carpet remnants. *I bet there are nests of mice underneath.*

The foul smell became overwhelming as the man led them into the kitchen, where a big pile of accumulated trash was stacked by the door. Nora gagged but tried to hide it. *Oh geez, I hope I don't throw up. If I did, he wouldn't even notice.* At the end of a cluttered counter, the man pulled up a carton box containing a stack of CDs. "Edgar died in November two years ago. I burn every closed-circuit video onto a CD and have done that since I got the cameras installed ten years ago." He chuckled. "I told you that I don't throw anything away, not even what's on my computer. Everything has a use. Most people don't understand that. But often, when I need something, I've usually got it. I know exactly where everything is."

"If you have the video that we need, then I'm all for it," Hawk said. Nora noticed him breathing into his hand to help survive the stench.

"Ah, here it is." He stuck the disk into an ancient IBM computer which was extremely slow in booting up. Then, when the disk finally came up, he slowly scrolled down to the evening of the murder. As he did so, he hummed a familiar Broadway tune from the musical, "Oklahoma." Hank and Nora were barely holding on. They needed fresh air.

Finally, the evening in question came up, and Hawk asked if he could locate 8:00 o'clock for them. He did so, and they asked him if they could view it now. "Yup, beat yourselves silly." He laughed as he stepped away from the computer. Both Nora's and Hawk's eyes focused on the old monitor. There was nothing to see for a couple of minutes. Then, suddenly, a figure of a woman wearing dark clothes, her head covered by a hood, appeared coming out of the alley. She was in a hurry as she sprinted to a car where only the front portion was shown in the video. She quickly jumped in, as evidenced by the dome light flashing on and then off as the door was opened and closed.

"Mr. Fairfield," Hawk asked, pausing the video. "Do you recognize this person here?"

The man put on his red-framed glasses and looked carefully. "Yeah, I remember seeing that. I thought that it was the neighbor's daughter. They live in that corner house across the street. They've got some rambunctious teenagers that are constantly coming and going. They park their cars on the side of the house. I think that is their girl's car. She drives a small Nissan. Isn't that a Nissan?"

Nora squinted to get a closer look. "No, I believe it's a Honda product, judging by the grill and logo."

"Well, I'll be dammed. Maybe that is who killed Edgar."

Hawk said, "Mr. Fairfield, could we borrow that disc ? I have a program on my computer that could clean up the image and enlarge it. We can go back and forth on the disc and possibly see her drive up and get a better view when she drives off."

"Nope. I don't give or lend anything." Hawk looked disappointed. "But I'll tell you what. You pay me for a blank CD, and I'll burn you a copy."

"Sure. How much."

"Oh, probably a dollar will do." Hawk gave him a dollar. The man chuckled and resumed humming as he made another copy.

The detectives almost ran out of the house after they thanked him. Both breathed in as much fresh air as their lungs would hold. As they walked back, Nora looked at Hawk and shook her head in wonderment. I can't believe what happened. As I told you before, you're just an unbelievably lucky guy."

Hawk laughed. "You know what they say, 'Better to be lucky than good.' Anyway, I hope with an enhanced video we can get a clear picture of that woman. She looked sorta familiar to me. But don't ask me who it is until we watch the CD."

As they walked back to the car, Hawk's cell phone played the familiar ring of *Bad to the Bone*. The number was unfamiliar. Upon answering, a nervous voice said, "Hello, Detective Hawk, this is Ursula Hamlin. You know, Mr. Visser's paralegal."

"Yes, Ursula, I remember. What can I do for you?"

"I wish to apologize for my standoffish attitude when you asked me all those questions. I was really upset with the horrible deaths of Mr. Visser and Mrs. Durand, and talking about it was difficult. I have now had time to calm down and would be willing to answer whatever additional questions you may have."

"No problem," Hawk said as Nora listened to the speaker. "I understand how tough it must've been for you after working for Baxter Visser for so many years. It must've been a great shock. How are you holding up?"

"I still can't believe that this really happened. The more I think of it, the more depressed I become. You asked me who I thought might be angry enough to kill them."

"Yes, do you have someone in mind?"

"Well…it's probably nothing, but Brit Larsen seemed really upset when the two lawyers were at it. She heard it through the door, she said, and it made her sick. She told me recently that 'I'll have to do something about it or just plain quit.' I honestly believe that she wanted to change places with the woman that Baxter was playing around with."

"Do you think she was jealous enough to kill them?"

"No, not really. And I feel bad now that I said anything about her. Compared with the many receptionists over the years, she's a class act."

"Anyone else, such as another woman, that had an affair with Visser that you can think of? Perhaps a client or a friend that would come to his office without a legal issue but just to see him for a rendezvous?"

"No. I can't remember anyone like that. Whoever did it must have really had a reason, don't you think?"

"Yes, for sure. And that's our job to find out."

"So, do you have any leads right now? I assume that whoever shot them was careful and didn't leave any physical evidence behind, so it would be hard to find who killed them. Am I right?"

"We have several suspects, and we're working on finding the perpetrator. I think that it's just a matter of time."

"I imagine that you don't have much to go on…unfortunately."

"Oh, there is always evidence out there. We just have to find it."

Ursula hesitated for a moment, "Well, I hope I'm not one of your suspects. I wouldn't have hurt Baxter. We worked so long and so well together…I miss him."

"Ursula, at this stage of the investigation, we hadn't ruled anyone out."

She seemed disappointed at first but then recovered, "If there's any way that I can help you, Detective, I'll be more than willing. I liked Baxter and want you to find his killer."

After they both clicked off, Nora curiously asked, "What do you think that was all about?"

"I don't know. I'll have to think about this conversation."

"Maybe she really misses her boss and wants to make sure the killer is found. Or she's pulling the wool over our eyes."

CHAPTER 37

ORLINSKI AND Holliday made their way around the law office building to the alley in the back. The house next door was converted into several apartments and had no visible cameras. Scanning the residential house directly across the alley for any sign of a camera turned out to be disappointing as well. Orlinski began proceeding further down the alley, but Mortimer remained standing, his eyes intensely studying the top eave of the two-story structure.

"Mortimer, let's go. We must double back and talk to the people in these houses yet. What's so interesting up there?"

"A camera pointing toward the law office parking lot and the alley."

"Where? I didn't see a damn thing."

"It's barely visible. Look there," he pointed a crooked finger at the eave. "It's painted in the same gray color as the trim of the house and barely an inch over the clinging vine hugging the wall."

"Wow, buddy, you're right. What an eagle eye." Orlinski patted his partner on the shoulder and Mortimer nodded as though that's the way it should be as the two detectives proceeded around the corner to the front of the house.

As they climbed up the three concrete steps to the wrap-around wooden porch, two men wearing expensive suits, one blue and the other dark gray, white shirts with matching gold cufflinks, were exiting the house. One had a key out, prepared to lock the front door.

"Oh, you startled me," the man with the key wearing the gray suit said. "May we help you?"

Orlinski said, "Yes, as a matter of fact, you can." He opened his suit coat to display the police shield. "My name is Detective Orlinski, and this is Detective Holliday."

"What would the police possibly want with us?" The blue suit said, his tone aggressive. "We need to go to an appointment. We have no time for whatever you're here for."

"We'll be brief, but we're investigating the murder of the two lawyers across the alley, and this is very important," Orlinski said.

"We have nothing to do with that."

"Oh, no worries about that," Orlinski chuckled. The men did not return a chuckle or a smile. "Sorry to bother you, but we see that you have a CC video camera facing your backyard. Does it work?"

"Yes, it does, but the videos are only saved for a few days. Really, though, we need to be downtown in a few minutes. Can't this wait?"

"When will you return?" Mortimer asked, his voice sharp.

The man in the gray suit seemed friendlier and more relaxed. "After the appointment, we'll join some friends for lunch and should be back around three this afternoon."

"Long lunch," Mortimer commented.

"I'll tell you what. If you give me the date and approximate time you are investigating, I promise that I'll look it up and have it ready for you after three."

Mortimer was not pleased and showed it, but Orlinski agreed and told the men that they'd be back after three.

As they parted, Mortimer commented, "They'll forget to do it. There's something about them."

"Mortimer, you don't trust too many people, do you?"

"And I'm usually right."

"That's cynical. It's tough to live that way. But you said that you trust Josephine, and you really don't know her that well."

Mortimer remained silent as they made it back to the alley, searching for more cameras. "You know, Stan, I want to trust her." After saying that, he began to sneeze three times without covering his mouth. Orlinski stepped away from the spray.

At the end of the alley stood an eight-story apartment building. Noticing that it had video cameras set up on each corner of the building, the men entered the foyer from Pennsylvania Street. A small sign directed them to the manager's office in the back of the hallway.

As they walked in, an Indian woman wearing a sari and thick-lensed, heavy-framed glasses informed them coldly that there were no vacancies.

"We're not here to rent an apartment, ma'am," Orlinski said with a pleasant smile. "We're Denver Police detectives and would like to view your videos of last Friday, if we may." He introduced himself and Mortimer to the woman. Both opened their coats to display their badges.

"Why do you need to see them? What happened?"

"Ma'am, this is a murder investigation, and your cooperation would help us," Mortimer said, his typical frown etched on his long face.

"It must be the murder of those two lawyers that I read about. Lawyers! I wouldn't mind killing the one that represents a tenant we evicted. He has made a living nightmare for my husband and me. Imagine suing us for unsanitary conditions. We take care of our apartments and—"

Orlinski interrupted her. "I'm sorry to hear of your situation. But, ma'am, we're on a tight schedule. May we see your feed from last Friday ? I see that you have everything already set up behind you."

The woman blew out a deep breath and turned around. Without looking back, she asked, "What do you want to see? I have eight cameras on the outside of this building."

Mortimer said, "We're mostly interested in the ones facing the alley and the side street."

It took her a few minutes to bring up the videos. "You want all day or what time?"

"Start with 5:30 to 8:30 o'clock."

She grumbled but complied. Orlinski could see that to view the two cameras, one facing the alley and the other the street, would take all afternoon. "Could you email me the videos or make a copy of them for us, please?"

"I'll email them to you. Give me your address."

Orlinski watched as she copied both camera feeds for the requested times. After thanking her, they proceeded on.

Mortimer's feet burned from walking. "Stan, I need to rest and eat. *Here we go again,* Orlinski thought. *Watch him cajole lunch out of me.* Sure enough, he did. They ate at a greasy breakfast place on Colfax Avenue. As Orlinski expected, he ended up paying for both.

After Mortimer devoured a triple hamburger with cheese and Orlinski tried to spoon a salty, watery chicken noodle soup, the two detectives continued in their search for video cameras. This was the second time in the last three days that they were assigned this task, and Mortimer continued to complain that his feet hurt. At one point, he stumbled over an uneven sidewalk only to be caught by Orlinski.

"You need to get better shoes," Orlinski advised. "Those shoes with thin leather soles are crap for walking a distance. Get some like mine with thick soles and a good insert."

"Oh, I know you're right. I have some sneakers that are comfortable, but they don't look professional. Captain MacGregor would get on my back if I came to work wearing them. I'll have to ask Josephine if I could have a pair like yours. What brand are they?"

"These are Rockports, but I also like Bass."

"Josephine will scour the thrift stores, but if she can't find them, I don't think she'll want to spend the money."

"Geez, Mortimer. You have a problem; you're working and earning money."

"Oh, I give my paycheck to Josephine so she can budget it. She says she's good at it."

Orlinski shook his head and then glanced at his watch. "It's after 3 o'clock. Let's see if our friends who promised us a copy of their video footage came through."

As they approached the house, the man in the grey suit quickly rushed out, clutching a flash drive in his hand. "Here you go," handing it to Orlinski. "I hope it helps you."

After thanking him and returning to their vehicle, Mortimer said, "I just get this bad feeling about them. Did you notice his glassy eyes and how fidgety he appeared ? He made sure that we didn't go inside. I bet they're into cocaine."

"We're here for a murder investigation. You should refer your suspicions to the drug unit."

"Oh, good idea. I'll ask Josephine what she thinks first, though." Orlinski again shook his head hardly waiting to blab to Hawk and Nora what Mortimer said about his mysterious Josephine.

CHAPTER 38

WITH THE disk of the video in hand and wondering if there might be a breakthrough in the Hendrix murder, Hawk and Nora rushed back to their vehicle. Hawk seemed overly anxious to enlarge the image of the woman in the footage. Nora couldn't quite understand the fascination that her partner exhibited with the Hendrix case. It was Carpenter's case, but Hawk wanted to pursue it. *Why? Does he really believe that the Hendrix unsolved murder is connected to ours?*

When she pressed him on the issue, his reply was, "I don't know. I just have this gut feeling that the two cases might have a connection."

"Do you really think it was the same murderer? And would that be Goldie Hendrix?"

"Nora, I just don't know. But the fact that all the victims were shot in the forehead makes me wonder."

"It would certainly be interesting if the slugs from both cases match."

"It certainly would. We must get the one from Carpenter's case to the crime lab right away."

"What set you off to focus on Goldie anyway? She seems like a nice lady. Doesn't strike me as a killer."

"That's just it. She was a little too nice and cooperative."

"Clint, it's just southern hospitality."

As they strode from the parking lot to the police station, Nora noticed a black Ram pickup with a large grille guard. It was backed into the nearest parking slot across the street. She gave it a second look before grasping Hawk's arm and pointing at the truck. As Hawk turned to look, they both saw the driver's window roll down, and the barrel of a rifle protruded. They barely had time to hit the ground when they heard the sound barrier shatter with the slugs whizzing past just a few inches over their heads. The two projectiles exploded into the stucco-covered cinderblock wall of the building, bits and pieces of plaster flying.

As officers piled out of the station, the truck peeled out. With squeaking wheels, it flew through a red light, barely missing the traffic on busy Colfax Avenue, then recklessly proceeded south on Washington Street. The officers hustled over to the two detectives as they rose from the asphalt, breathing hard as they brushed themselves off.

"What the hell?" An officer exclaimed. "What was that all about?"

Nora shook her head in disgust. "Just another day in paradise. Someone else that tried to kill us, that's all."

Still shaken, their legs feeling like rubber, they slowly made it up to the second floor. "I don't think that was a professional hitman," Nora said. "Some punk that has made two attempts on us. I hate to say it, but I think the captain's right. He's some ex-con who was promised money at the jail by Bradford or O'Leary if he kills us."

News traveled fast at the station, and instantly, Hawk and Ricci were summoned to MacGregor's office. She looked irate as she told them that until that man is found they will have desk duty. "You stay put right in this building except to go home. Do you understand my direct order?"

Both detectives attempted to protest, but the captain cut them off. "I've made my decision. Now go to your desks. Work on the lawyers' murders from here."

"Captain," Nora asked, "Can we at least call witnesses to come to the station for interrogation?"

"That'll be fine. Just don't leave the building until it's time to go home. Stay together for protection. It might even be a good idea to decide to bunk down in the same house for the night. There's a BOLO on the truck, and Nancy and Harry will be assigned to track down the shooter…that will be all."

As soon as they sat down at their desks, Hawk inserted the CD they brought back from the hoarder. Once he had it up on the screen, Nora rolled her chair to join him. They began from the beginning and fast-forwarded the video until a car stopped and parked near the entrance to the alley behind Hendrix's house. It was an older model Honda Civic with the front license plate missing. A person in all black, wearing a hoodie, got out of the car and casually walked down the alley. Hawk magnified the figure as much as his program would allow, but the person was careful in concealing their face, and neither he nor Nora could make out the features. Both decided, though, that the person was a thin woman by her walk the shape of her body as outlined in tight-fitting athletic wear.

There was no other activity on the video except for a few passing cars until a few minutes later. They saw the woman sprinting back toward the car. As she rounded the corner to the driver's side, maybe because of a breeze or because of her abrupt turn, part of her profile appeared. Hawk again enlarged the image. The two partners stared at it for a long moment.

"I agree. She does look familiar." Nora paused and wrinkled her nose, "It can't be who I think it is, can it?"

CHAPTER 39

AFTER DRIVING one-half hour to the city of Federal Heights, a northwestern suburb of Denver, detectives Salazar and Ling pulled up in front of John Dickerson's tri-level house. According to DMV records, he is the registered owner of the black Ram truck that tried to run down Hawk and Ricci.

Nancy tensed up as she climbed out of the vehicle. All the hits on Hawk and Ricci made her realize how vulnerable she was in her chosen work. She knew that the job of a police officer was dangerous when she joined the police department immediately upon graduating from Red Rocks Community College with an associate degree in criminology. As a patrol officer, she often sensed danger, but her nerves were not shattered as they were now. It was part of the job, and she did not dwell on it before, even as a detective. But now, after all the attempts on Nora's and Clint's lives, she has become more than ever nervous and squeamish.

The two detectives were about to confront Dickerson. It was assumed that he was the one who tried to run her colleagues off the road. The same truck was involved in the brazen shooting directed at Nora and Clint right in front of the police station. Nancy felt a pit in her stomach. *Who knows how he'll react when we start asking questions about the incident?*

Approaching the house, neither she nor Harry saw the black Ram pickup parked anywhere. Instead, a Chrysler minivan was sitting in the driveway in front of the double door of the attached garage. "The truck might be garaged," Harry said. Both unsnapped their holsters as they approached, just in case of trouble.

"Should I cover the back?" Nancy asked. He may run out the back."

Harry, too, was dubious about confronting the man by himself. "No need," Harry said. "This is his house with a family, judging by the kid's skateboard propped up against the wall. He won't go anywhere."

It took three pokes on the doorbell before a little girl, around the age of eight, opened the door. "My daddy said for me to find out what you're selling."

Nancy smiled, "We're not selling anything. Please tell your daddy that we're Denver police detectives and would like to talk to him."

They heard the girl tell her father, and soon after, the TV was toned down, and in a couple of minutes the man opened the screen door and stepped outside.

"Yeah. What's this about?"

The detectives introduced themselves and asked if he was John Dickerson, the owner of a 2013 black Ram Truck.

The man hesitated as he thought whether to answer or not. Harry repeated the question.

"Yes, I'm John Dickerson, and I do own a Ram. What in the hell is this about anyway?"

"May we see your truck, please?" Nancy asked.

"Not until you tell me why you're here."

"Were you in Parker yesterday?"

"No. I never go out there. Why do you want to see my truck?"

"Because someone in the truck tried to force another vehicle into a concrete barrier to cause harm. Also, your truck was seen at a shooting at the police station. Can you explain that?"

"Well, it wasn't me." He shook his head in disgust. "That sonofabitch moron of a brother took my truck three days ago, and I hadn't seen him since." Obviously upset and becoming angry, his face turned red. "He's at it again…getting in trouble and all. I wondered if that bastard was going to steal my truck and steal it out of here. Shit! He just got out of jail…that idiot."

"Had he done something like that before?" Nancy continued to ask questions.

"No. He begged me to loan him the truck because he's got a job to do where he'll get paid a bunch of cash. I hoped he had found a job, so I tried to help him out. He's been hit in the head too many times playing football and getting into fights, and he just doesn't think straight. I thought maybe if he got a job for a change, he would stay out of jail. And now look at what he did. Shit!"

"What's your brother's name?" Harry asked.

"James. We call him Big Jim."

"That's James Dickinson?"

"Yes."

"What was he in for?"

"Burglary and assault. He told me that his case was dismissed. Not enough evidence or somethin' like that."

"Did he tell you who it was that gave him that job?"

"Not really. Just someone he met in jail. He hooped and hollered that he'll get paid enough money where he didn't have to work for a year."

"Do you know what the job was?"

"He wouldn't tell me. Said it would be best if I didn't know."

"Didn't you think that was odd?"

"Yeah, but frankly, I don't put much stock into anything he says. Most of it makes no sense, and I just don't pay much attention to him."

Harry continued, "Mr. Dickinson, do you have any firearms?"

"Yeah. It's a huntin' rifle, a 308 Winchester, but I have it locked up in a gun safe in the basement."

"Can we see it?"

"I'll bring it out. Wait here."

The man went back into the house, and Nancy asked Harry if he believed him. "I do. He doesn't really have a reason to go after Hawk and Ricci from what I can see. But the brother does. I bet Bradford or O'Leary knew he was to be released and offered him cash if he'd kill them. It sounds like they're getting desperate and asked a dumb amateur to do it. If the guy is caught and squeals, it would leave them wide open for witness tampering and conspiracy charges."

"I tend to agree, Harry. We need to capture Big Jim alive so that he'd testify against those corrupt cops."

Dickinson came back shaking his head from side to side. "Shit! My rifle's missing. Big Jim must've taken it. I keep the combination to the safe on a piece of paper high at the top of the safe. He must've found it." He looked devastated and concerned. "Find him before he hurts somebody."

"Any idea where he might be? Who does he hang around with?"

"Oh, I see why you thought that I was driving the truck in Parker. Big Jim has a sort of a girlfriend— on and off—that works at a dive in Parker. I think the name is Duro's or somethin' like that. Big Jim also told me that she has an apartment in southeast Denver, where he crashes once in a while…I think he said it's by Havana and Florida or somethin'. Don't know anything about her, though, except that she's a big woman, the kind he likes. He might be shacked up with her now."

"Can you think of her name by any chance?" Harry asked.

"No, I can't remember. Wait, it's some name that started with an 'S' like Sally or Susan or somethin'."

Before they left, Nancy asked Dickinson to open the garage door. She wanted to make sure that the truck was not parked inside. It wasn't.

As they drove away, Nancy said, "Harry, what if we head to Parker and check out Duro's Bar ? See if there is a big waitress there with a first name that begins with an 'S'."

"Nah, I wouldn't do that first. If she sees us snooping around, she may tip off Big Jim if they're together. I suggest we drive around the apartment houses in the border area of southeast Denver and Aurora and see if we can spot the truck."

"Now?"

"No better time than the present."

"Isn't that just like looking for a needle in a haystack?"

"Maybe. But I know the area pretty well, and I have an idea where to look."

"Okay. I guess we're going for a long ride. I'll call Nora. Remember Clint, and she told us about the strange conversation they had with a waitress at the bar? Maybe she remembers her name and fills us in as to what to expect."

CHAPTER 40

NORA RICCI quickly clicked "accept" when Nancy's name and number appeared on the screen. She had been thinking about both Nancy and Harry as to whether they had any problems with John Dickinson. She understood how dangerous Dickinson would be if he were the same man who tried twice to kill Clint and her. She had warned her colleagues to be extra careful and not take any chances. Nancy promised to call her the minute they left him.

"Are you guys okay?"

"We're fine, Nora. But John Dickinson doesn't appear to be the shooter. His brother, James, took his truck for a big job he had to do. A Winchester rifle is also missing from the house. Frankly, I'm relieved that he wasn't there. The more I think about it, it was foolish for Harry and me to show up without backup."

"Well, we just weren't sure that John Dickinson was the one. Do you believe it's his brother that we want?"

"It sure looks like it…um…Nora, do you remember the name of that waitress at Duro's Bar that you told me about?"

"Yeah, her nametag showed 'Shirl'."

"Shirl, yeah. That must be the one John Dickinson was talking about. He thinks that James is shacking up with her in an apartment somewhere in the vicinity of Havana and Florida in southeast Denver. We're on our way there now."

"Oh God! You'll need help. She's a big woman that easily outweighs you by fifty pounds. And if James Dickinson is the one, he's armed and dangerous. Here, let me put you on speaker so that Clint can hear."

After Nancy quickly summarized the narrative, Hawk said, "We'll be there as soon as we can once you locate the truck. How close to the area are you now?"

"We just left Federal Heights. It'll take us at least forty minutes."

"Don't go looking for the people. Wait until Nora and I arrive. You might want to notify the local District for backup at that time as well."

"I don't want to start a false alarm. We may not find him anyway, and he might not be the one who shot at you. I think we need to locate the truck first and then go from there."

"Alright, then," Hawk said. Call us the moment you see the black Ram. Wait for us, and we'll be there in probably twenty-five minutes."

"Wait a minute. I thought you were restricted to your desk. You'll violate a direct order."

"Don't worry about us. Your safety is number one."

CHAPTER 41

IT TOOK LONGER than they thought, but after about an hour in heavy traffic, Nancy and Harry finally pulled up to the intersection of Florida and Havana. They started their search to the west of Havana so that they'd have jurisdiction while in Denver. To the east was the City of Aurora, and there'd be jurisdictional problems if they had to make an arrest, Nancy thought. There were several complexes of apartments in every direction. It looked hopeless to find Dickinson's truck just by driving around, but they decided to give it a try.

After driving through three apartment complexes, Harry grumbled, "This is crazy. We're wasting time and gas. You were right. We're looking for a needle in a haystack."

After snaking through the parking lots of yet another complex to the north of Florida, Harry grumbled again in frustration. "Chances of finding the truck just by driving around are slim to none. Let's wait until we get a definite address on this Shirl woman."

"Harry, just park the damn thing and let's wait for Nora to call. She's working on getting an address, okay!" Nancy showed her frustration, especially since she could not shake the bad feeling of impending doom in her gut.

Within ten minutes after they parked and waited, Nora finally called. "Nance, I contacted Norman Durand. With a little persuasion, he finally cooperated and gave me Shirl's last name and address. I'll text it to you. Call us as soon as you see the truck, but wait for us to get there before you confront Dickinson."

Receiving a definite location was not a relief to Nancy. Her stomach continued to feel full of agitated, fluttering butterflies. *Why do I have this rotten feeling that things will not go well for us…oh well, a job is a job. This is what I signed up for…great!* Her thoughts kept her silent as she nervously rubbed her forehead back and forth.

Now that they had the address, Harry drove into the parking lot of rows of apartment buildings. He wound around several structures on the lookout for the truck. At the last, secluded, smaller lot with just one row of parking, Nancy spotted a black Ram taking up two spaces. Harry backed the police Tahoe at least a hundred yards away, leaving a narrow view of the truck. He didn't want Dickinson to see their vehicle. Even though it was unmarked, it still advertised "Police" to an observant person.

"I'll call Hawk and Ricci," Nancy said.

"Wait before you call. Let's make sure it's the right truck." He slid out of the Tahoe and nonchalantly walked toward it. The license plate numbers were etched in his brain. They matched, and so did the bumper guard that Hawk had described. Hurrying back to the Tahoe, he gave Nancy the go-ahead to call both their colleagues and the backup from the local Denver Police District.

Unfortunately, in her state of unusual anxiety, one that she had never before experienced, Nancy mixed up the address numbers to the dispatcher, sending the patrol officers miles away.

Accompanied by Mortimer, who insisted on joining them, Nora and Hawk wasted no time driving through traffic, lights strobing and siren wailing. Nora attempted to reach both Perez and MacGregor and tell them of the urgency, but neither one picked up their phones. She remembered that they were at a meeting, so she texted them both to let them know where they were headed. As a rule, she obeyed her superior's orders diligently. In this case, she knew that there would be unpleasant ramifications for disobeying a direct order to remain behind their desks. But both she and Hawk sensed that they would be needed, judging from Dickinson's previous behavior. He was dangerous, and they knew that Harry and Nancy might not be able to handle Dickinson on their own. They just had to take their chances with the brass.

In the meantime, Harry and Nancy stayed in the Tahoe. After twenty minutes, Harry became anxious. Exhaling forcefully as he hit the steering wheel, he complained, "Nancy! This is ridiculous! If that's the guy, he's not after us. He's after Clint and Nora. What are we so worried about? We need to find him and arrest him before he has a chance to arm himself or flee."

"Harry, have patience. Let's wait for backup. They should be here anytime, as should Hawk and Ricci. Actually, I don't understand why backup isn't here yet."

"I just can't sit here any longer. At least I'll disable that truck so he can't get away?"

"How?"

"I'll deflate the front tire."

Before Nancy could object, Harry slid out of the Tahoe and quickly made his way to the truck. Nancy saw him squat down, unscrew the tire cap, and insert a key into the air release valve. Harry was ready to return when he heard footsteps. He sneaked a peak and froze. A tall, broad-boned, barrel-chested man with an unshaven angular face was walking towards him.

To add to her anxiety, Nancy saw the man as well. She stiffened in her seat. *That's gotta be James Dickinson.* The man was much bigger and heavier than her slim partner. In a struggle, should there be one, Harry would be no match for Dickinson. She stopped breathing for an instant, speculating whether Harry had seen or heard him. To her relief, she saw that he did. Harry quickly moved away from the left front of the truck, crouching low along the bed, and squatted behind the rear of the truck. Dickinson walked up to the driver's side and immediately noticed the flat tire. He swore out, banging his large fists on the sheet metal of the hood. Enraged, he flayed his arms and roared like an angry lion.

Kicking the tire, Dickinson lumbered around the front of the truck to the front passenger side, whipped open the door and stuck his head and shoulders into the cab. Nancy knew from her son's Dodge Ram that the jack and tools were underneath the seat.

Now that the man was occupied in the cab, Nancy assumed that her partner would nonchalantly walk away and wait for backup to arrive—or, at the very least, wait for her to join him so that they could confront the man together. That is what she would have done. Instead, Harry believed that he would be able to arrest the man while he was in a vulnerable position retrieving the jack.

Just as Harry pulled out his gun and was about to surprise Dickinson, Shirl walked out onto the parking lot. The solid-built, unpleasant woman was taller, sturdier and outweighed the thin five-foot-nine detective just as did Dickinson. Seeing Harry approach her boyfriend with a gun, Shirl bellowed, "Hey you! What the hell you doin'?"

She quickly made her way toward the detective while Dickinson, hearing his girlfriend's raspy voice, jerked out of the cab. He first appeared stunned, and then his anger boiled over when he saw the gun and the police shield on Harry's belt. Harry stepped back five steps, still pointing his weapon at Dickinson. But as Harry retreated, the man stepped forward. Identifying himself as a Denver Police detective, Harry commanded Dickinson to stop, turn around and place his hands behind his head.

Out of the corner of his eye, Harry noticed Shirl circling around behind him. He twisted his torso toward her, the gun now pointing at Shirl. He yelled for her to stop in her tracks. She slowed to a creep. At the same time, Dickenson was inching his way toward Harry. Harry stepped back again, but Dickinson and Shirl continued forward. Harry shouted for them, "to stop, or he will shoot." However, that's the last thing he wanted to do because they needed Dickinson to testify against Bradford and the others.

With fear clutching her heart, Nancy realized that her partner was in trouble and needed instant help. She leaped out of the Tahoe and raced toward Harry, tugging at her holster to pull out her Glock. As she ran, she saw with horror the couple leap, in unison, at Harry. She heard the gunshot as Harry fired his weapon. But the shot must have gone wild since neither the woman nor the man fell to the ground as she had expected. Instead, it was Harry who suffered the attack of the combined power of the two heavyweights. They pummeled him with their bodies and their fists. And it was her partner now lying flat on the asphalt, not moving, his gun knocked out of his hand and sliding along the pavement. As he lay there, she saw the woman kick Harry in the ribs and was about to kick him in the head while the man lifted Harry's gun and stuck it inside his waist.

Nancy's heart was about to break out of her chest at what she saw develop so rapidly. And now the woman was about to kick Harry again. Nancy screamed. Her piercing cry surprised the couple, and they turned toward the running detective. She was now near them but stopped short of ten feet away when she saw Dickenson go for the gun in his waist. Nancy shrieked, "You pull out that gun, and you're a dead man! Get on your knees with your hands behind your back!"

With a mocking laugh, he didn't comply but stayed in place. "Now! You asshole," Nancy screamed, "take the gun out slowly and throw it on the ground."

"Okay, you got it, little lady," he smirked, his hand moving toward the weapon.

"Slowly!" Nancy yelled. "Slow and easy. Two fingers on the handle and throw it down!" The man appraised the detective, battling in his mind whether to throw the gun down or take a chance and go for her.

"Now!" Nancy hollered.

Dickinson opted not to take a chance on being shot—the cop appeared raging mad, dead serious and would have no qualms in blowing him away. So, he complied, and at the same time, he purposely took a step toward her.

With the attention on the man, Nancy failed to notice Shirl inching closer to her, now just a few feet away. Nancy immediately stepped back and swung her pistol at Shirl. That gave Dickinson the opportunity to step closer as well. Becoming aware of them trying to box her in, she now pivoted the gun at him, then fanned it back at Shirl, then again back from one to the other. "Stop! Both of you! On the ground! Now!"

They stopped for a second, then started to creep closer to Nancy. Nancy backed up a few more steps. She hated the retreat she had to make, but she had to keep her distance. A couple more steps, and she'd be where Harry lay on the asphalt. At this point, Dickinson stood about seven feet away while Shirl was five feet apart. They would not listen to her order that they move closer to each other. Generally, she lost all authority because no matter how much Nancy commanded and threatened them, they totally ignored her and continued to slowly shuffle forward with that taunting smirk on their faces as if challenging her. She yelled again, "This is your final warning. Get on your knees and place your arms behind you! Now! "You're both under arrest!"

Both stood glaring at her for a minute before they began to laugh. "You think you're able to arrest us, little lady?" Dickinson said. "We eat people like you for breakfast."

Shirl bellowed out a louder laugh, "That's funny, Big Jim. Get rid of her and then that Asian, and let's get out of here. We're attracting a crowd."

Nancy was totally at a loss for what to do at that point. She had never come across anything like this before. They were not afraid of her. She wished she had a taser gun or at least mace. If she shot them, she would have to prove that her life was in danger. In this situation, it would be only her state of mind with no real proof that they would have harmed her, especially since they were unarmed. It scared her that these people did not take her threats and commands seriously, only laughed in her face. *They see the fear in my eyes and my trembling hand, but I can't help it.*

"You know, lady, you're annoying," Dickinson said, his laughter turning to anger, his face becoming beet red, his fingers clenched into fists.

"You take a step toward me, and you're the first one I'll shoot."

In a way, Nancy wanted him to take an obvious threatening step toward her. That would perhaps be the justifiable reason for the need to shoot to protect herself. But she knew that if they rushed her, she would not be able to kill them both. If she shot the man, the woman would pounce on her immediately. And from the corner of her eye, she noticed the crowd gathering, cell phones pointed at her. She understood that whatever she did would wind up on several video recordings to be scrutinized and her actions criticized. She needed to defuse the situation and avoid firing the weapon, if possible. The couple almost dared her to take a shot. *They are unarmed, and firing on unarmed people always leads to questions. Was it justifiable? Was it excessive? If I were to kill one, or by chance both, or wound or miss, I'd be blamed. Then there are a ton of questions, paperwork, administrative leave, personal liability and maybe even worse, a criminal charge leading to prison. Where in the hell is the backup, and where are Hawk and Ricci?*

Suddenly, Harry moaned as he was beginning to regain consciousness. And instinctively, Nancy turned her head toward him, taking her eyes off the couple for about two seconds. That gave Shirl the break she watched for. She took two quick, long steps close enough for her fist to pound the detective in the right shoulder, mostly underneath her armpit. The torque in the attack in such a vulnerable spot sent tingles and numbness in Nancy's arm, causing her to lose control of her grip and drop her weapon. At that same instant, Dickinson shoved Nancy hard to the ground before lifting the Glock and pointing it at the crowd that quickly scattered.

Nancy regained her footing and avoided another punch from Shirl. She was able to strike Shirl in the side but unfortunately missed the solar plexus, the spot that she was trained to hit to disable the assailant. But the punch to the side only made the woman angrier, and she lashed out with a blow to the stomach, then the shoulder, then to the ribs. *So, this is how I die?* The best Nancy could do was to shield her face with her arms.

Dickinson watched his crazy girlfriend hammer the detective. He smiled in delight. "Kill her, kill her," he encouraged. Then he caught Harry struggling to get up to save Nancy. Dickinson grabbed the man, pulled him up to his feet and decided to pound the life out of him.

Both Dickinson and his girlfriend were so engrossed in ending the lives of the detectives that they did not pay attention to a white Explorer that made an abrupt turn in the parking lot. The vehicle barely stopped before Hawk and Nora rocketed out, flying toward the melee with Mortimer not too far behind. Nora saw Shirl throw a hard punch at Nancy's face, knocking her to the ground. With her attention focused on Nancy, Shirl did not see Nora do a spinning cartwheel whose centrifugal force struck Shirl on the side of the face. She stumbled backward, not knowing what hit her.

In surprise and disbelief when she saw the same detective that she talked to at Duros Bar, Shirl seemed pleased to beat her up as well. She lunged at the slim detective, but Nora spun around and, with an outstretched leg, hit the heavier woman in the chest, pushing her back. She jumped again and instantly spun in the opposite direction with the leg lifted head high and, with the power of whirling motion enabled her foot to smash into Shirl's jaw. Shirl was stunned but not down. She threw a punch, but Nora dodged the blow and instead leaped again. Using her leg as a catapult, she sank her foot into Shirl's chest, then spun again and connected her leg behind Shirl's knee. Her knee buckled, but Shirl managed to remain on her feet, though unsteady. Nora twirled again and struck Shirl in the side of her head and, with a jump and a strong kick knocked her to the ground. Shirl lay stunned, breathing heavily and obviously in pain. With Mortimer's help, Nora rolled the woman over and handcuffed her.

While Nora was busy with Shirl, Hawk dove into the big man while he beat on Harry as if he were a punching bag and tackled Dickinson to the ground. Dickinson pushed Hawk off as though he were a feather. Both catapulted to their feet. Dickenson came at Hawk with a punch that Hawk avoided and instead plowed his fist into the man's kidney. The man cried out in pain. Infuriated, Dickinson roared like a bear, eyes shooting fire. He went for Hawk, swinging wildly. One of the punches hit Hawk on the shoulder, but he was able to dodge the others. Hawk danced around Dickinson as if he were a boxer looking for an opening to jab his fist into the man's throat to disable him. He saw an opening, but instead of striking the windpipe, his right fist undercut the man's jaw, and in quick order, his left fist plowed into the abdomen, right underneath the ribcage. He hit the solar plexus. In pain and unable to breathe, the big man keeled, giving Hawk a chance to use the back of his elbow to hammer the back of the shoulder to bring him to the ground, his face striking the pavement. He tried to get up, but by then, Mortimer, having already helped Nora cuff Shirl, rushed over, shoving his big shoe on the back of the man's shoulders, pushing him flat on the asphalt while Hawk cuffed him.

Panting, shoulder burning with pain, Hawk helped Mortimer pull Dickinson up to his feet and guided him to where Nora had Shirl in custody, standing by the Ram. Mortimer kept an eye on the two arrestees while Nora and Hawk went to Harry's and Nancy's aid. Harry was barely alive but breathing. Nancy was somewhat alert. She tried to say something, but her friends could tell she was in such bad shape that she could not speak, barely able to breathe.

Finally, two patrol cars sped in, followed by an ambulance. A few minutes later, both MacGregor and Perez showed up. *Oh, oh. We're in deep doo-doo,* Nora thought.

CHAPTER 42

MACGREGOR AND Perez were not pleased. Harry and Nancy did not follow the procedure and found themselves in a life-or-death situation. Hawk and Nora disobeyed the order to remain at the station. Perez barked that this incident probably would go on their records, and they should expect further consequences. But in the meantime, Hawk and Nora were given permission to accompany Salazar and Ling to the hospital.

Perez was particularly angry at the poor response for back-up that Ling and Salazar received. As soon as he and his superior headed out to the address provided by Nora, Perez called the local District station to inquire whether the backup had arrived, and everything was going well. To his dismay, he was told that the patrol officers had gone out, but the address given to them was wrong. He yelled at whoever he talked to, gave them the correct address, and demanded that they send someone out ASAP. Only at the scene did he find out that Nancy had messed up on the address. She inverted some of the numbers. "The dispatcher should've cross-referenced the location with Nancy's phone or simply called her back." He complained to MacGregor.

Now MacGregor was angry and threatened to take it up with the brass at that District.

Nancy and Harry were taken to the closest hospital, Medical Center of Aurora, the same hospital in which Nora and Hawk captured Devin O'Leary, the murderous, corrupt cop. The incident brought back unpleasant memories to Nora. That and the fact that her colleagues were being treated for their severe injuries made her absolutely miserable. Hawk paced back and forth worrying about the detectives, driving Nora crazy.

"Clint, would you please sit down ? You're wearing out the floor. The doctor said he'll be out to give us a status report as soon as she's able."

"Sorry. I hate what happened. I feel as though I am to blame, Nora."

"What are you talking about? We saved them from death."

"That's just it. It was our case. Dickinson was after us. We should've been there, not them."

"We had no choice. Listen, get your mind off that. What do you think MacGregor is going to do with us?"

"I just hope she doesn't demote us back to patrol."

Nora looked surprised. "Do you think that that could actually happen?"

Hawk shook his head and exhaled with force. "Who knows ? I'm not ruling anything out."

At that moment, the ER doctor walked in. "Your friends are stable right now," the black woman said. "But we're admitting them for further observation. Both might have some internal bleeding. Detective Salazar has a broken jaw and two fractured ribs. Possibly a concussion. Detective Ling has three fractured ribs, multiple contusions, abrasions and severe head trauma. We'll watch them both carefully." The doctor hesitated, then added, "Go home. There isn't much that you can do here. We've called their spouses, and I understand they're on the way."

"If you don't mind," Nora said. "We'll wait at least until their spouses come."

"Suit yourselves."

After the doctor left, Nora looked at Clint, who sat slumped in the chair, holding his left shoulder. He looked exhausted and in pain. "Are you all right, Clint? Your shoulder is bothering you, isn't it?"

"I'm okay. A little pain, that's all."

"You should see the doctor. Go into the ER and have it checked out."

"I'm fine, Nora. Don't worry. I'm glad we're waiting for Julie and Gus. We need to tell them what happened and fill them in on what the doc said."

They sat in silence for several minutes until MacGregor, Perez and Mortimer walked through the waiting room door. Both Nora and Hawk jumped to their feet. There were no pleasantries exchanged before the captain asked what they knew of Salazar's and Ling's status. After Nora explained what they heard, MacGregor said, "What a freaking deal this had been." Still obviously angry, the tone of her voice was brief and abrupt.

Directing her comments to both Hawk and Ricci, she said, "I understand from talking briefly to several witnesses and reviewing a videotape one of them took, which she forwarded to me, that if you and Ricci and…Holliday, I suppose, hadn't come when you did, Salazar and Ling would probably be beaten to death. Who would've thought Salazar messed up on the address ? And why did Ling jump the gun and couldn't wait for backup to arrive?"

Hawk and Nora glanced at each other. Was there hope of a reprieve, based on MacGregor's comment, about them saving the detectives from death?

"I'm going to think hard overnight about your actions today and give my decision of what I'm going to do with you tomorrow. But I'm wrestling with the good you both had done versus the bad." The detectives saw her lips curl up into a faint smile, giving them hope that perhaps their punishment would be minimal. "So, go back to the station and get to work. I don't care if you work all night, but I want all the incident reports for this fiasco today and the ones for the last few days filled out and on my desk by the morning." She tried to look sternly at the detectives, but somehow, her face belied that look.

"Oh, I don't think that Josephine would like it if I had to work all night, Captain," Mortimer intervened.

The captain's face flushed with a touch of anger, "Detective, I don't give a damn whether Josephine likes it or not. I'm your boss, and you do what I say. Do you understand?"

"Oh, yes, of course. I just wanted to avoid the unpleasantness at home…anyway, why am I being punished? I wasn't ordered to desk duty?"

In a highly irritated voice, MacGregor barked, "You're late on a couple of reports, and I want those detailed reports before you go home."

Seeing the Captain's building anger and Mortimer putting his big foot too deep in his mouth, Nora quickly said, "No problem, Captain, we'll work as long as it takes to catch up on all the reports. But we'd like to explain to Julie Ling and Gus Salazar what transpired and that the doctor told us that their spouses are stable. They should be here anytime."

"I'll let you wait with us for half an hour, but if they're not here by then, you are to return to the station. And take Holliday with you. He needs a ride."

The five sat in awkward silence, waiting. Nora happened to glance at Perez, and their eyes met. He smiled and winked before saying, "Captain, with your permission, I'd like to put in a good word for Ricci and Hawk. Dickinson posed a danger, and they knew it. My God, he was so brazen as to actually try to shoot them right in front of the police station. Before that, he tried to run them down with the truck.

That's a man out of control that doesn't care what happens to him or anyone else. Nora and Clint understood the danger that Salazar and Ling faced. They tried to contact us, but we were unavailable. Sure, they violated a direct order to remain at the station, but as far as I can tell, thank God that they did. Instead of the hospital, we could've been at the morgue. Thinking this through, I don't think that they should be punished or notations made in their record. As far as Ling and Salazar are concerned, we can't second-guess them. They were at the scene and obviously thought that they could handle the situation. Things just didn't go according to plan. It could've happened to any one of us."

"Nice speech, Lieutenant. It's obvious that you're defending your detectives, but I must have discipline in my units." She turned away from the others and concentrated on a painting of a gentle brook flowing through a green pasture, a red barn in the background. A couple of moments later, she turned her head toward Hawk and Nora. "I'll have my decision by morning." A moment later, she demanded that Hawk and Nora return to the station now and get to work since the spouses weren't there yet and time was wasted.

As they rose to leave, MacGregor said, her voice still harsh, "One of you needs to drive Ling's vehicle back to the station from that damn parking lot. Hawk, go ask if you can get the key from the nurse. It's got to be with Ling's belongings."

It was already 6:30 PM when the three detectives returned to the station. Before getting to those blasted reports that Nora hated to fill out, she called Angie Visser and demanded that she come into the station for an interview at 10:00 o'clock in the morning. As agreed with Nora, Hawk called Norman Durand and ordered that he meet with them at 1:00 o'clock tomorrow afternoon at the station. Durand at first objected, but after Hawk told him that he'd otherwise be picked up by a squad car, he relented.

Not having as many forms to fill out, Mortimer said his goodbyes at about 8:00 and hurried home to Josephine, muttering that he was certainly going to get a ration of tongue from her. Smiling broadly at the way Mortimer phrased it, Hawk commented to Nora, "Poor guy. He's under Josephine's thumb."

"I know. We need to do something to help him with that."

"Nora, he's a big boy. Let him work it out on his own. I do believe that he's starting to question his relationship with her."

"I just hope that she doesn't kill him first."

"Not until she's able to get her fingers on that inheritance."

"Gads! That doesn't make me feel better."

Finally, at around 11:00 o'clock, Hawk took Nora to his place. They followed MacGregor's advice to stay under one roof for protection. They were exhausted from the strenuous day, both mentally and physically. The mental stress of seeing their colleagues beaten up and the fight with Dickinson and his girlfriend wiped them out.

Discovering his garage booby-trapped a couple of days earlier, Hawk parked the Jeep a few feet away from the garage doors, just in case someone did it again. Both Nora and he squirmed as the door opened. With the light from the phone, Hawk examined the garage for any visible explosives. Seeing none, he slid back into the seat and parked the Jeep in the garage. He shook his head, chuckled, and told Nora, "I'm just a little paranoid, don't you think?"

"I don't blame you. As a matter of fact, we need to search the inside thoroughly."

"Or are we being silly? Nora, how many people could there be trying to put us away?"

"Clint, I don't know. But I'm too tired to think about it. I just want to sleep and dream pleasant thoughts, like you and me picnicking next to a rushing creek high in the mountains, far removed from anyone trying to do us away."

"Absolutely. Just to escape everyone, at least for a while, would be terrific."

Once the Jeep was parked and the garage door closed, both exited the vehicle. As they walked toward the house, Nora turned to face Hawk and quickly passionately pressed her lips against him. She left Clint smiling broadly as she headed toward the back door, thinking, *I love him. Am I a fool?*

CHAPTER 43

REMEMBERING THE killer, Finn O'Leary, lurking in the basement of Nora's house, Hawk gingerly stepped down the basement steps of his townhome, gun in hand, to check it out, just in case. Nora made her way upstairs. After Hawk accomplished his mission, he stopped at the refrigerator. He was suddenly hungry, not having eaten since lunch. He called up Nora to join him. But there was no answer. He called her name again. Still no answer.

Thinking that she was in trouble, he high-tailed it up the stairs to the second floor. He peeked into his bedroom. It was empty. Then he looked in the guest room. Nora was still fully dressed, lying prone on the bed, her peaceful face turned to the left and resting on her arms. She was fast asleep. He smiled, taking in the picture, and reflected on how much he relished having Nora in the house and near him. He began to realize that he would miss her when it was safe enough for her to leave. Grabbing an extra blanket from the closet, he covered Nora, planting a soft kiss on her cheek. She didn't stir, still in deep slumber.

Suddenly, his exhaustion overwhelmed him as well, and Hawk barely made the few steps to his bed before collapsing. It wasn't until 3:00 o'clock in the morning before he awoke. He looked in on Nora and saw that she had changed positions but still slept soundly. With his stomach grumbling that it was empty, he made his way down to the kitchen. The moon was bright. He didn't need the kitchen light. Before opening the refrigerator next to the unshaded bay window, he happened to glance at the side street. There, a worn-out, discolored blue GMC Jimmy pulled up near the entrance to the alley—a vehicle that he knew did not belong in the neighborhood. As he continued to peer out and as the man exited the vehicle, the light from the streetlight illuminated a heavily bearded man. The guy was medium built, with a black baseball cap, wearing blue jeans and a black sweatshirt. He looked around before slowly began strolling toward the alley. Hawk watched as he turned into the alley until he was no longer in view.

To all appearances, the man certainly looked suspicious. Hawk hurtled up the stairs, grabbed his Sig Sauer pistol from the nightstand and raced down to the back door. Scouring what he could see out the small window of the door, Hawk's heartbeat pounded wildly when he saw the man leap up to the top of the cinderblock fence and propel himself over. Then, hugging the side fence, he was at the door in an instant. Hawk moved to the side so that the man wouldn't see him through the glass. He heard the man insert something into the deadbolt to pick it open. As the man fiddled with the lock, Hawk swiftly unlocked the deadbolt, turned the doorknob, and swung the door wide open.

The man yelped from sudden shock and received a bigger shock when Hawk plowed into him, shoving him off the small cement landing and down the two steps. The man landed hard on the flagstone pavers of the patio. Hawk was on top of him in an instant with his weapon stuck in the man's ear. At the same time, he saw a gun sticking out of the man's waist. He quickly pulled it out with his left hand and threw it in a juniper bush not far away.

"Who the hell are you, and what are you doing here?"

Panting, the intruder mumbled, "Sorry, man, I must have gone to the wrong house. I was going to a party at Sal's place."

"Bullshit. Get on your knees and put your hands on your head."

"Hey, sorry, man. I told you it's a mistake."

"You got that right, maaan. Now you're under arrest, complements of Kent Bradford and Devon O'Leary." Hawk pulled his arms back and cuffed him.

"Who?"

"You know damn well 'who.' Weren't you just released and promised a bunch of money if you kill me ? That's right, isn't it, punk? Fess up, it'll go easier on you."

"I'm not saying a word."

"Good idea. Don't say anything until I advise you of your rights. You have the right to remain silent, the right to an attorney—"

"Listen, man, I know all about my rights, and I'm not talking."

Hawk paid no attention and continued with the advisement. He noticed Nora at the door with fluttering, sleepy eyes. "Can't I leave you for a moment without you—"

Hawk interrupted. "I just read him his rights. Do you have your phone with you?"

"Yes." She quickly understood why Hawk wanted her phone. She pulled it out of her back pocket and began recording.

Hawk said, "Nora, this man was breaking into the house. He had a gun, and I suspect that he was sent here by Bradford to try yet again to kill us. He just told me that he made a mistake by coming to the wrong house."

Nora chuckled, "I'd say he made a mistake. I suppose he's denying knowing Bradford and denying that he was promised money if he killed us. Am I right?"

"Hey, man, I'm not here to kill nobody. I ain't a killer…okay, I'll admit that I'm a burglar, but that's it. I'm here to rob your place, man. And I need to stand up. My knees are killing me."

"You admit that you were just released from City Jail."

"I admit to nothing. I need to stand, bud."

"You know, bud, that all we have to do is call, and we'll find out. And find out that you were in the same jail block as Bradford and O'Leary."

"All right. I admit that I was just released on bail for a trumped-up burglary charge. I know those guys, but I know nothing about being paid to kill you."

"Sure, you do," Hawk said. "That's why you're here and about to be picked up and thrown back in the same jail with them. Wait till Bradford and his cohorts hear how cooperative you've been with us, fingering them."

"Hey, man, I told you nothing."

"You think he'll believe you after we hold you for a while?"

The man did not reply. But the detectives saw his shifting eyes and contemplative expression, indicating that what they said began to sink in.

"Too bad for you," Nora said. "We can see how worried you look. You realize that if you're thrown in with them in the same cell block, you won't live long—whether you tell us what we need to know or not. So, do yourself a favor and talk. We can protect you and make sure you're placed somewhere safe away from them."

"I'm not squealing on nobody."

"They wouldn't know that, would they?" Nora said, finally sloughing off her sleep and becoming more alert.

Still standing over him, Hawk said, "That's right, all we have to do is let the word out that you cooperated."

"You wouldn't do that."

"Hey, man, you came here to kill us. Why wouldn't we do it? Don't you realize that we're trying to help you stay alive?" Hawk let him mull things over for a few minutes before he continued, "Tell us exactly why you're here, implicating whoever offered to pay you to take us out, and we'll talk to the DA to reduce your charges. No guarantees, but at least you would have some hope that the district attorney will. And move you away from Bradford, O'Leary, and Jeffries. We know that they promised to pay you big if you killed us."

Hawk helped him stand up and pulled his wallet out of the back pocket. "Buddy, that's it. Say hello to Bradford and O'Leary when you get back. Tell them that you didn't cooperate with us and see if they believe you. You know darn well that that won't fly." Hawk looked at his driver's license and saw the name Martin Zimber, home address in Commerce City. He passed the wallet to Nora.

"Well, Mr. Zimber, I called the patrol officers, and they'll be here in a few minutes," Nora said. "Once they get here, you'll be taken to the police station for interrogation. We'll keep you as long as we can, then send you back to City Jail. By that time, it'll be too late. Bradford will already be suspicious, and you might end up with a shank up your belly."

"No way."

"That's fine," Hawk said. "We'll give you time to think about what's best for you—City Jail or someplace safe."

"I'm not saying another word. I want a lawyer."

"All right. I hear the doorbell; your ride is here. You know, you'll probably be charged with a whole bunch of crimes all the way from attempted murder conspiracy to commit murder to trespassing. So good luck to you."

As the officers began to haul him away, Zimber cried out, "Hold off," a forlorn, agonizing expression was etched on his face. "I want a lawyer and hear what deal I'll get for cooperating. And if I tell you anything…you gotta protect me…I want a good deal, with no time served."

"We'll work on it," Nora said. "See you tomorrow morning."

After Zimber was taken away, Nora looked at Hawk, shaking her head. "I can't believe another idiot out to get us. Or…do you think that he might've just been a burglar, and that was all?"

"Nah. He was out to get us. The fact that he's afraid to face Bradford points to that."

"What are we going to do? I mean, there'll be more idiots lined up out there."

"Actually, I'm encouraged. He'll roll over on Bradford, which I'm sure he will. And I think Dickinson will cooperate as well. Once we have actual proof that Bradford and the others are behind all of this, we'll get a court order to keep them away from other inmates, at least until their trials are over."

"But we don't know how many more are out there," Nora said.

"They'll be easier to track now that we know who to look out for."

"Hopefully," Nora whispered softly as she thought, *but what if there was another professional hitman that had been hired and not these amateurs from the jail?*

CHAPTER 44

MARTIN ZIMBER sat downcast as he awaited interrogation. By the time they transported him, booked him, and threw him into the holding cell, it was already 5:30 o'clock in the morning. He had no chance to sleep or even snooze and felt groggy. Then, at 7:00 a.m., he was handcuffed and escorted to Interrogation Room 2 and told to wait.

As he sat behind a walnut Formica-topped table with his hands restrained, he had plenty of time to contemplate what a stupid thing he had agreed to. *But I had no choice but to agree. That sonafabitch Bradford threatened me if I refused to kill Hawk and Ricci. Even if I were on the outside and he was inside, he said he'd get me. Then he offered me ten thousand dollars each. That would've given me enough to pay off the loan shark for my shitty gambling debt. Gads, I'm a fool. Such a freaking fool. But he warned me. If I were to give him up to the cops or testify against him, I'd be a dead man. What am I to do? Can I trust the cops or the DA to protect me?*

At exactly 8:00 o'clock, Hawk and Ricci walked into the room. Kimber looked defeated and worn out. The forty-year-old looked as if he was about to cry. "Where is my attorney?" he asked, attempting to be forceful but somehow failing as his voice was frail out of despair.

"She's downstairs," Nora said. "Be up in a minute. I'll go check on her."

Nora left, and Hawk and Kimber sat silently across the table from each other, the prisoner's dull-blue eyes staring at his handcuffed hands. Three minutes later, a young public defender was escorted by Nora into the room. The attorney was a Latina with shimmering long black hair. Trim in build and pleasing to the eye, she walked in with authority. She wore a stylish black pantsuit with a soft pink collared shirt with a dainty gold star necklace.

She introduced herself as Crystal Montoya and asked the detectives if she could see her client in a private room before the deputy district attorney arrived. A police officer escorted Kimber while Nora led the way to a slightly bigger than a closet-sized room down the hall.

At 8:30, the deputy district attorney, Mona Clayton, walked in lugging a bulging red leather briefcase, files sticking out. She was a pleasant-looking black woman with short hair. She wore a yellow long-sleeved dress with a reddish-brown leather belt that matched her high-heeled shoes. "So, my understanding, detectives, is that I'm to offer a deal to the suspect if he gives you the information that you're looking for. And what is it you need out of him?"

"We need Kimber to finger Bradford or O'Leary, who we think offered him money to kill us," Nora said. "I'm sure you know that we have been targeted by them to eliminate us as witnesses in the trial that's coming up. We seem to be the star witnesses against them. If they get rid of us, the case falls apart, we're told."

"Yes," Hawk added, "We expect that once Kimber fingers the corrupt cops, you would charge them with tampering with witnesses and conspiracy to commit murder to add to the other charges they're facing."

"And how will that protect you?"

"Counselor," Nora said, "If we obtain statements from Kimber and possibly Dickinson that Bradford or O'Leary have hired them to eliminate us and the fact that they also hired professional hitmen to kill us as well, you'll be willing to file additional charges against them. Once done, the sheriff's office would take us more seriously and make sure that the men are kept separate from the general jail population or prevent them from communicating with someone on the outside until the trial is over."

"Okay," Mona said. "I don't see a problem with that now. Didn't the two hitwomen give up who hired them?"

"No," Hawk said. "Their attorney, Marlene Linkletter, told them not to say a word, and they haven't, but the case is pretty solid against them with enough evidence to prove that Bradford and O'Leary hired them."

"All right, then," the DDA said. "Bring the man in, and I'll decide whether to give him a deal or not."

Kimber's attorney wanted an agreement in writing that if her client tells what he knows regarding Bradford, O'Leary and Jeffries, then he would only be charged with attempted burglary and granted probation with no additional jail time. All other charges, including his prior burglary charge, would be dismissed.

Mona laughed. "Do you want me to throw in a two-week vacation in Cabo San Lucas while I'm at it?"

"That would be great, "Crystal said. "But Mona, I'm being realistic. You need his testimony. He's just a small fish in the sea of barracudas. But this little fish can help you win your case against those corrupt cops. He's insignificant when you look at the big picture."

"Sorry, counselor," Mona said. Nothing doing. He's not insignificant. He is one of the barracudas, as you put it. He was at Detective Hawk's door, ready and willing to kill him and Detective Ricci. No, you're dreaming. The best I can offer you is I'll drop all the other charges against him, including his previous case, but he'll have to plead to attempted murder, and I'll recommend the minimum sentence for a class 1 felony."

"That can't work for him. His life is in danger, and if incarcerated, he'll be killed. Listen, he's not really a killer. He was desperate for money to pay off his gambling debts. Go easy on him. He fears for his life from Bradford and from some loan shark that he got involved with."

"Well, that's his problem. Sorry, no can do. You're being too unrealistic. I guess this meeting was a waste of everyone's time, and I'm leaving."

"Hold off, let me talk to my client." She went to the corner of the room and whispered. Two minutes later, attorney Montoya and her client sat back at the table. "He's willing to compromise if you are. Look, Mona, he's in desperate shape. He truly is afraid to be sent back to the jail where Bradford is awaiting trial. Can't you come up with something that will work here? He's willing to listen."

The DDA thought hard for a few minutes. "Fine, and this is my only offer. Take it or leave it. He pleads guilty to burglary, a class 4 felony. I'll recommend the minimum sentence for that charge. I'll dismiss all other charges. You should be happy that I'm in a good mood today. I'm giving him a gift. Under the circumstances, that's a great offer, and he better grab it before I walk out the door. You know I could charge him and win with the class 1 felony of conspiracy to commit murder." She stared hard at the defense attorney for a long few seconds, then added. "But, and this is a big but, the detectives must be satisfied with his answers."

"We need to have a private conference over this," Montoya said. Again, they were escorted to the attorney-client room. Fifteen minutes later, they were ready to agree to the prosecutor's deal if she would recommend probation or at least minimum time to be served in a facility away from Bradford.

Mona would not agree to probation but did agree to recommend a minimum sentence in another facility away from Bradford. Kimber accepted the deal.

When Kimber was questioned by Hawk and Ricci, he sang like a bird, admitting to being promised by Bradford $10,000 each for the deaths of the detectives to be paid by a friend on the outside. He was also warned that if he squealed, he would be killed whether Bradford was in prison or not. He knew of no other men who were solicited by Bradford or by anyone else.

After hearing what Kimber said and watching him voluntarily sign a full confession, Montoya left. Mona said, "We'll file additional charges against the men and again try to get the Sheriff to make sure that the men do not communicate with anyone else. If solitary confinement is necessary, then let their defense lawyers argue that it violates the Eighth Amendment of cruel and unusual punishment."

While Nora and Hawk were interrogating Kimber, Lieutenant Perez assigned Orlinski and Holliday to interrogate James Dickinson. Present also was yet another young public defender assigned to his case. He looked like an inexperienced kid, as if he just graduated from high school, let alone law school. He sat there fidgeting with his collar and tie and generally appeared nervous, as if this was his first case.

Orlinski began by asking innocuous questions such as Dickinson's full name, address, and date of birth, but the suspect remained silent with a smirk on his badly bruised face. Orlinski would have loved to put a fist through his face if he could. He was getting hot and bothered thinking about what this dumb low-life did to his friends, Nancy and Harry. He thought he should cool his heels for a moment and told Mortimer to take over while he walked out of the room.

Mortimer began pressing him to answer questions, outlining the many charges he faced, including assault on police officers, attempted murder and conspiracy to commit murder, along with being in possession of a firearm while on parole. In his typical intimidating manner, he stood over the man glaring through him.

"Before my client gives you any valuable information," Dickinson's attorney from the Public Defender's Office said, "What kind of a deal can you give him if he provides you the information you need concerning who hired him to cause harm to the detectives?"

After taking some deep breaths and being lectured by Perez to keep his cool, Orlinski strode back into the room. He sat down across from Dickinson but looked at his attorney and said, "There is no need for a deal as far as we are concerned. We already know who hired him to kill Hawk and Ricci. Both of you know that Mr. Dickinson won't see freedom for decades to come, if ever."

"I'll tell you who offered me money to kill the detectives," Dickinson said, not waiting for his attorney. "But you better lower my sentence and keep me away from the men."

"I suppose that if you sign a statement that Kent Bradford offered you money and confess that you took him up on his offer and then attempted at least twice to kill them, then the DA will take that into consideration and perhaps dismiss a charge or two. But that's the only offer you're getting."

Dickinson was about to say something, but his PD cut him off. "I want a plea agreement for my client with a guarantee."

"Nope. There are no guarantees here. The judge decides but sometimes follows the recommendation of the prosecutor. So, is he willing to sign the confession? At that point, his cooperation will be noted by the DA, and perhaps she'll be more lenient with him and ask for less time to be served."

"Yeah," Mortimer said. "You better do as we ask because you'll need any break you can get from us or the DA's office. You and your girlfriend beat up two police detectives, causing them to be hospitalized with serious injuries. You'll have a hard life awaiting you in prison."

"Better take that offer," Orlinski said. "You won't get anything better. You'll save yourself a few years in prison."

"Mr. Dickinson," the PD said, "don't make any decisions until I try to talk to the DA myself."

"We're in a cooperating mood today," Orlinski said. "Tomorrow, we might take a hard-nosed approach and give you no breaks and recommend that the DA do the same."

"What if I tell you that I know who shot those two lawyers?" Dickinson said with a smirk.

CHAPTER 45

AS HAWK and Ricci returned to their desks, pleased with Kimber's successful interrogation. They felt a sense of relief that Bradford would face additional charges. They could now assume that he and his co-conspirators would be kept separately from the general population, cut off from any communication with the outside world, at least until they testified against him in a trial. Of course, the defendants can communicate with their lawyers. But surely, they thought, the lawyers would not participate in dirty deeds such as hiring hitmen.

Captain MacGregor had not yet called them into her office with a decision as to what she decided concerning their disregard of a direct command. *No news is good news,* Nora thought. Both Hawk and she hoped that they would just receive a slap on their hands with a reprimand to not do it again.

A few minutes later, Orlinski and Mortimer walked up to them. "Dickinson is acting as though he has an upper hand," Orlinski said.

"Why in the hell is that?" Hawk said, seeming genuinely puzzled.

"Wants a better deal from the DDA because he said that he knows who shot the two lawyers."

"How would he possibly know?" Nora asked. She thought for a second. "Unless he did it, which I doubt. But he knows his girlfriend, Shirley Macon…do you think that Durand hired her to kill his wife?"

"Wow, that's kind of far out," Orlinski said. "What do you think, Hawk?"

"I think that we need to find out more about Shirl's background. I doubt that Durand hired her. If she did it, it must be personal."

"I'll do a check as soon as I get a chance," Orlinski offered. "Hard to believe, though, that she did it."

Mortimer finally spoke up. "I'm with Clint. I also sense that if she killed the lawyers, it would be personal. I bet that one of them represented her at one time, or she was on the other side and blamed them for her loss."

Orlinski and Mortimer returned to their desks. On their way, Hawk overheard Orlinski ask if Mortimer wanted to hear a funny joke.

Mortimer answered quickly, "Oh, no, that's not necessary. I won't understand it anyway."

Nora and Hawk continued to discuss the unlikely possibility of Shirl as the killer. She was aggressive and violent enough to carry out something like that. Nora reminded Hawk of her not-so-subtle attempt to pin the murders on her boss, Durand. Just as Hawk was to respond to that, the detectives were informed that Angie Visser was downstairs waiting for them.

"I'll run down and get her," Nora said. "We'll meet you in Interrogation number 1." Hawk nodded as he gathered up his notes, his laptop and the CD of the video provided by the hoarder on Hilltop and headed for the room. At the same time, Detective Carpenter arrived at Hawk's invitation to join Nora and Hawk since the questioning concerned his case, the death of Edgar Hendrix two years ago.

Angie seemed obviously nervous about being called to the police station for questioning. She did not sleep all night, tossing and turning, wondering what this was all about. She was also surprised that there were three detectives in the small room who would question her. After sitting down as requested, she meekly asked, "What's this all about? I told you I don't have a clue as to who shot my husband."

"We understand," Nora said soothingly. "We have questions of another nature that go back two years." Upon hearing that, Angie straightened up, breathing shallowly. "You've met me and Detective Hawk before, but I'm not sure whether you know Detective Carpenter." She pointed to the man. Carpenter gave Angie a quick half-smile.

"Mrs. Visser," Hawk began, "I'll get right down to the nitty-gritty." He turned his laptop towards her and hit the enter button, then walked around the table and leaned over the computer, punching a few more keys. A video appeared, and after he scrolled through it, he stopped when a car parked on the side became visible.

Angie Visser didn't say a word or give any indication that she knew the car, "Do you recognize the vehicle in the video?"

You could tell how reluctant it was for her to admit that she did; nevertheless, after a long hesitation, she answered meekly, "Um, um, yes. That was my son's first car. We bought it for him when he turned sixteen."

"And why was it there?"

"I don't know. He must've been visiting someone in the neighborhood. Where was this, anyway?"

"In the Hilltop area of Denver."

"Well, I do know that he has friends that live over there. You know, high school kids, they seem to party and get to know other kids."

"So," Hawk continued, "You were not driving the car then?"

"No, I don't think so. I rarely drive his car unless I absolutely need to."

"Let me refresh your memory, then. Let's forward the video a tad."

An image depicting a woman running out of the alley appeared. "Do you recognize that woman? Here, let me enlarge the image for you to get a better look."

She sat back in the armchair, her elbows on the armrests and began rubbing her eyes. Looking back at Hawk, she muttered, "I knew this day would come. Yes, it was me."

Nora took over the questioning while Hawk returned to his seat across from the suspect, "What were you doing there?"

"Um, um…I'm so ashamed. Um, I had an affair…with Edgar. We'd been seeing each other for about six months before he died. I was devastated. That night, he asked me to come to his house to show me a high-priced painting. Said that he purchased it at an art gallery at the Broadmoor resort. He was so proud of it. Um, he told me to come over at exactly 8:00 o'clock and use the alley to the backdoor. I followed his instructions and was on my way to meet him exactly at eight. He said he'd meet me at the gate. I knew he'd be there. The man lived by the clock. Everything had to be precise."

"His wife was your friend," Nora said.

"I know, I know. Oh God! I'm going to regret my weakness and indiscretion until the day that I die." In a low voice, she continued, "Um, he was so different from Baxter—wonderful, warm, respectful and understanding. All the things that Baxter forgot early in our marriage. Um, it wasn't so much for the sex. We just enjoyed each other's company. He complained that Goldie had become too much of a socialite and seemed to have lost interest in him. We both felt that way about our spouses—we felt isolated."

"Did Goldie Hendrix know of this affair?" Hawk asked. He noticed that Carpenter was taking notes.

"She must've known the more I think about it. But she never said anything or acted like she knew. Instead, our friendship grew after her husband's murder."

"What made you think that she knew?" Nora asked.

"Um, she began to talk more about Edgar, about his habits, and then she'd say something to the effect that I know his habits as well. There were other things that just led me to believe that she was aware."

Carpenter said, "You were seen in that video a minute or two after Hendrix was shot. You were running away. That only leads me to believe that you killed him."

Angie's eyes flew wide. "No, no, I didn't kill him. I loved him. I enjoyed every moment I was with him. We even talked about divorcing our spouses. I know he was older, but I could see living with him the rest of our lives together."

"Well, it doesn't look good for you as far as Hendrix being murdered." Carpenter persisted. "All the evidence points to you. And I'm sure that my fellow detectives, Clint and Nora, would agree with me that since you killed once, it would be easier the second time to kill your husband as well."

"No! No! This can't be happening! It's a nightmare! You've got it all wrong!"

"Then tell us what happened," Nora said.

"All right. I drove my son's car so that no one would recognize my car. I started to walk toward the back gate of Edgar's house when suddenly I jumped when I heard a bang like a gun going off or a car backfiring. The shot sounded like it came just a house or two away. I immediately thought of all the shootings between gangs. I was so scared that I ducked behind some trash cans sitting next to the fence. When I looked up, I saw a person walking rapidly down the alley away from me."

"Was it a man or a woman?" Hawk asked.

"Um, I believe it was a woman. She was dressed in a black jacket and wore dark pants."

"Do you know who it was?"

"Um…no," brushing her brown eyebrow with her finger.

Hawk continued, "You recognized her, didn't you?"

"I really can't say for sure." Hawk continued to glare at her.

"Who do you think it was?"

"Oh God! I don't want to get my friend in trouble because I'm not sure, but…um…she kinda looked like Goldie. I think I recognized her shoes more than anything else."

"What about her shoes?" Hawk asked. "Were they special or something?"

"She always told me that unless she has to wear dress shoes, she will wear Kuru sneakers because they give her the arch support that she needs."

"And were they Kuru sneakers?"

"Um, um…I'm not sure, but they looked like the kind that she wore—mauve with a patch of light blue at the heel."

"How could you see that?" Hawk asked. "Wasn't it dark out?"

"Well, um, the moon was out, and there's a streetlight at the end of the alley. I think what caught my eye was the shiny light blue strip on her heel."

Nora asked, "Thinking that your friend killed your lover, you continued to be good friends. That's remarkable. I'd been really pissed off and had gone to the police right away."

"I know. Um, I'm a very weak person. First of all, I'm not sure that it was Goldie. I really didn't want to believe that it was. I guess I repressed who I saw in the alley, wishing it wasn't her."

"It might not have been her," Detective Carpenter spoke up. "Mrs. Hendrix had a receipt from a store in Cherry Creek Mall that confirmed her alibi that she was in the store at the time of the murder."

"You're trying to lay the blame on someone else when, in fact, you're the one that was in the alley at the time of the murder, and you're the one seen running from the scene of the crime, dashing into your car, and speeding away. What are we supposed to think?"

"No. I told you that I wasn't sure who it was, but when that gun went off, and I saw a woman running away, I took a quick look at her, then I took off so that people wouldn't think that I did it. I did not shoot Edgar. I loved him!" She was breathing hard, her chest heaving. "Maybe you should check out the credit card machines that the store uses. Sometimes, the time isn't adjusted for daylight savings. I believe Goldie told me that once. I did not kill anyone—not Edgar or my husband."

"We'll check that out," Carpenter said.

The three detectives finally dismissed Angie Visser. They didn't have enough to charge her. Her story was plausible. She denied carrying a gun or even having a gun in the house. But Hawk and Nora remembered that Goldie must have had guns since she is a champion marksman.

CHAPTER 46

DETECTIVE CARPENTER was now determined to reinvestigate Hendrix's murder with Goldie as the prime suspect. Nora and Hawk told him that they also needed to talk to Goldie Hendrix about the murder of the two lawyers.

"Well, if you talk to her before I do, get a confession out of her for her husband's murder, although my money is on Angie Visser. But why do you think that Goldie is involved with the murder of the two lawyers?"

"Visser seemed to sleep with any pretty skirt," Hawk said. "Goldie is not a bad-looking woman, kind of sexy, actually. I wouldn't put it past them to have had an affair as well. And if she shot her husband, she might have no compunction to shoot Visser and the woman he was screwing that night. Whoever shot them, I believe, did it out of overwhelming jealousy. We need to explore that line with Goldie."

"Okay, that's a stretch, but good luck with that."

After Carpenter left, Nora teased Hawk a little, "Oh, so you think Goldie is good-looking and sexy, do you?" Nora chuckled. "I told you that you're fascinated with her." She continued to snicker.

"What's so funny? I'm being serious. Don't you think my reasoning is possible?"

"Okay. I'll give you that. Actually, it might be very plausible that the two of them hooked up. After all, she attracts you, so why not Baxter?" Nora pointed the finger at him in jest and continued, "And I noticed how friendly she was with you. And you liked it—you li—iked it," her smile was broad, accentuating her mischievous eyes.

"Will you stop ? I have you to be attracted to. I don't need anyone else."

"Oh my God! Clint, that's the nicest thing you ever said to me." She placed her hand on his shoulder. Hawk glanced at her gleaming eyes as he covered her hand with his own.

Next, Hawk and Ricci interrogated Norman Durand, who reluctantly came into the station visibly upset. After sitting in the room by himself, cooling his heels, he finally calmed down and just wanted to get it over. After Hawk and Ricci came in, he now seemed to be more cooperative. When they told him that his waitress, Shirl Macon, had strongly insinuated that he would be the logical murderer, he erupted, "That's bullshit! She's full of crap."

"Well, it's possible," Nora said. "Your alibi doesn't hold water. You were not at the bar, as you claim, so what are we supposed to think? You certainly had a good reason to kill your wife and her lover because of her affair."

"That's impossible. I told you I really didn't care who she screwed."

"Why is it impossible?" Hawk asked, his eyes boring into the man.

He remained silent for several minutes. The detectives could almost see the cells in his brain doing contortions. Finally, he looked at them and said, "I hope what I will tell you doesn't go any further than this room or at least the police station."

"We'll try to keep it here, but that's the best we can do. No promises."

Durand again hesitated, then said in a quiet, soft voice, "I had to lie about my whereabouts because I was with my boyfriend late in the afternoon and into the night. I'm gay. But if my customers find out, I'm sure I'll lose my business. They are not very accepting of gays, constantly joking about people like me."

Hawk and Nora seemed stunned at first. If that truly was the case, then he would be eliminated as a possible suspect.

"How can we confirm that?" Nora asked.

"Ask my boyfriend. His name is Richard Rivera. He has a ring camera by the door. You'll see me walk in around 4:30 last Friday and not leave until I had to get back to the bar to close."

"All right," Hawk said. "We'll check it out. You're free to go for now. Thank you for coming in."

After they returned to their desks, Orlinski and Mortimer ambled into the homicide unit and made their way to Nora and Hawk. Holding a green and white flash drive between his fingers, Orlinski waved it in front of Nora's face.

"We supposedly have a copy of last Friday night's video from the house directly across the alley to the law offices."

Mortimer added, "And also, we finally were able to talk to all the tenants in the apartments across the side street. One of them had a video camera set up in the window that showed the street and part of the yard of the law office building. She was able to find the feed for last Friday and sent it to Orlinski's phone since my flip-top phone doesn't have internet." Mortimer then threw his head back, took in some quick breaths, then belted out a thunderous sneeze. Nora jumped, as did the other detectives. "Oh, sorry," Mortimer said. "I don't know what got into me. So, together, we should watch both videos, okay?"

Still chuckling from Mortimer's sneeze, Orlinski asked, "Which one do you want to see first, the back or the side?"

Nora took the thumb drive from Orlinski and plugged it into the USB port. Immediately, a video appeared portraying the alley behind the law office building and part of its small parking lot. They fast-forwarded the feed to closing time for the law firm. At exactly five o'clock, Melody Elmers, Brittany Larsen, and one of the upstairs paralegals were seen scurrying to their cars. A few minutes later, White and Garcia walked out together, laughing hard. White patted Garcia's shoulder as they parted, his face flushed from a good laugh. Then, White checked his watch before climbing into his silver Cadillac Escalade. Garcia drove off in his blue BMW Five-Series. Then, eleven minutes later, White's second paralegal walked out and took off in an old Saab convertible.

"Is this everyone except for the victims?" Nora asked as she leaned her head closer to the screen. No wait. I didn't see Ursula Hamlin. Did you?" The question was addressed to the men viewing the monitor behind her.

"Let's back it up and go through this again," Hawk said. "This time, let's take inventory."

"I've got my pad," Orlinski said. "Call out the names again, and I'll write them down."

Nora did, and she was right—Ursula Hamlin was not seen coming out of the building with the others.

"Do you think that Hamlin walked out the front?" Hawk asked, remembering, though, that Ursula told him that the staff used the back door to go in and out per company policy. He asked her that question the other day when he came up to her desk to obtain a sample of her writing.

"Orlinski said, "That means that Ursula could be the killer."

"Is her car in the parking lot?" Mortimer asked.

"No," Hawk said. "All that's left is Durand's Nissan Pathfinder and Visser's Range Rover. Maybe she parked it out front somewhere, and that's why she might've left out the front door. She must have the keys to both doors."

"Maybe she parked out front," Nora said, "but I want to run the video again. I thought I saw somethin'."

She ran the feed back and forth until the notation 5:35 p.m. was displayed in the lower corner. Then, she slowed the video to a crawl, one frame at a time. At 5:38 PM, at the very upper corner of the screen, the sole of what looked to be a wide black sneaker barely appeared about a foot off the ground.

"Look at that," Nora said. "Someone was running away. That looks like a pretty big shoe; it could be either a man's or a woman's."

"I'm guessing that the person stayed hugging the house and was out of the range of the camera," Hawk said. "But when he or she made a wide turn, probably to go around the corner of the place, part of the right shoe fell within range of the camera. I bet the person ran down the side of the building and onto the street. Good work, Nora. Can you blow it up even more?"

After Nora enlarged it without making it too distorted, Hawk took a photo off the monitor with his phone and sent it to Chet Watkins, the expert on shoe soles. He included a text message for Chet to study the sole and part of the heel and see if he knows what shoe that is.

Chet answered within a minute that he'd get back to him as quickly as he could. "I enjoy the challenge," he texted.

Mortimer said to Hawk and Nora, "It's remarkable how you two always come up with something." They were surprised by that comment, as Mortimer was not known for throwing compliments around.

"Well, thanks for that," Hawk answered. "But most of it is luck."

"Oh, um, I have to go," Mortimer said. "Nature calls. I'll be back soon. Don't watch the other video without me." With that said, the man ran out of the Unit, leaving Orlinski standing with Hawk behind Nora, who was at the computer.

In a whisper, Orlinski said, "Wait till you hear what I heard Mort say about his Josephine."

"What is it?" Nora asked, interested.

"Oh, he's back already. I'll tell you later."

The gossip is at it again, Hawk thought,

Hawk's ringtone played the tune *Bad to the Bone.* Chet's name appeared on the screen. Without any salutation, Chet said, "That was an easy one. Give me a harder one next time. The sole is from a Reebok Sublite work shoe. I'd guess size 10w. The foot slants to the right, as indicated by the right side of the heel, which is more worn. Anything else?"

"Not right now, Chet. Thanks."

After he clicked off, Hawk seemed to fall into deep thought. "What are you thinkin'?" Nora asked.

"I'm thinkin' that I saw someone wearing that type of shoe just a few days ago. But for the life of me, I can't remember who or where. It'll come to me. So, are we ready to watch the second video, Orlinski?"

"Yeah, I'll transfer it to Nora's email."

"I got it!" Hawk shouted. "Shirl Macon!"

"Shirl Macon?" Nora repeated, surprised. "She wore shoes like those? Oh, yeah, you're right. I remember now. But why would she be at the place?"

"Good question. She's still locked up, and I bet if we check her shoes, they match." Hawk turned his attention to Orlinski. "Stan, did you have a chance to check on her as far as court cases she might've been involved in? I tend to agree with Mortimer that she might've been involved in a case that involved Visser."

"No, I haven't had a spare minute yet. I'll get to it after we watch the video of the sideyard."

The feed was a little grainy, but enough could be seen to make out an image of a woman at approximately the time of the murders. She was dressed in black pants and a light gray top. She wore mauve or light purple sneakers with a patch of another color on the back of the heel. Her hair was black and curly, but it was hard to make out her face. The woman seemed to be in a hurry as she quickly strode from the direction of the law office building onto the street which she crossed before turning towards Logan Street, and then was out of the range of the camera.

Nora enlarged the image; it became somewhat distorted, but it was enough for Nora to shout out, "Oh my God! Hawk, you're right. She was involved. That's Goldie Hendrix, isn't it."

The three men behind Nora bent to see the image. "I never met this woman," Mortimer said. "No one asked me to join them when she was interviewed," his voice bitter.

"Sorry, Mortimer," Hawk said. "You and Orlinski were gathering good evidence for us here."

Nora said, "So what does all this mean? That law office on the night of the murders was a busy place. We're thinkin' that Shirl was there and maybe also Goldie? What's that all about? Does that mean that one or maybe both are the killers?"

"Strange, isn't it," Hawk said. "We'll have to figure it out. You know, those shoes she's wearing look expensive. I haven't seen a pair like that before. If Chet can identify them and Goldie does wear those kinds of shoes, then that'll help confirm that it was her." He took a photo of the shoe and sent it to Chet. "Wait a minute! Aren't those shoes similar to the ones described by Angie Visser that she saw on the woman that was walking down the alley when Edgar Hendrix was shot?"

"It sounds like it," Nora said. "Same person then and now. I think your Goldie has a lot of explaining to do." Nora laughed teasingly.

"What do you mean, my Goldie?" Hawk returned the laugh while both Orlinski and Mortimer had no idea what could be so funny, not knowing that Nora teased Hawk about his fascination with Goldie.

"Okay then," Orlinski muttered. "I think we're making progress. I'll check on Shirley Macon to see whether she has any court cases. This is becoming interesting."

Orlinski returned to his desk, and Mortimer declared, "Anyone hungry? I could use a hamburger."

"Aren't you required to go to lunch at home?" Hawk asked. "What will Josephine say?" Nora snickered to herself knowing that the man hated the food that his fiancé prepared.

"Oh, I guess you're right. She did say that she's going to prepare a salad with chopped cucumbers, tomatoes and olives on a bed of hummus."

"That sounds yummy, Mortimer," Nora said.

"Oh, you think so. I'm not sure that I'm up to it. Can't you say that you need my help to interview someone for an excuse? Oh, wait, I need to go home after all. I'm anxious to tell her about the two women who could've killed the two lawyers. See who she thinks is the one."

Hawk said, "She's been wrong every time so far. Maybe you should just go to lunch with us."

"Oh, that will be great." He patted his back pocket. Oh, darn, I forgot my wallet this morning, so I can't go after all."

His face looked so sad that Nora said, "I'll buy you lunch, and you can repay me back later."

"All right, then. I'll go. Not sure when I can pay you back. Josephine keeps a tight tab on how much I spend."

CHAPTER 47

LUNCH WAS at Charlie Brown's Bar and Grill in the Capitol Hill area. It was one of Hawk's favorite restaurants because of its historical character. It had been a staple in the area since 1933. Every time he visited, he imagined what life was like decades ago during the economic shock of the Great Depression when the restaurant first opened. It was a marvel that the restaurant had survived the hard times. Hawk just loved the place. He never ceased looking at the unique rectangular bar surrounded by polished brass railings and the knick-knacks on the shelves above the bar counters.

Nora enjoyed the atmosphere as well and was pleased that they came. At first, Mortimer admired the place and even pointed to the paintings of the restaurant, as it looked years ago, with some interest, but then he became more enthusiastic looking at the menu. When the waitress came to the table, he quickly ordered two hamburgers with fries and a large Coke. Hawk took a gyros sandwich while Nora ordered a salad with chicken.

Waiting for the food to arrive, Hawk and Nora quietly discussed the case. However, Mortimer was more interested in the food the servers were carrying to individual tables. Hawk glanced at Mortimer and smiled. With raised eyebrows, he pointed out their friend's enthusiasm to Nora. They winked at each other. Mortimer sat erect on the edge of his seat, licking his chops as servers with trays of food walked by them.

When their order arrived at the table, Mortimer dug into his first hamburger. "Oh, oh, ah. This is so good. I love it." And as always, before Hawk or Nora took two or three bites of their food, Mortimer had gobbled up the hamburger. He stuffed a handful of French fries into his mouth and seemed to have swallowed them whole without the appearance of chewing. Then, he quickly grabbed the second burger. Hawk and Nora watched in amazement as he devoured the second one with equal gusto. After the last of the fries were gone, he wiped his mouth with the napkin, threw his head back and closed his eyes in satisfaction. Then, suddenly, as if he thought of something, he opened his eyes and fixed them on Hawk's and Nora's plates.

"Oh, I ate a little too fast. You, guys, barely started eating. But I was hungry."

"Yeah, we better get to it, all right," Nora said. "Times a wasting."

"Well, if you can't eat it all, I'll finish it for you." Hawk and Nora laughed, but unfortunately for Mortimer, they were hungry as well, thus leaving him disappointed.

After lunch, the three detectives headed out to interview Goldie Hendrix. On the way to the Cherry Creek area, Hawk received a call from Chet Watkins, who informed him that the shoe in the video was a tough one to analyze since he couldn't get a good look at it. The best information available seemed to indicate that it was a Kuru Atom shoe that is popular for people who have foot aches, such as plantar fasciitis.

"Okay, Chet," Hawk said, "you're beginning to sound like Janeel with her fancy words. What in the hell is that?"

Chet chuckled, "That's heel pain, to put it simply…oh, don't hold me to this, but I think that this shoe is the same shoe or at least the same brand as the one you sent me to look at before."

"You mean to tell me that the shoe the woman wore walking from the law offices is the same as the one worn by the woman walking down the alley right after the Hendrix murder two years ago?"

"Let's just say they're both Kuru shoes. Made in China but headquartered and designed in Salt Lake City. At least that's my opinion, even though they were not the exact shoes since the color was different. But then, the video was grainy."

"Wow! Thank you, Chet, you're the greatest. By the way, were you able to get a DNA off the blond hair strand that I gave you last week?"

"Yeah, I didn't forget. We should have the results back any day now, and we'll see if we can match it up with someone."

Hawk had his speaker on, and both Nora and Mortimer heard the conversation. "Clint," Nora said, "you had a hunch all along that the same person was involved in both murders. I thought you were nuts, but you might've been right all along."

"And you two believe that the woman in both cases was this Goldie that we'll be interviewing?" Mortimer asked.

"Looks like things so far are pointing in that direction, ace," Hawk said.

"Oh, Ace? I guess it's okay to call me that…maybe. Actually, I like the name. I'll ask Josephine what she thinks about that."

"Let us know," Hawk said. "We'll be on pins and needles until then," he added jokingly with a chuckle.

"Oh, yes, I'll let you know tomorrow."

Goldie Hendrix became concerned after Hawk called for an appointment to see her again. She wondered why . What did the detectives have in mind? They already talked to her and even though she was nervous as could be, she thought that the interview went well. What did they know now that required them to return?"

After all, she was trained as an actress and should be able to mask any mannerisms that would portray guilt or insincerity. She was good, one of the leading actresses in a promising play off-Broadway in New York. And soon, she would be on the big stage on Broadway, her future bright. Considering herself to be a talented actor, she believed that her performance with the detectives was perfect. She really did not think that she would be seeing them again. *Maybe I'm not as good as I think, and I didn't fool them at all.* She noticed how Detective Hawk seemed especially interested in her husband's murder. *It wasn't his case so why all the questions? What did he suspect?*

She sat back in her easy chair and tried to relax. It didn't help. The knot in her gut was still there. A daytime soap opera was on TV, but her mind wandered from the show to the night when Edgar Hendrix first entered her dressing room at the theater in New York. He was all smiles, so handsome and debonair, standing with such authority by the door with a large bouquet of flowers. Even though he was several years older, they went out afterward to one of the most expensive restaurants in Manhattan. For several weeks, they met after her performances, and he continued to wine and dine her on tenderloin steaks, lobster, caviar, and white truffles, all carefully prepared by the best gourmet chefs in New York. She was hooked on the good life and his gentle and understanding personality. She readily agreed to accompany him to his suite at the Ritz-Carlton. That was the first of many nights together.

Then he sprung it on her. He was returning to Denver and would like to take her back as his bride. He promised her that he'd build a mansion in her honor with large closets so that she could fill them up with whatever designer clothes and jewelry she wanted. She'd have a butler and as many servants as she required. She would be the grandest socialite of them all, his pampered princess. It sounded so wonderful for a girl who came from a poor family and moved from Brooklyn to

South Carolina when she was a teenager. The wealth that he displayed while he wooed her was absolutely intoxicating.

But by marrying the man, she'd have to give up her dream of being a big star on Broadway. Goldie sweated over what she should do. Did she really love the man? He was obviously smitten with her. But what about her career, the applause that she craved ? She would have to give it up. But then, she thought, sadly, how really realistic was her dream of becoming a star on Broadway? There was so much rivalry. For a big show, her singing was not up to par compared with some of her competitors. Neither were her dancing skills. She tried to keep up with the dance steps the choreography required, but she struggled. There was always someone better. Then there was the anxiety and stress over auditions that, at times, physically made her sick, even made her vomit. She thought about all the negatives: the long hours late into the night, the travel for weeks away from home, the memorization, the tedious rehearsals, the backstabbing, the waiting anxiously by the phone whether she was picked for the part and the general phoniness of it all. And that is why, for all those reasons she began to consider accepting Edgar's offer of marriage and moving to Denver.

When she moved to Denver, she thought that she might join an acting group, one requiring less stress than a Broadway play. After all, why not? Her acting skills were good, learned through drama classes in high school and a couple of years of college. She had several roles in plays before audiences in high school, college and small community theaters before the big break came to play off-Broadway. But why would she want to go through all of that again if she were to live as a "princess." So, she was swept off her feet by the charming Edgar Hendrix and now she resides in Denver and possibly is in very deep trouble.

In trouble because Edgar lied to me. He had a cozy yet large house in a good neighborhood surrounded by other beautiful homes. But they were not mansions on estates as she had pictured them in her mind. There were no butlers or maids except for a cleaning woman who came once a week. Instead, Edgar had turned out to be a tightwad, unlike the man who threw money around as though he had it to burn when he wooed her in New York.

After a year of marriage, she asked him to add her name to the title of the house as his wife. He refused and later insisted that she sign a postnuptial agreement, which she refused. That's when they seemed to drift apart. They moved into separate bedrooms. He placed her on a strict budget. However, she admitted that it was still generous in the amount of 4,500 dollars per month for her personal expenses, such as clothing and jewelry. He also promised her that she would be his beneficiary on his substantial life insurance policy, but that was it, and not to expect any other assets that he may have at the time of his death. The thought of the insurance calmed her even though she felt that he treated her like a child or a kept pet. Even though she was able to continue to have perks such as a luxury car and a Denver Country Club membership, she no longer felt as if she was his wife and partner in life. She began to resent him, maybe even hate him. Him! For him, she gave up her career, her family, and the city that she loved and moved to Denver. Her only consolation was her friends and the deepening relationship that slowly developed with Baxter Visser.

Baxter and Angie became best friends with her and Edgar, enjoying each other's company. Baxter often appraised her with his hungry eyes. She enjoyed the attention and the casual flirting. At some point, it went too far. At first, she resisted his advances, but then, when he placed his hand on her knee at one of the dinners out as two couples having fun, she didn't brush it away. He had this animal magnetism that turned her on, and she allowed him to take further liberties at every opportunity. Now that Goldie's marriage was in the dumps, she looked forward to trysts with him. They were careful. Meeting in his office late at night when no one could possibly be around. When she asked about cameras in the place, he laughed and told her, "That, my dear, is why this building has no cameras."

She knew it was wrong, but the fun and excitement of making love to a wild man in secret was exhilarating. She felt a tinge of guilt when she was with Angie but rationalized that Baxter was a sex addict and she was just one of many of his conquests. But then, after several months, she began to develop deeper feelings for him and no longer liked the idea of sharing.

It was a little over two years ago that she heard a voicemail message on their landline from Edgar's insurance agent. She could still remember the exact words, "Hello, Mr. Hendrix, I won't be able to meet with you tomorrow to change the beneficiary on your life insurance. I truly apologize for the inconvenience, but I have an emergency that has come up, and I'll have to leave town for a couple of days. I'll call you when I return. Thank you, Alan."

She went to his home office and searched the filing cabinets. Under the tab of "INS," she found the whole life insurance policy in the amount of three-million dollars payable on death. As he promised, she was named the beneficiary. *Now, the bastard wants to cut me out altogether. I'll be destitute!* She had to come up with a plan and fast. But what?

Now, as she waited for the detectives to arrive, she wondered what they knew, particularly of her affair with Baxter. *But how? I was so careful.*

CHAPTER 48

AT THE BUILDING, Goldie buzzed them in and met them at the door of her extravagant condo. "Please come in. I'm pleased to see you both." *You won't be so pleased after we question you,* Nora thought. Goldie wore a tight-fitting light beige skirt with a flowery, low-cut bright top that accentuated her breasts. Nora hated to admit it but conceded that she looked amazing with her black curly hair, the right touch of makeup and bright red lips. The suspect asked them to follow her, and as they did, Nora glanced at a gold tray atop a glass table with stamped letters yet to be mailed.

Nora halted briefly as she took a closer look at the names and addresses written on the envelopes. She immediately recognized the beautiful cursive writing. *Wow! She's the one! The mystery woman who wrote that note to Baxter Visser. That's the same handwriting as on the note, I'm sure of it. Man, that Baxter sure got around.*

Nora and Hawk sat down in the same positions that they sat in when they last visited her. Mortimer, though, refused to sit. Once again, Goldie offered tea with cookies. After they refused, she, nevertheless, went into the kitchen and poured out four tall glasses of sweet, iced tea from a pitcher. As Goldie fussed with the tea, Nora whispered to Hawk that she noticed the writing on an envelope that matched the note found under Visser's computer. Hawk's eyes widened while his mouth flew open.

Goldie lifted the tea glasses off an elegant silver tray, handed one to each and said, "I hope you'll like the tea. Summer is almost over, but it's still a very hot day today, and this should hit the spot. Please enjoy." She looked at the standing Mortimer and asked him to sit down. He reluctantly complied and sat down in the other side chair.

"Well, thank you, Mrs. Hendrix," Nora said.

"Oh my, sweetie, just call me Goldie. Every time I hear Mrs. Hendrix, it reminds me of my poor husband's tragic death. Anyway, I hope you'll like the tea. Not all sweet tea is brewed and sweetened alike, you know." She then turned her attention to Hawk, giving him a wide smile. "So, I understand that you have some more questions for me."

"Yes, Goldie, but I'm afraid that they won't be very pleasant questions since we now have more information to work with."

"Oh my, honey, you're scaring me." Her perpetual smile since they walked in suddenly faded.

"We'd like to know more about your relationship with Baxter Visser."

"Sweetie, as I told you before, we were friends. The four of us got together for dinners, went to concerts, that sort of thing."

Hawk nodded to Nora to take over. "Goldie, weren't you seeing Baxter romantically?"

Goldie displayed a fair amount of shock and a look of outrage. She was a former actor, and neither Hawk nor Nora was fooled. "Certainly not! Angie is my best friend, and I would never, never hit on or allow Baxter to hit on me…although I must confess that he tried to hit on me a few times, but I certainly discouraged that."

Nora asked her if she'd allow her to take one of the envelopes to be mailed from the foyer side table. Surprised at the request, she said,

"I don't know what you're getting at. It's so unusual, but I'll get it for you."

When she left, Mortimer whispered to the other two, "She did it. I feel it."

In the meantime, Nora took out her phone. She had a photograph of the note that Hawk found and needed now to see if it matched the writing on the envelope.

After Goldie returned, she reluctantly handed the envelope to Nora. "I don't understand what in the world you would want with it."

The detectives didn't answer immediately. Nora and Hawk were engrossed comparing the handwriting while Mortimer eyed a plate of cookies on the counter. After a long minute, Nora glanced at Hawk, who nodded for her to continue questioning the woman. "Goldie, do you want to change your mind as to telling us whether or not you and Attorney Visser had an affair?"

"No. Certainly not. What does that envelope have to do with Baxter ? It's addressed to a friend whose birthday is in a few days."

Hawk said, "In that case, would you compare the handwriting on the envelope with what's on Detective Ricci's phone."

He gave the envelope to her along with Nora's phone with the photo of the handwritten note on the screen. Goldie attempted a fake smile and said as confidently as she could, though inside, she trembled, "I don't understand your games. But, sweetie, if it'll make you happy, sure, why not."

Her breathing remained shallow, and her chest heaved as she read the note on the phone. With her dark eye noticeably twitching, she said, again with obviously fake bravado, "Oh, that. It was just a joke. There was nothing serious between us."

Hawk said, "Why is it so hard for you to admit that you had an affair with the man? That's not against the law. But if you shot Visser and Elizabeth Durand in revenge that he was with another woman, then that definitely is unlawful, and you're in big trouble."

"Yes, big trouble," Mortimer suddenly spoke, startling Goldie. "We know that you were in the alley behind your house at the exact moment your husband was shot."

Goldie sat back with a shocked expression. "I most certainly was not!"

Nora said, "We have an eyewitness. You lied when you provided a receipt from a store whose clock was an hour behind. That means that you could've shot your husband and afterward walked around the Mall and purchased a piece of jewelry, knowing that the time on the receipt would give you an alibi." Goldie's breathing continued its a rapid pace as a bead of sweat appeared on her forehead. "We can only come to one conclusion. That is, you killed your husband, and if you killed once, the second and third killings would come easier." Goldie fell back in her chair and put her hand over her forehead. Nora continued, "And now that we know you had an affair with Visser, a logical conclusion would be that you killed Baxter and Elizabeth out of sheer jealousy and revenge."

Goldie screamed, "You have no idea who killed Baxter. You're just trying to pin this on me, and all you have is a note that I wrote him. You better have more proof than that."

Hawk said, "Unfortunately for you, we can place you at the scene at the time of the murders. We have you on tape walking away from the law offices." Goldie's eyes and mouth flew open.

"How can that be? I wasn't there! I was with Angie Durand at the restaurant."

"Well, Angie said that you came late. She had to wait for you."

"I got stuck in traffic, as I told you before."

"No, you told us that you had to wait for Angie since she came late."

"Well, I just can't remember who came first. I thought I did. I want to see the tape of me supposedly being at the scene, as you call it."

Hawk showed her on his phone. She stared at it and then laughed. "That's not me. You can't see that woman's face clearly. It could be anyone with black curly hair."

Nora said, "Goldie, it's time for you to stop lying to us. The case against you is very strong. We're expecting a warrant to arrive any minute to search your condo. And if we find the shoes you were wearing the night of the murder, as shown in the video, in your closet, then that's you for sure. Chances are that we'll find a 9 mm pistol or revolver used in the killings as well. You are an expert marksman, and I bet you have a variety of weapons—"

"Okay, okay. Oh God!... I was there. Baxter and I had been having an affair. You're right. But, please believe me, I did not kill Baxter or that woman lawyer...I went to see him because he hadn't called me for several days and wouldn't return my calls. I knew that he worked late on Fridays. At least, that's what he always told me. I thought I could catch him and discuss where our relationship was heading. I didn't necessarily want to lose him, as he was fun to be with. Can't say I actually loved him, though. It was just fun and an escape from living with boring Edgar."

"And when you heard or saw Baxter with another woman, you freaked out and shot them both ," Mortimer said in his deep voice. "You were emotionally involved with him, and it hurt."

"No, no, no! I was coming up to the building, and just as I took the first step onto the porch, I heard two muffled gunshots. Of course, you should understand that I didn't want to be found anywhere near there, so I quickly left and met up with Angie."

At that moment, a buzzer dinged in the kitchen, indicating that someone was at the front door. She stood up, straightened her shoulders, and proudly, with her head high, strolled toward the intercom in the kitchen. She glanced at the detectives, attempting a smile. But that smile was obviously very fake. "I'll signal him in. It's a police officer with the warrant you mentioned, although you really don't need one. I'd let you all look around. I have nothing to hide."

After a search of the premises, Kuru's shoes, like the ones visible in the video, were discovered in Goldie's closet. However, no 9 mm weapon was found anywhere.

CHAPTER 49

DRIVING AWAY from Goldie Hendrix's condo, the three detectives discussed Goldie's interview. She admitted to the affair with Visser but, of course, denied that she killed her husband or the lawyers. As far as her husband's murder was concerned, they agreed to leave it up to Detective Carpenter. His interest in the case had been rekindled. His chances improved dramatically now that Angie Visser claimed that she saw a woman looking very much like Goldie walking away a few seconds after she heard the fatal shots. *Yeah, let Carpenter solve the case,* Hawk thought.

"So, what do you think?" Nora asked. "Should we have arrested Goldie for the lawyers' murders?"

"Yes, we should have," Mortimer chimed in.

"Do you think we have enough probable cause?" Hawk asked.

"No, we don't have enough evidence now," Nora said. "Just common sense. Look, Clint, she had an affair. She must've seen or heard Baxter and Elizabeth at it when she came up to Baxter's door. She went into a rage, took her pistol out of her purse and blasted them away. Makes sense, doesn't it?"

"Um-hum. But unless we have other proof, it's all speculation. The fact that she just came to talk to Visser is plausible. But did she go in? We have her at the scene but nothing else to tie her to the shooting itself. Damn! If we only had found the murder weapon in her possession. I can't believe the cache of weapons in her gun safe. There wasn't a single 9 mm."

"She's too smart to leave a murder weapon around. She ditched it somewhere. That is if she is the killer. What does your famous gut say? Is she the one?"

Hawk laughed. "Famous, huh? Well, it's not telling me much right now."

"Well then, we're back to square one. I'm anxious, though, to question Sherl Macon since you think that the black shoe in the video could be hers…I must admit that is quite a stretch."

"Yeah, Nora, it does sound farfetched, all right."

"But, as I said before," Mortimer said, "there's got to be a connection."

"And what do you think of Angie Visser?" Nora asked. "I'm just not so sure that she is free and clear of all this."

Hawk looked at his reliable partner and said, "Why did we discount her so quickly? She was in the alley where and when Hendrix was shot. It's only her word that she saw someone else fleeing the shooting. And she's pinning it on her dear friend, Goldie."

"Yeah, again, our reasoning is that if she killed someone before, it'd be easier to do it a second time."

"This case is so frustrating. We just don't have anything solid to go on. It's all conjecture and speculation. I still believe that whoever shot the lawyers sat in the basement, waiting for the right moment to rush in and shoot. Both Angie and Goldie knew the building and knew where to wait. I wonder where Chet is on that hair strand. I pulled out of the bracket of the old chest down there. That's another long shot. Could be anyone's—a college student, a Goodwill clerk—anyone."

When the detectives returned to the station, Orlinski stopped them at his desk. "Hey, hotshots, do you want to hear about Shirley Macon?" The smile on his lips reflected through his bright blue eyes.

"Sure," Nora said, "must be something good."

"Maybe." He began punching keys on his keyboard, and a photograph of Shirley Macon appeared along with a case filing number.

Both Nora and Hawk leaned in to read the screen. "Look at that," Nora said. "There is a connection between Shirl and Visser." She read a little further. "And he was the lawyer that represented the father of her three children in a custody fight. She lost custody and all visitation rights. Wow! That's pretty drastic. Basically, she lost her children…she's gotta blame Visser for that. Losing her children—that's horrible."

Mortimer walked up to the desk and read the information on the monitor. "There you go, Clint. If you're right that that is her shoe in the video, then that places her at the scene of the crime on the day of the murders. She had motive and opportunity. I think we need to question her right away." A sense of excitement seemed to come over him. He began to pace up and down between the desks, raising his arms exuberantly in the air. His face, however, did not reflect his excitement but remained typically stoic. To the other detectives' surprise, it was a new mannerism of Mortimer's that they had not seen before.

"That's one excited guy," Orlinski said, chuckling. "He thinks that the case is solved."

Coming back to Orlinski's desk, Mortimer said, "Well! Aren't we going to interview her now?"

"We can't yet. She's been transferred to jail, and we'll have to make arrangements to bring her in. It'll most likely be tomorrow."

"Well, let's just go there and interrogate her."

"Mortimer," Hawk chimed in, "What's the rush ? She's not going anywhere."

"But, but, um, what if she posts bail?"

"Beating up on two cops, landing them in the hospital, the judge will surely deny bail or make the amount so steep that she couldn't bail out."

"Well, I'm going to talk to Josephine to see what she thinks. I bet she'd say we need to take care of it while the iron is hot."

"You do that, sport," Orlinski said with a little annoyance in his voice. "Besides, it's getting late anyway, and we need to get started on our paperwork."

"Oh, okay. I guess I need to put together something on my own observations. It doesn't take me long to put together a few words."

And Mortimer was right. While Hawk and Ricci were busy typing their reports, Mortimer proclaimed that he was finished and was going home.

Orlinski came up to Hawk and Ricci, "You know, I try to be civil to that Mortimer, but sometimes he makes it hard. This thing that he has with Josephine. What do you think that's all about? Why does he have to talk to her about every detail of our cases and then seek an opinion from her and then use it here as though she's some great guru who knows it all ? Who cares what that woman thinks!"

Hawk and Nora exchanged glances. Their mouths broke into wide smiles.

"Look, Orlinski, that's just the way it is. I think that neither one has anything to say to each other. Maybe his work is all they have in common to talk about."

"Not necessarily, Clint," Nora said. "They also have the vegan diet to discuss. That, and a large potential inheritance, is the bond that keeps them together."

They chuckled. Orlinski then said, "At least they have some kind of bond."

After finishing her report, Nora grabbed her black Michael Kors purse, threw a glance at Hawk, waved her hand to signal a goodbye then started to walk out. She suddenly stopped dead in her tracks as she remembered that her car was still in her garage and some of her clothes were at Hawk's house. "Whoops! Clint, with all the commotion of this long day, I forgot that you brought me to work this morning. Man, I'm losing it."

"Oh yeah! Good. Give me five minutes to finish up, and I have an idea. What if I treat you to a cheese and butter baguette sandwich followed by a slice of Tiramisu at my place ? I have something important to discuss with you,"

I wonder what he wants to discuss with me. Is he going to tell me that he wants a serious relationship? Should I play coy? Should I push his buttons and say that I'm going to have dinner with Seth Morgan, even though I'm not ? Geez, I'm being silly. Probably wants to talk about the case. "Alright, that sounds terrific."

Nora returned to her desk and threw herself into her maroon vinyl upholstered office chair. She opened the internet to see what the latest news headlines were. Just as she came to the middle of a story, Hawk said, "Okay, I'm done, let's go."

Before making it home, Hawk ran into Safeway to buy a long loaf of fresh French baguette and a package of butter while Nora waited in the Jeep. Once at the house, by habit at this point, they searched the three levels of the townhome to make sure no one was lurking about. They've become paranoid. Each hated the fact and hoped that with time, the bad feeling would go away once the past incidents became pushed back in their minds.

Afterward, Hawk called Mrs. Rose Lucero, his neighbor, to let her know that he was home and Stella could now return. In less than a minute, he heard his dog and Rose at the front door. Once the door was opened, Stella rushed in, jumping excitedly at Hawk. Then, the yellow Lab spotted Nora in the kitchen as she was pouring water into a coffee pot. She instantly forgot about Hawk and rushed to greet Nora. Hawk gave Rose heartfelt thanks for watching Stella, and after she left, he proceeded to feed the dog.

While Stella attacked the dog dish, Hawk pulled out a couple of deli packages. Baby Swiss cheese was in one and a Lithuanian low-fat cheese in the other. With the combination of the French bread, butter and cheese, Nora thoroughly enjoyed the sandwich with a cup of coffee. Hawk did as well, but Nora noticed that he appeared anxious, perhaps even nervous. *What's up with him?*

Nora said, "Can't say I enjoyed a sandwich more than this. But I really should be heading home, no matter how good the food around here is." She laughed briefly. Hawk still appeared on edge. "What's this somethin' that you want to discuss with me? Is it about the case?"

Hawk let out a nervous chuckle, "No, far removed from work. Why don't we get more comfortable in the living room ? Oh, I forgot to offer you the Tiramisu."

"Oh, I couldn't."

Nora sat down on the couch, and Hawk slid in next to her. Facing her, he mumbled, "Nora…um…I've been doing a lot of thinking about us the last few days."

"Um-hum."

"I mean to where I'd like our relationship to go. Um." Nora waited patiently. *This could be very good or very bad."*

"Hawk, spill it out. What's the problem?"

"Okay, here it is. I love you." He suddenly froze, appearing shocked by what just came out of his mouth.

Oh my gosh! "And."

"And I want us to be together. I want you here or there, doesn't matter where, as long as we…we're together."

Nora grinned widely. "What does that mean exactly? Do you want to move in together?"

"Yes, yes. That's what I mean. I miss you when you're not with me."

Well, it certainly isn't a marriage proposal, but knowing Clint, that's a big step. I don't think he ever asked anyone before to live together. What should I tell him? I love him, and if this is what it may take to get married to him eventually. At least he's committing himself to that. "Let's say we do. How do you want to work it? I mean, your house or my house or a whole new place?"

Hawk scratched his head, still a little dazed at this life-changing arrangement that he proposed. "Geez! I really don't care. You pick."

"You know, we'll have to keep it under wraps. No specific rule with DPD against fraternization as far as I know, but it is probably highly frowned upon if we continue to work as partners."

"Yeah. That could become a problem. Let's keep our individual houses, but we can still arrange to live together in one or the other— your choice. Maybe even alternate for the variety of it. No one needs to know where we spend the night. Just need to make sure that gossip, Orlinski, doesn't know."

Nora thought about what Hawk had said. She bit her lower lip indecisively. Finally, a wide smile broke out on her excited face. Stretching her arm out to pull him closer to her, she showered him with kisses. Hawk didn't mind as he returned the kisses until they found themselves upstairs in the bedroom.

CHAPTER 50

WITH EAGERNESS, the new chapter in their lives continued into the next morning. Since they were told to come in late, Hawk and Nora were in no hurry to rush out from underneath the sheets. Breakfast was fun, working together to prepare a Denver omelet containing eggs, diced ham, mushrooms, bell peppers, shredded cheese and onions. Whole wheat toast, orange juice and a special blend of coffee from Costa Rica, one that Hawk liked, were also on the table. They laughed and giggled as they played house for the first time under the new arrangement.

"So," Nora asked, "where do we go from here?"

"We better decide where to live. I have a wonderful arrangement with Mrs. Lucero to take care of Stella. She loves the dog, and Stella is great with her. But I'm sure we could maybe find someone in your neighborhood that would do the same—watch her while we're at work."

"Yeah, that's a consideration I hadn't thought about. Then there is this issue with clothes, makeup, and extra towels. You know, all that mundane stuff."

"Honey, we'll solve all that. Just tell me where you'd rather live. I really don't care. We'll find a sitter for Stella."

"Clint, geez, um. I guess I'd prefer to spend more time at my house. With my big yard, Stella would have more room to roam."

"Okay, that's the plan. Anybody in mind that might watch the dog?"

"Yeah. The lady across the street, Joanie Carmichael, loves dogs. She just lost hers, and I'd bet that she would agree. She's a retired bookkeeper, and I don't think she leaves the house much."

With that decided, Hawk loaded up some of his clothing along with a few toiletries in the Jeep. He took Stella to Mrs. Lucero and explained what he was up to. He told her that he'd pick the dog up after work. She looked disappointed but nodded in understanding. "Love rules the day," she said. "You two make such a nice couple. I wish you much luck." Hawk hugged her and asked if she would still be willing to watch Stella whenever necessary or when they stayed at his townhome. She readily agreed.

Finally, after unloading at her house, Nora took her own car, and Hawk followed her to the station. When they arrived, Orlinski told them that Shirley Macon was in Interrogation Room 2.

The first thing that Hawk did when they entered was to look carefully at her shoes. They were tucked under the table, and he couldn't see them. As he walked around to the side, the shoes were more visible. He quickly determined that they were the same ones he had seen her wear at Duro's Bar. He would have to ask her to remove them so that he could compare them closely to the ones in the video.

Upon seeing Nora, who had brought her down in the fight, Shirl's scowl deepened. Hatred shot out of her hazel eyes. She was mad and looked enraged. If her handcuffs were not tethered to a bar on the table, she would have pounced on Nora. They suspected that they would get no cooperation from her, at least not initially.

"Screw you!" she screamed at Nora. "And you too." That was directed at Hawk.

"Thank you," Nora said as calmly as she could manage. "Now that we got that out of the way, we have questions for you."

"I'm going to give you shit as far as answers, you freakin' bitch."

"Now, Shirl," Hawk said, "you don't understand how much trouble you're in. It's one thing to be charged with assaulting detectives, but it's quite another for murdering two lawyers."

Shirl's mouth flew open. "What in the hell you talkin' about, you idiot. I never killed no lawyers."

"Sure, you did. We have you at the scene of the murders."

"You're full of it."

"Yeah, you were there at the precise time the lawyers were killed. And you had a beef with Mr. Visser because you blamed him for losing your children. That's motive."

"Go to hell! I did not kill nobody."

"We got you cold," Nora said. "A double murder like that. You'll die in prison. Never see the freedom to beat up on people again." Shirl threw Nora a look that could kill.

"I ain't never been there, and you can't prove a damn thing."

Hawk said, "Sure, we can. Shirl, take off your right shoe."

"I ain't doing no such thing. I know my rights."

"You want me to call an officer in to pull it off of you?"

"Hell," She pulled her black Reebok off. "Take a good sniff of it, you sonofabitch."

Hawk smiled as he and Nora examined the sole carefully, even using a magnifying glass, which he brought, knowing that he would need it. They then compared the sole to an enlarged photo of the back portion of the shoe taken from the neighbor's video at the time of the murders. Shirl stared at what Hawk and Nora were doing. Nora noticed that for the first time, Shirl's hands trembled, her breathing more labored. "Alright," her voice suddenly became quieter and calmer. "I was there, but I didn't kill nobody." She hesitated and took some deep breaths before continuing. "I have a bad, mean temper.

Got it from my old man. I started missing my kids really bad Friday afternoon after work. After I got some liquid courage from a tequila bottle. Without thinkin' things through, I decided to barge into that prick's office and beat the crap out of that slick bastard lawyer. Teach him what it's like to be in pain for a change…I need some water."

An officer brought her a bottle of water. Shirl chugged almost half in one gulp and then continued, "I walked up the side of the place and looked through windows that weren't shaded to see if that bastard was in and alone." She took a big swig from the bottle and deeply inhaled through her nostrils, exhaling hard through her mouth. "Just as I looked through a window that had the shade not down all the way, I saw this woman come out of a door, one that looked like it might lead to a basement or someplace like that. She was tiptoeing slowly toward some office. She, not me, was the killer. She had a gun in her hand. When I saw that, I skedaddled out of there as fast as I could, going around the back of the house and down to the street on the other side of the building. Just as I got to the street, I heard a couple of gunshots comin' from the building. So, you can't pin those murders on me."

"And why should we believe you?" Nora asked although she thought that Shirl was telling the truth.

"Because that's what happened. I'm not makin' this shit up."

Nora continued on while Hawk was making entries in his notebook, "So what did this woman look like?"

Shirl gave them a fairly good description. Hawk even asked her to sketch the type of hairstyle as she depicted it. Afterward, Hawk and Nora glanced at each other. They knew exactly who that woman was."

CHAPTER 51

CAPTAIN MACGREGOR and Lieutenant Perez seemed relieved that the lawyers' killer had finally been identified—maybe. The source of the information, a felon who was herself at the scene of the crime, bothered them.

"I hope that's enough to get a warrant," Perez said. "Do you have other evidence to go along with Shirl's statement?" Hawk looked at Nora for an answer.

"We have another call out to Chet Watkins about that strand of hair that I found tucked in a metal strip on that chest in the basement. Hopefully, it'll match the suspect's DNA. Also," Nora continued, "we know through a video that the woman must have been at the scene of the crime."

"Okay," Perez said. "I'll try to get the paperwork. Go pick her up. That may be enough. I'll get an arrest and search warrant based on the facts that you told me, but I may have to wait for Chet's analysis. Call me as soon as you hear once we get the warrant. Find the weapon. That'll clinch it."

As the two detectives walked out of MacGregor's office, Mortimer lumbered into the unit. "Oh, are you going somewhere?"

"Yes, Mortimer," Nora said. "We're going to make an arrest of the lawyers' murderer."

"Oh, wait for me. I'll tell Perez that I'm going with you."

"Don't you want to know who we're after?"

"Oh, Josephine and I had a long discussion regarding who killed the lawyers. She didn't agree with me that Shirley Macon was the killer. She convinced me that it was Angie Visser. It makes sense to me. She has the most to gain from her husband's death. Josephine made a point that they shouldn't have had, as she puts it, carnal knowledge of each other. She also did not like Baxter Visser as I described him, and finally, I told her that we found them naked with the man on top of the woman. Josephine told me that that was absolutely disgusting and that I should've walked out of the building. But then she said that Visser deserved it."

"I don't know if anyone deserves to be murdered," Hawk said. "But both of you are dead wrong."

"No, you must be wrong. Who do you suspect to be the killer then?"

"It's Ursula Hamblin."

"You mean the loyal paralegal?" Hawk nodded. "Nah," Mortimer said, shaking his head. "She wouldn't kill her boss. She would protect him first. Why would she want to kill him anyway?"

"She harbored romantic feelings for him all those years that she worked for him," Nora said, "Then it got to a point where she couldn't take it anymore with him screwing around with so many women but never giving her the time of day romantically. At least, that's our conjecture since Clint told me after he first questioned her. You suspected her as a strong candidate, didn't you, Clint?"

"Yes, I did, but then we ran across more, possibly even more obvious suspects, and I put Ursula away in the back of my mind. But I tell you both, the fact that she didn't come out of the building through the back door as she usually said she did, got me to thinkin' that we need to revisit her as the prime suspect. After all, who had the best opportunity to shoot the lawyers at the exact moment that she wanted to."

"That's crazy. I'll run it past Josephine if that's a woman's way of thinking."

At that moment, Hawk received the expected call from Chet. Chet confirmed that the strand of hair belonged to Ursula Hamblin. That meant that she had been in the basement and sat on that bench waiting. He didn't want to make a big deal of it, especially since Nora teased him about it, but as far as he was concerned, unscientifically, the butt impression on the dusty chest most likely belonged to Ursula.

"I'm going with you anyway. You might get into another fight and may need my help."

After clearing with Perez and after Perez gave them a copy of a faxed arrest and search warrant, the three detectives made their way to the law office building, assuming that Ursula was still winding up Visser's cases. They planned to search first her desk and cabinets for the gun. If they couldn't find it, then they would proceed to her downtown condo with her. With Hawk remembering her uncooperative interview, he expected that she would put up a fight.

He was right. "What in the hell?!!!" She screamed. "You have no freakin' right to look through my things. Get out of here! I don't give a damn if you have a warrant or not. This isn't right. More police abuse and harassment is what this is. I'll have your badges and sue you for everything you own." Her voice was loud and shrill. She picked up a heavy-duty paper stapler and hurled it at Hawk, barely missing his head. Seeing that the woman was out of control, Nora, with Mortimer's help, restrained her arms and handcuffed her before she was about to heave a jar stocked with peppermint candy. Mortimer led her into the conference room, advised her of her Miranda rights and stayed with her while Hawk and Nora continued their search for the gun. All of this turmoil was witnessed with shocked expressions by the other paralegals and staff. Even attorneys White and Garza hustled out of their offices to see what the commotion was about.

It was important to do a thorough search for the weapon because, on the way to the offices, the three detectives arrived at the conclusion that Ursula would not have taken a chance of walking out with a murder weapon in her possession in case she were stopped. She had the opportunity to hide it and retrieve it later after the dust settled. After not finding it at Ursula's workstation, Nora suggested doing a thorough search of the basement before heading out to the woman's condo.

There are all kinds of places between the beams: cross beams, loose bricks, and some hanging ceiling tiles where a weapon could be hidden. But once she got there, she saw the numerous cobwebs and shuddered at the thought of sticking her hands into all those spider webs. *Yuck! I'm glad I'm at least wearing gloves.*

"Okay, let's chase some spiders around," Hawk chuckled.

And for at least thirty minutes, he and Nora searched every nook and cranny they could find, all to no avail. They had to give up. As they began climbing back up the steps, Nora paused, "Wait. We never looked that carefully behind the staircase."

"It's all open," Hawk said. "The stairs have no risers, except for the bottom one—just the two stringers holding up the open threads."

"That's just it. Why is there a riser on the bottom step and not the others ? I'd like to check it out." She shined her flashlight at the back of the stairs, shedding light on each thread. When the light shone on the bottom thread, the only one with a riser, she noticed a little shelf between the step and the floor. She lay down on the dirty floor, pushing her arm underneath the step and feeling with her hand for whatever she could find.

"Bingo!" she called out. "Clint, I feel some cloth with what feels like a gun inside."

Ursula's jaw dropped when she saw Nora holding her 9mm Ruger pistol. She never thought anyone would find it in that special spot that she discovered while moving boxes underneath the staircase. She believed that it would be safe there until she was clear to take it out of the building and dispose of it. Her arrogantly held head slumped onto her drooping shoulders. Not a word did she mutter as she was escorted out of the building. But as they sat in the car, she said quietly, almost to herself, "They deserved it. Baxter deserved it. After all the years, I've waited for him to come around. I was the one of those bimbos who truly loved him. All the years, I've helped him with his practice. In the end, he didn't even know I was there waiting for him. He used me. He had no real marriage with that stupid wife of his. They didn't love each other. He needed me. Then, under my nose, he made love to all those women but never even thought of me. He deserved it, and I'm glad I did it. Now, he won't torment me any longer."

EPILOGUE

WITH ANOTHER case solved, both Hawk and Nora had a wonderful feeling of satisfaction that comes with a job well done. They were positive that the Ruger pistol would be a match to the slugs that killed the lawyers, and later, it turned out that it was indeed. On the advice of her attorney, Marlene Livingstone, Ursula Hamlin entered a plea of not guilty. On further advice, she refused to cooperate. Counselor Livingstone was up to her tricks and threatened the police department with an illegal arrest and search illegally obtained confession, setting the case up for a fight in court.

Detective Carpenter arrested Angie Visser for the murder of Edgar Hendrix. He found out that Angie had practiced at a gun range for weeks prior to Edgar's death and became quite a proficient shot. The gun used to kill Edgar was found hidden in the attic of the Visser house. While conducting a thorough search of the Visser house, he ran across a letter written by Edgar to Angie stating that he was tired of their relationship and asked her not to bother him again. That was the motive Carpenter needed for her arrest. Needless to say, Goldie and Angie were no longer bosom buddies.

"Well, we did our job," Nora said as they returned from work to her house. "Now the district attorney's office can handle it and put Ursula away. So, what should we have for dinner? I'm not very hungry, are you?"

"I wouldn't mind just something light and fast."

"I've got some goat cheese and veggie flatbread from Trader Joe's. It's really pretty good. Only takes a few minutes to bake."

"Excellent. I'll make the salad. You know, honey, it's great having you near me."

Nora smiled, spun quickly around, and planted a long kiss on Hawk's full lips. He laughed, "I do love having you near."

After dinner and the dishes put away, they settled on the couch to watch the local news. The arrest of Ursula made the top story, and both Nora and he were mentioned as the arresting detectives. Mortimer was not, and they knew that he, particularly Josephine, would be upset.

While Nora and Hawk were enjoying their new arrangement of living together, Mortimer became more interested in Josephine's background. She had always been secretive about her past, and Nora's comments to him that he really did not know her well began to sink in. Josephine didn't like Mortimer's continued questions about her background and answered by haranguing the poor man that neither of them had to share personal information with each other. "I don't want to hear any more of it. Do you understand me?"

"Oh, yes, of course. I was just curious."

"Okay, then. Sit down and eat the breadfruit steaks that I prepared as a surprise. That breadfruit is expensive and hard to get. I splurged to give you a special treat because you've been injured so much lately, so you better love it." After Mortimer sat down, a knife and fork in his hands, Josephine shouted out, "Don't forget, Mortimer, that we agreed that what's in the past is in the past. We look only to the future. So don't ask me any dumb questions about the past." Mortimer made a mental note to ask Nora to find out all she could about his fiancé.

James Dickinson and Shirley Macon remained in jail, unable to post the high half-a-million dollar bond for each that the judge ordered. A week after the ordeal with the two, Detective Nancy Salazar was released from the hospital, her jaw wired up. Nevertheless, she was anxious to return to work as soon as possible. Harry Ling suffered a traumatic head injury, and his prognosis for complete recovery was guarded. He was scheduled to be released from the hospital a week later.

Nora and Hawk continued to keep their living arrangement secretive. They understood that the gossip mill around the station was very active, and people talked about them. It didn't help when Hawk asked Captain MacGregor for a few days off, and then Nora did the same a day later. They thought that MacGregor and Perez both suspected a romantic relationship between the two, but so far, neither had said a word. They hoped that they could avoid any rumors as they took off together to a beach resort in the Caribbean Island of St. Thomas. They were afraid that if the brass found out, not only could they receive a reprimand for fraternization, but also, it could be worse. One of them could be transferred to another district. So, Nora's excuse for days off would be that she stayed with her parents in Pueblo, Colorado, and Hawk would say that he went camping and mountain climbing. "Just make sure that we don't say too much to Orlinski," Hawk cautioned Nora.

"Anyway, Clint, the fact that we're living together now could be the fault of Captain MacGregor. Ever think of that?"

"How so?"

"She's the one that wanted us to stay in the same house for protection from the hitmen."

"You're right. We can throw that back at her if she makes a fuss of it."

Upon their return, Hawk sauntered into the station five minutes ahead of Nora. Orlinski appraised them both and made a comment that both looked fit and suntanned, as though they spent time under the sun. Then he told them that they looked good and refreshed. "MacGregor and Perez both want to see you immediately," he added.

Nora tensed up as they made their way to MacGregor's office. She whispered, "Clint, we may be in trouble. Why would both MacGregor and Perez want to see us?"

Hawk inhaled deeply as he and Nora walked in. MacGregor was behind her desk while Perez sat on the couch. "I'm glad you're back, refreshed and raring to go, I hope," MacGregor said. "Looks like both of you got some sun. I told you that you needed some time off considering the fisticuffs and attempts on your lives." Both Hawk and Nora felt a sense of relief. MacGregor was cordial and said, "I hope you both had a nice vacation."

Perez said, "I'm glad you're here now. It's been hectic around here with you gone and Salazar and Ling recuperating. Never seen Orlinski and Mortimer work so hard. And now we have yet two more dead bodies at a hotel that we must deal with. So, head out pronto to the Cambridge Hotel, not far from the Union Station. If Mortimer is here, take him along so that he won't whine like a puppy when he's not with you. Now go!"

HOTEL MURDERS

The author invites you to take a SNEAK PEAK of part of the first chapter of the forth book of the Clint Hawk and Nora Ricci murder mystery series.

CHAPTER 1

Present day: Denver, Colorado

THE WEATHER in downtown Denver that evening was turning cooler with the approach of autumn. The trees were beginning to shed their leaves preparing for winter. The moon was aglow as it shone down on Quincy Talbot as he scurried to the Cambridge Hotel in the LoDo—lower downtown—area, a backpack slung over his shoulder and lugging a suitcase filled with cash. He trembled as he made his way to the entrance, not from the cool breeze but from fear.

Quincy committed a crime. One that in a million years he would never have even thought of doing. He was desperate, all due to his dangerous gambling addiction. A mob bookmaker threatened to torture him and his children and watch them die a slow death if the sum of one hundred fifty thousand dollars was not paid by that night. Now he finally had the money. But it came at a price. He stole the heavily guarded plans and specifications of a revolutionary semiconductor chip from his workplace and sold the specs to a competitor of his company.

He now feared both his company and the shady broker that he sold the specs to. Quincy knew that once his company found out what he did, and they probably knew by now, he thought, they might or might not notify the police. But they would certainly send their goon security guard squad to retrieve the flash drive downloaded with the top-secret specifications. And more urgent to Quincy was the thought that they would have no qualms in killing him out of revenge and to keep the matter quiet. Afterall, billions of dollars were at stake.

Nor did he trust the slick-talking guy who arranged for the exchange—a lot of money in return for the specifications. Quincy wouldn't put it past him to find him, kill him and take back the cash. As a bonus, he'd get rid of me as a witness, Talbot imagined as he looked around to see if he was followed. Oh God, I'm becoming more paranoid every minute. He was glad that at least he demanded that the exchange be made at an open public place. He knew he was dealing with perhaps the devil, but he was so desperate to get hold of the money. He realized that he was in grave danger, and he had to hide. The thought that he really messed up forced the insides of his stomach to twist into a pretzel.

But first he had business to attend to before he could totally disappear. He frequented one of the new boutique hotels and that's where he checked in, hopefully for just a few hours to meet with a money expert and the bookie that he owed money to. His room was on the fifth floor, and he waited. As arranged, Quincy nervously expected the mobster to meet him there and collect his money. Also, as coordinated by him, he was to meet Tina Dionisio, a highly recommended investment banker, to come and help him shelter the cash in offshore accounts. Fearing that the cash sitting in his room or him carrying it around would hasten his demise. He had to get it out of the room as quickly as possible. As far as he knew, those were the only individuals that had knowledge that he was at the hotel.

A half-hour later, Mika Kochak, the bookie mobster he had expected, banged on his door. Quincy opened it with trepidation. "Do you have the dough?" The man bellowed and Quincy hoped that no one else on the floor heard him.

Quincy handed him a paper bag with one hundred fifty thousand in cash. Kochak moved his fat butt over to the bed and plopped down. He slowly counted the money. "I want another five per cent for a service charge."

"What service charge?"

"You made me come all the way over here to get my money. If you had paid me as you should've, I wouldn't have to be here. So, give me the extra ten grand now if you don't want your legs broken."

"But, Mika, you said five percent. That's not ten grand."

"The extra fee is because I want it. Now hand over the money!"

His body shaking, Quincy pulled out the suitcase from underneath the bed. The last thing he wanted was for Kochak to see the two million dollars less the one hundred fifty that he had paid him, stacked neatly in the suitcase. He took the bag into the bathroom, closed the door, and took out another ten thousand to pay the bastard, his forehead and underarms were drenched in sweat. "Here's the money. Will you leave now?"

"Maybe I should take a look at what's in that suitcase."

"Look, Mika, I paid you what you wanted. Please leave, I'm expecting a visitor any moment now."

Kochak stared hard at Quincy for a long uncomfortable minute. Then gave Quincy a hard punch to his right shoulder, causing him to stumble backwards. As he tried to straighten himself, Kochak started for the bathroom, obviously to look inside the suitcase. Quincy needed to block him from getting to that bathroom but knew that he had no chance with the heavy bully. He knew that if Kochak looked inside he'd see the money and take it.

Suddenly, there was a knock on the door and both men froze for a second before Quincy made it to the door and quickly opened it. Kochak didn't want any witnesses, so he decided that he had better leave and come back later. Pushing Tina Dionisio aside as he brushed past her, he shouted over his shoulder to Quincy, "I'm not through with you yet," as he stomped down the hall.

The shocked Tina didn't know what to do. She had never met Quincy before, and her first impulse was to turn around and walk away from what looked like a fight. But she remembered that she was here because of the two million dollars that the man seemed urgent to invest or secure. So, she thought she'd give him five minutes to convince her to stay.

"Ms. Dionisio, thank you so much for coming, particularly to this hotel room. I know you're suspicious of me and my intentions, but you are my lifesaver. As I told you I have a lot of cash and I must get it out of my hands as soon as possible. I've heard good things about you from a friend of mine, your client, that you are an honest woman and can be trusted."

"Thank you for the kind words, Mr. Talbot, but it's way past closing time and there is no way that I can invest the money tonight. It'll have to be tomorrow, if possible."

"I realize that, but I'm in deep trouble and may not survive the night. I don't think that anyone else knows that I'm here, but it seems there are eyes and ears everywhere. We are constantly surveilled by cameras."

The fact that the man didn't think he'd make it through the night scared her and she decided not to have anything to do with him. "I'm sorry, Mr. Talbot, I can't help you. Finding a good investment takes time and dealing in cash takes even longer. No U.S. bank would accept it without many questions."

"What about if you deposit the money into several offshore accounts? I understand that some banks do not require a name as they issue a number, or if they do, the name is always kept extremely protected. Or perhaps crypto currency where there are no questions asked. I don't have time to arrange anything like that or the know-how."

"I'm sorry, this is highly irregular."

"Please, please. I need your help. If you can't bank it right away, at least take the money, give me a receipt, and keep it safe for me until I contact you again." Tina shook her head in the negative and was ready to get up and leave. "I'll give you twenty percent commission. That's a lot of money for you considering that you get almost four-hundred thousand dollars. Well actually a little less since I paid off my bookie one-hundred-sixty thousand dollars and my past due child-support in the amount of twenty-three thousand."

That was a lot of money and all Tina had to do was to either set up a few offshore accounts, something that she had done for her clients several times or just keep it for a while until he contacted her. "All right, Mr. Talbot, I'll help you. But my fee is a flat half million. I feel that there is a risk for me involved here."

Quincy thought about it for a minute. That's awfully steep, but what choice do I have? I need to get the money out of here and then get out. "All right, Ms. Dionisio. I sure hope that I can trust you. Let me bring out the suitcase, you can count the cash and give me a receipt describing what you intend to do with the money. And," he hesitated as he swallowed hard, feeling the lump in his throat, "And if anything happens to me, I want you to set up a trust on behalf of my children. I'll give you their names and addresses. I just don't want my psycho ex-wife to know anything about it or for her to lay her grubby hands on any of it, okay?"

"Yes, sure. But why? Is your life in danger?"

"Let's just say that I have powerful people that are now out to get me…dangerous people…including the tech company I work for."

A chill ran down Tina's spine as she counted out the number of wrapped bundles of one-hundred-dollar bills. Each wrapped set contained five thousand dollars. Gads! What have I gotten myself into? The last thing I need now is to worry about my life. Would I be in danger as well? But it's half a mil. It's worth taking a chance. A minute later, Quincy's cell phone rang. He quickly answered. Tina could hear most of the loud conversation even though the speaker on the iPhone was off.

"I know what you did. You stole the specs. We worked on that Omnibus Project together and I want my share and I want it tonight. I can get pretty nasty if I don't get paid. I know that you met someone tonight."

"How in the hell would you know that, Simon?" Tina heard Talbot ask.

"I followed you. I spotted you downloading the specs and then handing over the flash drive to some dude. In return he left you a suitcase that I assume was full of cash. You got paid off and I want my share, Quincy. I watched you haul that suitcase into the Cambridge Hotel, and I know what room you're in."

"Okay, Simon, "No worries, I'll meet you tomorrow at City Park by the lake. Make it at 2:00 o'clock." There was a quiet response from Simon, but Tina couldn't hear what he said.

Visibly upset, his hands shaking, Quincy told Tina, "Hurry with the counting and get me that receipt. You've got to get out of here. Make sure no one follows you. I should get out of here myself. Let's meet in this room tomorrow morning at nine and give me details about what you did with the money. If you are able to bank it, I want confirmation of transactions."

Tina protested that there would be no transactions made in such a short time, but he seemed too upset to have that sink in. It took a couple of hours for Tina to go through every bill. After the money was counted, she gave him a receipt on the hotel's courtesy notepad and left in a rush lugging that suitcase heavy with cash.

About the Author

Victor Moss has been an attorney engaged in private practice of law since 1974 in both Pueblo and Denver, Colorado. Prior to that time, he had been an assistant attorney general for the State of New Mexico and assistant city attorney for Pueblo, Colorado. His prior books are Beware the Wolves: A Soviet WWII Love Story, No Return Home, The Soul Named Samantha, Coffee House Murders, The Murdered Wife and Country Club Murders. He lives with his wife in Highlands Ranch, Colorado.